TAKEN

BLOOD OF THE CHOSEN TRILOGY

D.L. BLADE

To my very supportive husband. You've been a rock throughout my writing journey.
Thank you, my love.
Enjoy the naughty content.

SOCIAL MEDIA

Goodreads:
@D_L_Blade
TikTok:
@authordlblade
Facebook:
@dlblade
Instagram:
@booksbydlblade
Pinterest:
@DLBlade
YouTube:
@DLBlade
Newsletter:
www.linktr.ee/dlblade

AUTHOR'S NOTE

Taken is a retelling, adult edition of my novel, *The Dark Under-world*, published in 2019, and features mature themes and content.

Full content warnings can be found on my website, www.dlblade.com

CHAPTER 1

MERCY

Deep breath. I'd been in far worse situations than this.

"Focus," I muttered to myself. "Just focus."

I sucked in a deep breath and slowly released it, hoping that would slow down my heart rate. Each breath I released burned my dry mouth. I assumed I'd been six feet under for at least two to three hours. I was unsure how long it would take for me to consume all the oxygen, but I couldn't imagine it being much longer than this. The air was thick within the wooden coffin, and it became harder to breathe with each passing moment.

It's not like I could die, but being buried in a wooden box for eternity would be worse than death.

I hadn't died and come back yet since I had become immortal. Though I wondered how that would play out. Would I pass out, open my eyes again, pass out, wake up, and repeat that again and again until I lost my mind?

My muscles quivered in anger just thinking about the two vampires who had put me down, but I also cursed myself for being such an idiot. I should've been paying better attention to my surroundings.

Fuck!

It wasn't about getting out of this situation, so I didn't suffer. It was about getting out so I could make *them* suffer. Very, very slowly.

Come on, guys. Where the hell are you?

I looked around the wooden coffin those assholes had forced me into after they'd injected me with God only knew what, which had crippled my powers. Once the drug had worn off, I'd opened my eyes to this nightmare—they had buried me alive.

This was going to happen, eventually. The vampires knew it was the only way to stop me, so long as we hid the dagger from their grasp. They had to put me six feet under, literally.

I held my palm open so that I could use my powers to light up the walls around me. I could barely raise my head before knocking into the lid of the coffin.

Man, it's fucking hot in here.

Sweat dripped down my forehead, and the taste of salt consumed my senses as it touched my lips and entered my mouth. I rubbed the sweat off my lips with my other hand and looked around the tiny and cramped space. The earth was slowly seeping through the cracks every time I shifted my body.

This wasn't one of those fancy metal caskets stuffed with the white cushion padding they use at most burials today. This was a tattered, wooden coffin that looked like it came straight out of the Dark Ages. The wood had split into several places, and I feared the entire thing would crumble on top of me if I so much as sneezed.

I placed my hands on the top of the lid and applied some pressure. When I pushed, even slightly, the wood cracked, causing the dirt to seep through again.

I couldn't use my powers at full strength; it would have only caused the ground above to crush me, then I'd die of suffocation repeatedly for eternity.

Now, that would be worse than passing out.

Slowly, the earth fell through the crack near my chest, the dirt and small round pebbles seeping through.

Oh, shit. That's it.

Earth.

Ezra's element.

Bingo! I can send a pulse through Earth to contact Ezra and share my location.

Without skipping a beat, the tip of my finger reached for the earth. I pressed my index finger deep into the soil through a small crack above my chest. I focused on Ezra and his energy. He *was* the ground we walked on. He'd feel it.

It wasn't as if I couldn't harness that power, but if I could connect my magic with his, I might be able to break through without crushing my body to a bloody pulp.

"Ezra, I'm right here," I whispered quietly. "Where are you guys?"

My pulse pounded faster when I closed my eyes and brought myself into a state of meditation, helping me focus on what I needed to.

This has to work.

I kept my finger on the soil for what felt like hours, but time seemed to move differently inside the little box, or the lack of oxygen messed with my head. I sent a stronger pulse of magic through the dirt. I was met with a loud cracking sound, and the wooden lid groaned.

Oh, fuck, I overdid it!

The coffin cracked further; the dirt poured in faster, and I had to remove my finger to shield my face.

Panic rose in my throat. What had I done?

I felt a jolt but kept my hands hovering over my eyes. As I peeked through my fingers, the coffin rattled, and the lid blasted high in the air in a violent explosion. I moved my hands to see the earth and wooden coffin parts swirling around the hole I had been in, as if I were in the eye of a tornado. I drew in a deep breath of fresh air and briefly shut my eyes while still in the center of the dust devil. When I opened my eyes again, I saw my coven standing around the whirlwind, with Ezra's arms spread wide. His eyes now shone a glowing, ashy brown color. As I reached for the top of the hole, Ezra lowered his arms, releasing the earth.

"Oh, thank God," Caleb cried out as he reached for me, pulling me out of the hole, then into his arms for a tight squeeze.

I finally released all the anxiety I had during the ordeal. "It didn't matter how much I tried to muster my powers; it wasn't enough. They shot me up with some kind of tranquilizer, and it knocked me out completely," I admitted. "For a moment there, I was beginning to think you'd not show up to my rescue."

Caleb flashed me a toothy grin and said, "Oh, come on. You'll feed Ezra's ego if you comment like that."

Ezra brushed off the dirt from his arm and looked up to meet my eyes. Only his tiny smile told me that helping me out of a bind was the best thing to happen to him all week.

The lightheadedness dissipated as my powers healed the trauma my body had experienced while buried alive. Being immortal didn't make me invincible. I still felt pain like any mortal would.

I also felt fear and anger, sadness, and hopelessness. Right then, I mostly felt anger. A fiery heat flushed through my body as I looked around to see if the vampires were nearby.

I'm going to fucking kill them.

The rest of the coven rushed my way and pulled me into a group hug.

"They're probably long gone by now," Simon said as he released our embrace. "Unless they're *that* stupid."

My attention left Simon when I heard a rustling noise, and I spotted the two vampires who had stuck me inside the coffin hurrying from the cottage next to us. "They're that stupid," I said through gritted teeth.

"Seriously, they buried you in their front yard?" Leah asked, pointing to the front of the cottage and then to the hole. She shook her head as the two blood-sucking shitbags made a run for the forest.

I frowned at that observation. Those idiots had been here the entire time, knowing I was suffering right outside their own door. They wanted to stick around and admire their handiwork.

Caleb gestured in their direction. "They're all yours, Mercy."

A slow smirk replaced my frown as I raised my hands, and an electrifying energy flowed through my fingertips. I threw down my arms, blasting my force in their direction. The strength of my magic slammed into their backsides, sending them airborne. It only took a moment for the pair to stand on their feet again, facing us with their fangs out and fire burning in their eyes. Caleb tossed me my stake as I ran toward the vampires. Once I reached them, though, they fell to their knees, pleading.

Oh, come on.

"Please don't kill me. I don't want to die," cried the one who had mocked me earlier as he grabbed my throat to toss me into the coffin. "Just turn us human."

I chuckled at his words. That was what I had offered them as they shoveled dirt over me for thirty minutes. I had given them an out, warning them that my coven would find me and that they'd be hunted down until I stuck a stake through their cold hearts.

They hadn't listened.

The second vampire, with blond tips and a stupid grin, held up his hands in defeat. "Please, I have a wife and—"

Poof! The simpering asshole was now dust.

Caleb stood there, holding his own stake while weaving flames between his fingers. The remaining vampire closed his eyes as if defeated, but when he opened them again, they were blood red.

"You'll pay for that, you fucking bitch! I'll make you all suffer," he threatened, flashing his sharp, deadly fangs.

I bent my knee, so we were at eye level, then placed the stake on his chest, right where his heart would be. He tried to snap at my throat, but Caleb had him frozen by a spell.

The vampire shook his head frantically from side to side before I said, "Have fun in Hell, you pathetic asshole."

My stake impaled his chest with a quick thrust, and I watched him turn to dust. He would now join his friend in whatever afterlife those creeps went to.

"Well, I'm ready to eat," I stated, but my voice cracked. "Actually, I could really use some water." After crying out for the last few hours in the scorching heat inside that box, I hadn't realized how dry my throat had become.

"Water, yes," Caleb said, "but food will have to wait."

"Why, what's going on?" I asked, placing my stake in the belt loop of my jeans.

"Something happened on Main Street a couple of hours ago," he explained. "There's police everywhere."

"In East Greenwich?" I asked.

Caleb nodded.

"Vampire attack?"

Leah shrugged. "We don't know yet, but Lily told us someone died, and she had overheard the police speak about an injury on the victim's neck."

My stomach twisted into a tight knot.

Was it someone we knew?

"What time is it?" I asked Ezra, who stood next to me.

Ezra looked down at his phone. "Midnight. Lily told us it happened around ten, just a few hours after you went missing."

Caleb reached into his pocket and pulled out my phone. I guess I had dropped it when they attacked me. I didn't even have a moment to defend myself before the needle pricked my neck.

I had planned to meet the coven for a couple of rounds of pool and beers when those two snatched me. We were right outside of downtown Providence. Not once since this all started had the vampires attacked so close to our hometown. I hadn't expected it and scolded myself for letting my guard down. I needed to be much more careful from here on out.

"Well, let's go, then," I said, and we hurried to Simon's car. As much as I didn't want the attack to be from a vampire, it was the only way we'd find the ones that needed to be eradicated—the ones that refused to turn human—like the two we had just killed.

Those who chose darkness were worthless, evil, and undeserving of our mercy.

CHAPTER 2

MERCY

"What happened here?" I asked an officer, my eyes narrowing on his badge. "Officer Shields?"

The officer looked to be in his late forties, strong in stature, and very handsome. His mustache was shaved thin, and his hair was light brown, with a few silver streaks along the sides of his head, right above the ears.

Officer Shields leaned against a Victorian-style steel light post next to Tippy's Pancake House, jotting down something on his little black notepad. They had wrapped yellow caution tape around the curb that stretched over to the other side of the parking lot.

The officer ignored me, of course. I was a nosey bystander, and he had orders to keep things quiet until they received the official report to be released to the public.

I glanced past him, but all I saw were a dozen cops inside the restaurant, moving around and conversing with each other.

"Is Tippy okay?" I asked. "I mean ... Ryan Harrison?"

Ryan was a resident who had lived in East Greenwich for the last four years. He kept to himself mostly, but the pancake house was new and exciting for him and a way to get to know everyone in town. It brought our entire community together when it first opened.

When Officer Shields didn't respond, I kept prying. "Look, I live right down the street. I just want to make sure it isn't someone I know." He glanced in my direction, shook his head, and walked away. "Don't worry," I mumbled to myself. "We'll find out soon enough."

The thought of the victim being Ryan, or as we called him, "Tippy," made my stomach ill. The attack had happened right around the time when he would have been locking up.

Lily appeared from behind the building. "I asked a few detectives, too, from the other side of the restaurant. They aren't giving me any answers. Only the parts they slipped up when they didn't realize I was within earshot. I'll sneak around to the south side of the parking lot and see what else I can find."

My stomach was in shambles again while I shook my head, thinking about it being someone I was close to, if not Tippy himself.

I turned my attention toward the parking lot to search for Caleb, who was trying to get answers, too, but when I shifted to the right, I bumped into him.

He crossed his arms over his chest and shook his head with a slight side smirk. "The Mercy I know wouldn't have given up so easily," he said, winking at me as he headed toward Tippy's, crouching under the caution tape near the front entrance.

"What the hell are you doing?" I uttered in a near whisper. "They won't let you in there." Caleb reached the doors as they opened, with the backside of the coroner pulling the front of a gurney. Once they emerged from the doorway, I immediately eyed the black tarp over the shape of what I assumed was the body.

A year ago, a corpse would have made my skin crawl, and I'd have cringed at the sight of it, but not anymore. This last year, we cleaned up or reported a few dead bodies, mainly between Boston and Salem. It was a change I had to get used to.

Bury whatever icky feeling you have, Mercy. This is your life now.

But why here? I wondered. *And why now?* The only time vampires had ever come to East Greenwich was because of me. We'd made a treaty with them six months ago that I would leave them alone as long as they didn't kill a human or turn one against their will. I even gave them a choice before driving a stake through their chest.

Well ... most of the time.

Their choice was simple—become human again or die at my hands. The ones that were just rotten to their core always chose death or tried to fight me before I ended it for them.

Vampires like Dorian were proof enough that good ones were among the fold. It had taken me a while to convince the rest of the coven, but eventually, they came to agree with me. Most vampire clans listened and obeyed this new "law," but there were still a few bad seeds. And those were the ones that kept us fighting.

Caleb moved to the side and let the cops walk by, but Officer Shields spotted him as they exited Tippy's.

"Hey!" Shields shouted. "Get on the other side of the tape before I arrest you. Now!"

Damn.

Caleb threw his hands in the air in defeat. "Alright. Alright."

Lily ran back around to meet us, slowing down as her eyes spotted the gurney. "Mercy, I managed to get a glimpse of the body before they fully zipped up the bag. It's Tippy, for sure, and there was blood completely covering his neck."

I felt my heart drop to my feet.

"No! Ryan!" a female voice shouted from my right. Caleb and I turned our attention toward Tippy's grandmother, Joanne, as she ran toward the restaurant. "No!" she screamed again, pressing her hands to her chest as if she were experiencing intense pain. Her legs gave out from under her, and her knees hit hard against the pavement. The officer manning the perimeter rushed over to Joanne, signaling to a medic to assist him.

Oh, shit.

I turned back to Caleb and slowly wrapped my arms around my waist, feeling a sudden coldness hit me at my core. When I looked up at him, I asked, "Why would anyone hurt Tippy?" I shifted my feet, letting my arms drop to my sides. "This isn't the typical pattern of vampire attacks that we've seen lately, Caleb. They've cleaned up their mess when there was a victim to cover their tracks since they know we're local here. What the fuck is happening?"

Right after the officer and medic assisted Tippy's grandmother, she tried to push past them and the lining of the caution tape, but before she could, her knees buckled, and she collapsed to the ground again. The same officer rushed to hold her shoulders, helping her to her feet. Joanne began to weep uncontrollably, and the officer escorted her away from the parking lot toward a police car.

"Would a vampire really do this right now?" I continued, trying to ignore the sound of her crying. "Knowing we're so close by? How stupid can they be?"

Caleb shook his head. "I don't know, but we'll find out soon enough."

⁂

We knew we wouldn't get any answers from the officers, so we headed home. I showered off all the dirt and grime from the involuntary burial and climbed into bed, exhausted from all the events of that day. However, sleep was impossible for me. It was four in the morning, and I still had Tippy and his poor, sweet grandma on my mind.

I browsed the news on my phone, and our local news channel had reported what they had learned from the scene. According to initial police reports, Tippy had been killed shortly after ten in the evening after he'd locked up the restaurant. A couple had come to eat there and hadn't realized Tippy had closed up for the night. They saw him sprawled out on the floor through the window, covered in blood.

Evidence showed that he was in the middle of mopping the floor when someone broke in and took his life. The killer had shattered the back window by a corner booth, and muddy boot prints lined the walkway leading to where they'd found his body.

They didn't release any information on how Tippy had been killed, but Caleb would follow up with our medical examiner contact, Melissa. She'd been helping us this last year whenever the supernatural arrived in the morgue.

"We need to have a connection that allows us to determine if it's a human or a vampire attack," Caleb had explained to me a year ago.

Brown University had invited Melissa to give a lecture to the medical students in forensic medicine. Given her credentials, Caleb thought she would be an asset to the coven. Though it was a bold move for us to fill her in on what we were, we approached her after the seminar and shared with her a world she hadn't known existed. Of course, she freaked out at first, but she was also happy to learn the truth. A whole new underworld seemed tantalizing to a medical professional like herself, so it was easy to get her on board.

We had to know if a vampire attacked the victim, so we could be the ones to handle it. It would put the police force in danger if they were tracking a creature they didn't know how to take down.

I shot a text to Caleb, as I was sure he wasn't sleeping, either.

Me: *I'm coming with you tomorrow. I want to be there for this one.*

Caleb: *Alright, I'll pick you up at ten. But try to rest. It's been a long night.*

Me: *Night.*

I closed my phone and rolled over onto my side. Whoever hurt Tippy was going to pay dearly. Whether it'll be behind bars or in a pile of ash.

CHAPTER 3

MERCY

Caleb and I reached the back door to the morgue, and we waited next to the brick wall for Melissa to let us into the building once she had the cameras down. Surveillance was on every corner of the morgue, and we couldn't risk Melissa getting in trouble for sneaking us in.

About five minutes went by when Melissa texted Caleb, informing him the cameras were finally down and that she was on her way to get us. Once the door cracked open, she waved us in and led us to the autopsy suite.

A cold snap of air hit me when we entered the suite, and a shiver ran up my spine, so I wrapped my sweater around my waist. The autopsy room had mostly steel tables and ceramic countertops, with fluorescent tube lights overhead. Two of the tables were bare, and the body bag from yesterday was at the center table. Melissa zipped open the yellow bag which held Tippy's body, and my heart sank when I saw his lifeless face.

"You were right, Caleb. Vampire," Melissa said. "See the bite marks?" She pointed to two red holes on the side of Tippy's neck.

I glanced up at Caleb and back at Melissa. "Was he drained to death?" I asked.

She shook her head. "No. I was at the scene last night taking photos. The amount of blood on the floor is about the same amount missing from the victim."

When I glanced up at Caleb, he looked as confused as I was.

Melissa saw our expression and continued. "He didn't drink from the body. His fangs pierced the carotid artery, and he bled to death on the floor. The vampire attack victims I've examined in the past were all drained." She pointed to the bites again. "The vampire who did this did it to kill, not feed."

My breath caught, and I stared at her wide-eyed. Caleb must have seen my shock. He inched toward me, bringing his fingers to mine and grazing my palm to help me relax.

I didn't mind Caleb touching me. I cared for him like family. Despite how our relationship was a year ago, I had to let all that shit go because we would always be in each other's lives.

Right then, though, Caleb was showing me he cared. Tippy was someone I knew, and even though I had to put on a brave face so I could focus on this murder with my coven, it still hurt that he was dead.

Not just *dead* but brutally slaughtered by a vampire.

I just couldn't understand why a vampire would randomly kill a human like this. Was there an unhinged vampire killing for sport now? Mostly we'd see them kill if someone betrayed them. They'd drink if *hungry*, but they never wasted blood in either situation.

Find the motive. There is always a motive.

Maybe they had been interrupted by someone approaching the restaurant and couldn't finish what they had started.

"Thank you," I said, pulling my focus back to her. "Once again, we appreciate everything you've done for us."

She zipped up the bag and grabbed a notebook off a metal desk in the corner of the room.

"Of course," Melissa said, clearing her throat. "My report will state that an ice pick was the weapon with two blows to the neck. Manner of death: homicide. Cause of death: blood loss."

Caleb glanced at me and shook Melissa's hand as if he had just completed a business meeting. "Thanks."

Jesus Christ, spare me.

I rolled my eyes, directing my attention away from them, so they didn't see. They were being ridiculous. I wasn't an idiot. I knew they had been hooking up in secret, but he was acting weird about sharing that with me and the rest of the coven.

"We'll be in touch," Caleb said and turned back to me. "Come on. We need to head back to the house and train."

Last year, after my mom died and I reached the age of twenty-one, I inherited everything she had, including what was already in my trust. I decided it was best to get my own place, so I didn't put Lily's life in danger within our "witches versus vampire" crossfire.

Yes, she had magic to protect herself, but even with her powers, this was too much for Lily to handle. I didn't want her involved and risking her life for me anymore, but she also had someone in her life now who didn't know about us.

That alone could put *him* in danger.

Lily had been dating Bradley since last December. He was cute, but he was the epitome of a computer geek. Bradley always wore these thick glasses high on his nose; his hair parted to one side. If he wasn't wearing a Star Wars shirt or his favorite black shirt with yellow vinyl lettering that read, "I'm Geeky, and I Know It," he wore a white button-down short-sleeve with suspenders and a bow tie. He was incredibly smart, and I didn't judge his lack of fashion sense because Bradley made Lily laugh, which was what mattered to her and to me.

Caleb had helped me and the rest of the coven find a property in East Greenwich. He still had his cabin in Salem, but he and his father mostly slept at Abigail's mansion in her spare rooms. Her place was massive enough, and once I turned Abigail and Desiree human again, they hadn't been back to the house. I guess being able to visit tropical locations and seeing a world in the daylight again were the only things that mattered to them anymore.

I don't blame them. If I were in their situation, I'd be long gone.

Riley and Amber formed their own pack and lived in Providence. Riley had finished up at Brown and then settled into an apartment near campus. His old roommate, Aaron, and his sister, Hannah, became werewolves shortly after their last semester. Riley explained no one had forced them into being werewolves like he had been but that they had chosen to be bitten.

Riley had informed me at a coffee shop a few months back that he and Amber were dating. They kept the pack a priority, though, as well as their allegiance to the witches. They'd assist us when we needed help to track down a vampire clan. I, of course, hated getting him involved, but the other four in the coven felt we fought better with a wolf pack by our side.

After graduation, Shannon moved to New Orleans, where her mother grew up. It didn't take much for Shannon to convince her parents they needed to leave East Greenwich as well. The danger she believed would reach her family was too much of a risk.

God, I missed her a lot. I mean, I understood why she left. Involving my friends in this life after what happened a year ago was a tremendous risk. The ones who were all too human needed to stay away.

Shannon was smart to pretend nothing supernatural was going on around her. We spoke a few times a week on the phone, but we kept the conversations brief, and she was careful not to ask questions that could lead to answers she didn't want to hear.

And then there was Cami ...

CHAPTER 4

MERCY

I quietly entered the doorway and spotted Cami in the corner of her dimly lit, gloomy bedroom, staring at a canvas painted with mist-like swirls surrounding a grove of trees.

"Oh, no," she said. "This is all wrong. It needs more black." She gripped the paintbrush and glided the black paint around the edges, making wide to narrow circles until she reached the center. "That's better," she added, turning around to face me. "Hi, Mercy." Her voice was flat and emotionless.

She had removed all the pastel colors that had covered the walls and furniture of her room the moment they'd released her from the hospital. "The bright colors are blinding me," she had once explained when I came to visit her. Cami had moved back in with her mother, Laurie, and since then, had only left her room for meals and psychiatric appointments.

"Hey." I stepped further into her room, scanning the walls that were covered in paintings like the one she worked on now.

Always black.

Always depressing.

None of her paintings made sense. Black paint covered most of the canvas, usually surrounding a forest or a river. It was unsettling.

After Cami awoke from her "coma," she wasn't Cami anymore. I knew she must have seen disturbing images or felt something during her possession that forever changed her. There wasn't a spell we could conjure to bring her back from that nightmare. I leaned down next to her and looked up at the painting.

"It's beautiful," I said. "Can I have this one? It'll look great in our training room."

She stared at her feet, avoiding eye contact with me as she nodded.

"I'll see you tomorrow, okay?" She looked up and grabbed my wrist to keep me from leaving. Cami's grip was fierce, and the expression on her down-turned face made my heart hurt. I held her hand and gently pried her fingers from my skin. "Caleb and I are going to train for the rest of the day with my coven, but I told him I wanted to stop by to see you. I'll be back. I promise."

I lowered her hand toward the paintbrush.

"Are you sleeping okay?" I asked her. Cami shook her head, keeping her eyes on her feet. "Okay." I pulled out two sleeping pills from my purse and placed them on her nightstand. I had been supplying them for her at least three times a week because every spell we had tried wasn't working. I grabbed the painting on the easel and replaced the spot with a blank canvas for her. She grabbed the paintbrush and started over.

Once I arrived back at my house, I entered the spacious basement where we had been training for the last year. Ezra and Simon shared a room in the far-left corner, sleeping on a bunk bed like two college roommates while we used the rest of the space.

We had lined the walls with steel hooks and racks on which we could hang our wooden stakes and silver daggers. In the center, a two-inch-thick pad stretched from one end of the room to the other. Ezra also bought a boxing bag we kept in the corner by the bathroom. He and I were the only ones who ever worked out with it. I may have been able to retrieve several memories back on how I fought in my past life, and the coven had been training me this last year, but I still needed to work on my endurance.

Leah descended the stairs with her hair pulled up in a short ponytail, barefoot, and wearing a tank top with yoga pants. She was tiny, especially without shoes, but she sure kicked ass when she fought.

"Was it a vampire or a human?" she asked us.

"Vampire," Caleb cut in as I opened my mouth to answer her.

"Sounds like a fucking party," Ezra beamed, coming over to the pad while pounding his right fist into his palm.

"Goddamn, Ez, be a little more sensitive. Mercy knew the victim," Leah snapped.

"It's fine," I said. "I need to detach my feelings from this case, so we can catch whoever did this. Caleb's having Roland investigate the Black Horse clan," I explained.

Leah nodded. "That's a good place to start. We've been waiting for that clan to fuck up something, so we would have an excuse to take them out."

The Black Horse Clan had moved to Providence shortly after I went through my Awakening, but they had agreed to stay out of our way. I hadn't met any vampires from the clan, but Roland had a friend, Marcus, who was part of their "family." Marcus never reported any mischief that went on within the clan. However, he promised they had changed their *questionable* behavior after my Awakening. Some bullshit about how they were the good guys now, trying to make a difference within their world. As much as I wanted to believe Marcus, I wasn't buying it.

The nightclub the clan built had broken ground this last spring and opened two weeks ago. Regardless of Marcus's reports and assurances, we kept a careful eye on them, and we would especially pay much closer attention to the clan now. Their reputation preceded them, and a nightclub would be the perfect hideaway in which to commit shady vampire crimes. It was dark; black shades hid the windows to keep the vampires safe from the daylight, and entry to the underground level was by exclusive invitation only.

"We haven't had a body in months." I tossed up a hand. "Then this happens. It's perfect timing, don't you think?"

Simon appeared from the bedroom, carrying a bag in his hand, and tossed it to the floor. "Are we assuming they're after Mercy again, given that it happened a few minutes from us, and she knew the victim?"

"It is our hometown," I said, facing Caleb. "This looks like something someone may do to get to me. Tippy's was a place I frequented a lot in the past. What do you think?"

Caleb was focused only on his phone.

"Caleb?" Leah called.

He looked up and sighed. "Probably, but we still need to investigate before we call them out and demand justice. I'll check it out, though. The last thing we need is to fuck this up and create a war after everything we built to form a peaceful agreement with them."

"Let me do it." The pitch of my voice climbed up a notch. "Sarah can come over tonight to help me. I just need to scope the place and leave. Once I see what we're up against, we can devise a plan and discuss whether we should focus on them or somewhere else," I explained. Still, I could already see Caleb shaking his head, because he couldn't help the control freak inside him. He hated it when I went undercover without him. "Quit shaking your head. We aren't making the same mistakes we did last year. I can do this." His mouth formed a straight line, and he flared his nostrils. "Stop looking at me like that."

Caleb rolled his eyes. "I'd feel safer if I were there with you."

"Absolutely not. The last time we investigated inside a bar, a vampire hit on me, and you beat the shit out of him and broke his nose."

His jaw muscles tightened. "He healed."

I huffed and shook my head as I kneeled to unzip the bag Simon had tossed onto the floor, ignoring Caleb's bitter response. I grabbed five sets of hand wraps, tossed them over to everyone, and put them on my own.

"We're sparring today. Leah, I'll pair up with you. Caleb, you can be the attacker this time. Ezra, you're the victim. Simon, you can help Leah if Caleb gets the upper hand."

"I'm always the fucking victim," Ezra whined. "Let Simon be the bait, and I'll be the dumbass vampire."

"You scream like a little girl," I teased. "You're the perfect target."

Ezra stuck out his tongue like a child, dragged his feet to the center of the mat, and laid down on his back. After a few more seconds of Ezra mumbling obscenities at us, he finally said, "Oh no. Is that a vampire?" His voice was flat, and he scrunched up his face at Caleb, who hovered over him.

Caleb pretended to show his fangs and dashed toward Ezra. Leah quickly leaped in his direction and pounced on his back like a tiger attacking her prey. She wrapped her arm around his neck and her legs around his waist. They struggled for a minute, with Caleb taking a few blows to the face from me while Leah twisted her body and pulled his shoulder to the right. He lost his balance and fell to the floor. I quickly shoved my foot into his chest, keeping him pinned along with Leah keeping her chokehold.

"Damn, Caleb. That was too easy," Simon mocked. "I would have jumped in to help you, but Leah took you down too quickly."

"I'm still not going to hit her," Caleb said. "But great job, Leah." He looked around at the coven. "We need to be able to fight with our hands and not rely on magic. The amount of training we've done this year has helped us more than simply practicing our magic all these years. Our physical strength will sometimes be our saving grace. But we still need more training."

"*You* need more training," Leah mocked and giggled to herself.

My phone rang, and I turned from the group. "Hey, Joel," I answered. "I was going to call you after we finished training."

"Lily told me what happened to Tippy," he said. "What did you guys find out?"

I explained to Joel what Melissa had discovered about Tippy's body and the recent updates on the Black Horse Clan, but I was only met with silence on the other end of the line.

"Joel?"

"Sorry. I'm thinking," Joel said. I heard Derek in the background saying something, but I couldn't make out what it was. "I'll do some digging on my end, but don't do anything until I find out more. Okay?"

"Sure. Got it," I lied, knowing we were going to that club tonight.

After hanging up the phone, I turned to Caleb. "I need Sarah if I'm going to go to that club." I took my gloves off and tossed them back into the bag. "You guys keep practicing. I'll send her a text now."

Caleb turned to the rest of the coven, and they paired up again. Ezra was more than happy to be the one attacking Leah this time, as he had no problem throwing a punch at her. I respected that he treated us as equals. We weren't fragile girls; we were vampire hunters.

I typed out a text to Sarah to let her know about our plans tonight.

> **Me:** *Hey, can you make me a blonde tonight?*

I waited a minute before she responded.

> **Sarah:** *Oh, boy, what's going on?*

How do I put this without freaking her out?

> **Me:** *There's a new vampire club in Providence. I need to scope them out. We think it might be tied to the murder in East Greenwich.*

> **Sarah:** *Yikes, okay. I'll be there at eight.*

Well, that was easy. The last time we went to a vampire lair undercover, someone had almost kidnapped Sarah again. I hated putting her life in danger, but she was adamant about helping us, because she had a power none of us possessed.

***

The water dripping down my back caused me to pause and press my hand against the tile. I shut my eyes and let my mind wander. The last year had been something else. The spell I had put on myself had removed my feelings for what I had for Caleb and the love I had for Dorian. It didn't, however, prevent me from *thinking* about them. And it did. Often. Sometimes both men at the same time.

Fuck, my mind is really in the gutter tonight.

I arched my back, letting my hand fall to my naval, lightly rubbing the bar of soap around my skin to wash it clean. I put the bar down, and my fingers gently pressed against my lower belly.

My mind pictured Dorian in here with me. His hard chest pressed up against my breasts, and his long fingers ran through my wet hair to push it back, leaving goosebumps in its wake.

"You're so fucking selfish," Dorian whispered into my ear before his fingers gripped my hair to yank it back, forcing me to look into his eyes.

Dorian was always gentle with me in my past life but not in my fantasies. No, he liked it rough, and I let him.

My fingers trailed down between my legs, finding my dripping wet folds. With a moment of hesitation, I let the water wash my hand before I slipped my finger inside of me. My inner walls clenched around it, throbbing in sheer need for a release as I began to move my thumb against my swollen clit. I leaned my back against the tiles; my head tipped back as I closed my eyes.

In my fantasy, it was Dorian's hand.

He was pinning me against the tiles, thrusting one of his fingers into my heated core while gripping my hip with the other. His calloused fingers moved at a curved angle, reaching that spot inside of me that made me so impossibly soaked, while his thumb provided the much-needed stimulation to my clit.

Dorian knew *exactly* how to touch me.

"I want to feel you come for me," he murmured against my ear, his icy breath tickling my skin as his pace quickened. His fingers were moving in and out of me in deep, slow strokes, sending a bliss unlike any other through my body.

Fuck.

My entire body was shaking for him, my breathing heavy and bothered as I did my best to stay silent.

My own hand rubbed my aching pussy harder, guiding me closer to the release I was aching for. It moved the way I would have wanted Dorian to touch me. Rough, desperate—with possession.

He pulled his hand back then, his knees hitting the bottom of the shower. His hands clutched my thighs, holding me in place, as his mouth dipped in between my soaked folds. His icy tongue moved with the utmost precision, circling around my clit. "Oh, God!"

A small moan left my lips as my hand flew to my mouth to ensure I remained quiet as the pressure that had been building inside me finally exploded. The feeling flooded my body, my knees buckling under the intensity of the pleasure that had overtaken me.

Moments later, I removed my hands—both from my mouth and the tenderness between my thighs, taking a few heavy breaths as my body relaxed, the hot water hitting my chest.

I shut the water off as I heard the bedroom doorknob click. Reaching around, I grabbed my robe, wrapped it around my body, and tied off a smaller towel around my hair.

"Hey, Sarah! Almost done!" I shouted through the door.

I didn't need to mess with makeup or do my hair tonight, as Sarah had those covered. After my Awakening, Joel performed a spell on me to mask my scent, as it lured vampires to me constantly. It worked out perfectly to go undercover in the vampire underworld, so we could take out the ones that were killing the innocent or had planned to. It also helped me find the vampires who yearned to be human again, so I could change them back.

After a few months, the plan wasn't working anymore. They knew of my existence, and they knew my face. Every time I'd get close, they'd run like scared little children in the opposite direction.

Or they would attack, and I'd have to kill them without getting any useful intel.

My friend Sarah, though, came up with another idea, and this one was brilliant.

"Okay, what look are we going for tonight?" Sarah asked as I came into my bedroom. "You said you wanted blonde hair tonight, right?"

I nodded. "Blonde, short pixie cut. Give me blue eyes, and bring them in slightly. Make them rounder, too … oh, and bigger tits."

Sarah and I busted out laughing. "This honestly is my favorite part of the weekend," she said.

She placed her hands on my face and chanted for a minute, and when she removed them, she clapped to herself.

"Look at you, beautiful!" she said, turning me around to face the floor-length bedroom mirror. She really did wonders with her power. Thankfully, we had a nice balance of what we could do between our coven and our fellow witch allies.

"Now, like before, you can't be more than twenty feet from me, or the spell wears off." She pulled out a sexy red spaghetti-strap dress from her bag. "You should wear this."

An occasional night out allowed me to dress up like this, but it was rare, especially now. The dress was stunning, so I'd have to bury the fact that I was about to show a lot more of my body than I was used to. At least most of how I looked tonight was created by magic.

"Well, what are you wearing?" I asked as Sarah pulled out another dress. This one was teal blue and strapless with sequins lining the bottom. "That's gorgeous, and it matches your eyes."

"Tilly's Place had a sale last weekend. I couldn't pass this one up," she said, glancing quickly at the clock on the wall. "Okay, get dressed. I'm eager to see what you look like in that." Sarah bundled up her dress and padded to the bathroom, shutting the door behind her.

As the door clicked, footsteps rounded the corner outside the bedroom doorway. I turned around as Caleb entered.

"Mercy, is that you?" he asked as our eyes met. Sarah always made me look different each time she cast a spell on me, so this face was unfamiliar to him.

"Yeah, it's me."

Caleb sized me up and placed his hand on my head, following the blonde strands down to my ears with his fingertips.

"I need you to be careful tonight, okay?" he warned. "From what I've heard, this clan is ruthless when threatened." He let go of my hair and looked toward the bed where the red dress was laid out. "Are you wearing *that*?" Caleb's tone was harsh and judgmental.

"Yes, Caleb. I'm wearing *that*." I rolled my eyes and moved toward the dress. I held it up and smiled to myself. "It's beautiful, isn't it?"

"You shouldn't wear that. You're supposed to be inconspicuous, remember?"

I stared at him, deadpan.

Since when did Caleb get to decide what I wear out?

"Yes, I'm aware, but I also need vampires to share their dirty little secrets with me. Maybe if I dress like this, they'll be more willing." I placed the dress on the bed again.

When I turned back around, he had stepped an inch closer and placed his hand on my cheek, caressing my soft skin under the pad of his fingertips. I stiffened and backed up. "What are you doing? Stop," I warned.

Caleb dropped his hand, but he didn't move back. If anything, I could have sworn he moved only in a blink, closing the space between us.

"Still nothing, huh? Just like that." He snapped his fingers and frowned.

"Are you back to this again?" I asked, becoming annoyed; he couldn't just let it go. "A year later, you're still giving me shit about what I did."

He stared at me, but it was distant. He lowered his brows and closed his eyes. "I'm not the one being selfish here," he said before opening them again. His hurtful words caused my body to tense.

I balled my hands into fists as a rush of heat coursed through my body. Just hearing those accusatory words come out of his mouth made my heart pound hard against my chest, and for a moment, I felt my powers tremble inside of me, just begging to come out and slap him.

"Removing my feelings for you and Dorian was the single most selfless thing I've ever done. I remember feeling something for you," I admitted, still not relaxing my fists. "I *still* remember it every fucking day. It's all there in my head, taunting me."

My shoulders finally relaxed when those words left my lips, as if I had been holding in a deep breath. Thankfully, letting out my frustration had weirdly calmed me, but only enough for my heart rate to slow down and my hands to loosen. I was still angry that he was bringing it up again, especially now. Did I have to hurt him so badly that he'd finally let it go and leave me alone?

"I sacrificed my feelings for you and Dorian for the greater good of the coven and for everyone who relies on us to protect them," I continued, trying not to glare so intently into his beautiful, sad eyes. Sometimes it was hard to look away, but I had to, so I turned my eyes to the ground. "I don't regret it." My voice was stern and level. "I don't regret any of it."

A stabbing pain ached in my chest as those words left my mouth. Did I mean them? No, I didn't. I regretted what I did every single day since it happened. Was I a better fighter because of it, though? Yes. Anytime those feelings stirred inside me, the spell would smother them out. It made me angry that I had to keep fighting it. But that anger was soon replaced with hope. Hope that Caleb would let it go, so we could complete the mission that drove me to cast that spell to begin with.

"Mercy—"

I held up my hand. "I also remember the lies," I said, hoping if I drove a nail into his heart, it'd make me feel better. Help him move on and let go of the past. "I remember the deception you showed me over and over again for your own selfish needs. Even if I could reverse this spell and feel something for you again, I wouldn't. I don't *want* to love you!"

Caleb slowly closed his eyes, and I felt shame flicker through me. Those words had to have cut through him like a knife. Those words may have been the worst thing I could have ever said. But I didn't know any other way to get through to him. It had been a year. He needed to move on.

"We're a *coven.* That is all we will ever be to each other. We will never have what we did over three hundred years ago. It's done. We are done."

I didn't mean for the words to come off so harshly. My own pain was shrouded under a mask I wore to keep Caleb from believing there was hope for us. In the end, it would hurt him more.

Caleb was more than just a coven member to me. He was a friend and even as close as family, but it had been a year, and he still hadn't stopped fighting for us to have what we had so long ago.

Caleb's face was unreadable, his mouth set in a flat line before turning away from me as we heard the bathroom door open.

Sarah appeared from the bathroom, her brown hair curled in tight waves and her dress snug against her thin frame, with high silver heels. "What did I just walk in on?" she asked.

I shook my head. "Caleb was just leaving."

He glanced at me but only briefly. His eyes stayed on Sarah's as if I were no longer in the room. "If the two of you don't text me on the hour, every hour, I'm coming out there to get you."

Caleb wouldn't even look at me. My words had hurt him so severely that he couldn't even respond to what I had just said. Instead, he stormed out, slamming the door behind him, which caused me to jump back.

"I really hurt him this time," I said.

"Can you blame him? Caleb's been in love with you for over three hundred and twenty years. You only remember the beginning of falling in love with him when the two of you were kids in your previous life and what the coven bond made you feel a year ago. Caleb remembers *being* with you, mind, body, and soul, during the gap of memories you lost. It's not easy for him to let something like that go," Sarah countered.

After Tatyana had rescued Dorian and the witches, all hell broke loose at the lair where Maurice had held me captive. Maurice and

Kyoko fled and went into hiding. Rumors had spread across the supernatural world that he and Kyoko had taken off to the west coast. Many of the vampires who resided in that mansion found new clans to join, and the human captives were finally set free. Some, though, came for help to turn them back, using my blood to save them.

Dorian and Noah stayed together, and it took me several days to track them down. Once I found them, I'd looked Dorian in his eyes, just as I had with Caleb, and I'd told him what I had done and felt. He understood why I had done it, but I still hurt him. The only communication I now had with Dorian was a few text messages every month to check in with each other.

That was our agreement. Other than that, we've not spoken to or seen each other in months.

I had offered Dorian my wrist to drink from that night, but he refused. He said he wanted to stay a vampire so that if I ever needed saving, he could be there for me to fight by my side.

I eyed the clock. "We have to go; the club opened an hour ago. Roland had his friend Marcus put our names on the list, so we shouldn't have a problem getting underground."

"Okay, let's go, then," Sarah said, grabbing my hand. "If anything goes south, I'll turn you back so you can fight in your own skin and put the fear of God in those vamps."

I smiled at her. "Damn straight, I will."

CHAPTER 5

MERCY

"Hold out your wrists," the burly man said at the front of the line of The Black Horse. He was twice as big as Caleb, towering over Sarah and me, but he had a kind face like a big teddy bear.

Before we arrived, I was confident everything would go as smoothly as planned, even though it rarely did. My nerves clutched my throat when the man reached out to wrap a black band around our wrists and stepped to the side to usher us in. Everything tonight relied on Sarah's magic holding to conceal my identity and the two of us getting the answers before it faded away.

A smile reached my face as all the tension I had been holding in was released when I heard the music. I had to lean close to Sarah's ear to talk to her, as the music was deafening.

"We need to find a guy named Marcus," I told her.

"What does he look like?" she shouted.

"Middle-aged Black man with a bald head. He told Roland he'd be wearing a gray silk suit and red tie. He's Roland's contact!" I shouted back in her ear.

"Is he a vampire?" she asked.

"Witch, actually." I looked around the room. "Roland said we could trust him." I raised one eyebrow.

"Ah, you don't, do you?" she questioned.

I shrugged nonchalantly. "I don't trust anyone associated with Roland, but I'll hear him out."

"Well, let's keep an eye out and tread lightly, then," Sarah said.

We scanned the bar, seeing only a few couples sitting beside each other and the bartender drying off the glasses. "Let's get a drink," I shouted over the music.

Sarah and I made a choice a year ago, once we reconnected after Tatyana rescued her from Maurice's lair, to stop drinking and stay sober. Alcohol and drugs suppressed our powers; if we were going in with magic on our side, we couldn't risk it. However, not having a drink would look suspicious in a bar, so we decided to each order a cocktail and pretend to sip it.

Over in the corner by the bar, leaning against green velvet curtains on the stage, I spotted a cute college-aged guy with hair so blond it almost looked white, staring right at us.

"Three o'clock," I said.

She turned toward the stage. "Alright, he's hot, though he looks human." With a shrug of her shoulder, she added, "Though I've been wrong before. Maybe try talking to him. See what you can find out."

I skipped in his direction just as the music changed to a song I didn't recognize, and thankfully, it wasn't as loud.

Looking over my shoulder before I reached him, I spotted Sarah moving closer so we could stay at least twenty feet from each other. She sat near the stage and pretended to drink her cocktail.

"Hey. I'm Cassy." I held out my hand for him to shake. "You seem kind of bored over here by yourself."

"Devon," he said with a playful smile. "Nice to meet you." Devon shook my hand and looked down at my drink. "And what are you drinking?"

"Cranberry and vodka," I replied.

"Did they not make the drink the way you like it?" he asked.

"What do you mean?" I asked in an uncertain tone.

"I've seen you *pretend* to drink that cocktail but not actually drink."

Observant.

If I didn't drink now, and this guy was working with the vampire clan beneath us, he'd know something was up.

Slowly, I sipped my drink, careful not to take too much. After flashing Devon a fake smile, I added, "Honestly, I'm too much of a lightweight. I've been taking it slow."

Devon smirked at me, then turned toward a pretty brunette walking by us. I used this opportunity to mouth the word "drink" to Sarah.

"Yeah." His voice pulled my attention back to him. "Most girls can't handle what we men can put down," he said.

Yikes. This guy is a fucking tool.

Devon grabbed my glass. "Wow, you really pounded that down in the last few minutes, didn't you?" he said. I looked at the drink he now held, and it was just as full as it had been moments ago. I glanced over at Sarah, and she smiled with a shrug.

Ah, she's making it *appear* empty in his eyes.

Devon set my full glass on the counter, which he saw as empty, and walked toward the bar. A minute later, he returned with another cocktail and a beer.

We clinked our glasses, and both sipped our drinks.

"How about we go downstairs and talk?" he suggested. "I mean, we can do other things if you'd like, but you look like the type of girl who needs a man to treat her like a queen first before she opens up to him."

My nostrils flared, and I felt my cheeks warm. I was doing everything I could to not smack the shit out of him.

Another forced smile. "Sure," I said. "Are you talking about the underground club?"

"Ah," he hummed, "you know about the club?"

"My friend and I are on the list," I said, tossing in a wink. "You have no idea how much we've been thinking about it tonight. To meet an actual vampire and—"

"Easy, wildcat," he interrupted, bringing his arm over my shoulder and pulling me in close, where I could smell his minty breath and strong cologne. "You don't want to appear too eager, or they won't let you stay. Remember, vampires enjoy the *hunt*. Act afraid, and they'll do whatever the fuck you want them to do to you tonight." Devon smirked, dropped his arm to his side, and took my hand. "Come on, let's go." After Sarah came over and introduced herself as Mandy, he gestured to a hallway that led to the back of the bar. "After you, ladies."

The hallway that led to the club was wrapped around the back of the building and descended underground. We came to a door with a shade pulled over a glass window that lifted when Devon knocked three times. A woman with sharp, feminine features whose obsidian hair was pulled in a tight bun on the top of her head pushed her face close to the little window to look at us with her bright emerald eyes. "State your name," she said.

"Devon Nordic." The woman waited before Devon placed two fingers on his neck and turned to face us. "They're with me," he told her.

"They're not getting in without their names on the list," she said, her red eyes turning brighter and her fangs protruding as if she was trying to intimidate us.

"I said they're with me," he shot back, his tone harsh and elevated.

"Cassy Thomas and Mandy Rain," I told the woman at the door, and we both placed two fingers on our necks. She looked down at a sheet of paper and back at us, then closed the window flap, and we waited again.

Devon turned to us and shrugged. My steady heart was the one thing that didn't give us away. We were about to enter uncharted territory and weren't sure what to expect. I held my breath and exchanged a glance with Sarah as the door swung open. The tiny woman appeared in the doorway, gesturing for us to enter. Once inside, we looked around. Colored lights flashed all around us, but the music was not as loud as it was upstairs.

I took another sip of my cocktail but just enough to show Devon I was drinking it. I leaned toward Sarah's ear. "Let's dance for a few minutes, so we can look somewhat normal before we snoop around."

"Good idea," Sarah agreed. We looked around to see where Devon had gone, as he was no longer standing by us. "Where did that douchebag go?" she asked.

I turned toward another stage where the club DJ was stationed and spotted Devon talking to a man seated in the VIP area. The man looked to be in his mid-forties, with jet-black hair and deep brown eyes that looked stark against his lightly tanned skin. He had a very handsome face, and even while he was seated on a large red leather couch, I could tell that he was tall.

At his feet was a human girl lying on the floor, surrounded by a group of vampires. Several bite marks ran along the side of her neck and inner thighs. The males had been feasting on her for what looked to be for hours. Two of the males took turns licking the clotting blood dripping down her legs, and a female vampire with golden-brown skin and rosy lips began to bite the human woman's neck again, creating fresh wounds to devour.

"Over there," I said, nodding their way. "It's fucking disgusting what they're doing, but we don't have a choice."

Devon caught our attention and waved us over.

This is too easy.

I didn't get less than ten feet near them before the middle-aged man he had been talking to locked eyes with me, and visions came rolling in.

Wait, a vision?! Here?

Shit!

The man ran by my side in a field next to my old home in Salem. I looked to be about six years old.

"Try to grab one, Mercy," he said. "Over here."

I looked above me as fireflies swarmed around us. I lifted a copper cup, and a few fireflies landed inside, so I cupped the top with my hand to keep them from flying away. "They're so pretty,

Papa," I said, and my vision returned to the beat of Ellie Goulding's song, *Lights*.

Oh shit!

"Cassy!" I heard Devon shout, and I realized I was still gawking at this man I now knew as my father from the seventeenth century: Alexander Winchester.

"This is Alex, ladies. He owns the club," Devon explained.

I looked over at Sarah with my jaw clenched. I had to turn away from them because I had difficulty concealing the shocked look on my face.

Yeah, Alexander looked a little different from my previous visions of him, but seeing him at the club was unexpected. I honestly believed he was dead.

Sarah held up a finger. "If you'll excuse us, gentlemen," she said, "Please give us a minute." Sarah gripped my arm and pushed me over to the side.

"What the fuck was that?" she asked. "What are you doing?"

"We need to go."

"Wait, why? What is it?"

"That's my father."

"Deadbeat dad?"

"No, that man sitting on that chair is my father from my past life. Alexander," I explained, running my hand through my hair. "Fuck! Of course, he'd look a bit different from how he did back then. I've had visions of him before, but they were brief. Vampires kidnapped him when I was a teenager in the seventeenth century." I looked over at Alexander, staring at us, along with Devon.

Fuck. We need to leave.

Sarah shook her head. "It's not like he'll recognize you. We came here to learn more about this clan, and what better way to do it than getting in close with their leader?"

"My fucking father!" I corrected, practically shouting.

"Shhh! Jesus, Mercy. Get it together."

"Okay. Okay." I looked over and smiled. "We've already drawn enough attention to ourselves since we've been here, so let's make the connection and get the fuck out of here."

She nodded and grabbed my hand, leading me back to the men.

"Welcome back," Devon said.

Alexander stood and reached out his hand. I held mine out, and he delicately grabbed it and kissed the top. I gulped and felt a hard lump slowly move down my throat. Sarah gave him her hand, and he did the same with her.

"Welcome to my club, little humans," my father said. "Drinks are on the house tonight, alright? Devon is my right hand, so anything you need, just ask him." His eyes lingered on mine.

If I weren't so overwhelmed with nerves, I would have been more thrilled to have gained the trust of Alexander's right hand.

Devon then gestured to the bar, and after an uncomfortable stare-down with my father, we followed. Though I was still in disguise, there was a tiny part of my thoughts that he'd still figure it out. I needed to get as far away from him as I could.

"Here's some water." Devon handed Sarah and me each a bottle of water. "It gets hotter down here than the rest of the club, so you need to hydrate. Those cocktails won't do it."

We thanked him and drank at least half our water before working our way over to the dance floor.

As we met at the center of the club, I spotted Roland's friend Marcus standing against the wall by the bar.

"Wait here," I told Sarah. "I found Marcus … I think."

Marcus wasn't far from where we were standing, so the distance kept me close enough to Sarah, so her spell didn't wear off.

"Are you Marcus?" I asked him. He nodded and gestured for me to follow him, but I shook my head. "Right here is fine, please." I glanced over at my father and Devon to make sure they weren't watching us, which they thankfully weren't.

Turning my head back to Marcus, I felt a wave of vertigo. I blinked and tried to focus, to pull my attention back to him. It *was* hot in the club, and the heat was getting to me.

"Roland said you're the guy I should talk to." I quickly glanced at Sarah, who was now dancing with Devon. He placed his hands on her hips as she moved back, grinding into him.

What the hell is she doing?

"I am," Marcus answered, pulling my attention back to him. "Mercy, you're going to need to act a little inconspicuous."

"I'm finding it a bit difficult," I said. "I just met my father."

Marcus grinned. "I can see that."

My eyes narrowed on his. "Did Roland know?"

Marcus shook his head. "I may be lifelong friends with Roland, but even I have secrets to protect my clan."

I nodded because I got it. Roland was a piece of shit, and I wouldn't trust him either.

"Sorry, I don't have a lot of time," I continued. "I need you to make up a story about how we've known each other for years and that my friend Mandy and I can be trusted. We need you to make us permanent members of this club. Keep us on the list and tell them we're humans with connections." I paused, a smile forming on my lips. "Oh, and tell them I love to let vampires drink from me."

"That's a great way to get caught," he pointed out. "Once they notice their vampire clan is getting smaller, your plan is over."

"You underestimate me, Marcus." I winked at him and took a step back. "But right now, I need to rescue my friend. We'll be in touch."

As I walked toward Sarah, my head pounded, and a wave of nausea hit me. The club spun, and I felt the bile reaching my throat.

We weren't even drinking.

When I reached her, her hair was sticky with sweat, and mascara smudged around her dazed eyes.

"Hey, are you okay?" I asked her. When she didn't respond, I said, "Alright, I'll go grab us some more water."

"How about some fresh air instead?" Devon suggested, grabbing Sarah by the arm and gripping mine firmly just as I was about to collapse to the floor. He helped keep us both steady and walked us toward the back of the club. Devon's grip tightened, his nails digging into my skin.

Shit.

I felt my dress loosen around the chest, and when I looked down, my breast size was shrinking. "Oh, fuck," I cursed to myself, knowing full well he had heard it.

As we walked past a mirror on the hallway wall, I quickly glanced up. Sarah was losing control of the spell. My hair was getting darker as we walked by the window, but thankfully, Devon hadn't looked down at me yet. We stumbled through a doorway, and I looked over at Sarah, whose eyes were shutting. She was clearly not herself, either, as she lost her balance and almost fell over. I barely caught her before she hit the ground, but I almost stumbled myself as Devon still had a firm grip on my arm.

Oh, great. The asshole drugged us through the water bottles.

"Right here, ladies." Devon gestured toward a black leather sofa. When I looked up, he grinned at me, flashing his perfect white teeth. This creep was a fucking rapist, and he wasn't going to get away with this.

Not tonight. Not to anyone, ever!

A moment later, I heard the unbuckling of his belt. I couldn't hold Sarah's slouching body anymore, so I lowered her to the couch next to us.

The curtain at the back of the room shielded us from the rest of the club.

Great, not that anyone would come to our rescue, even if they saw what was happening.

I looked around and then back up at him. My head fogged over, and nausea reached the top of my throat.

"Mmm," he hummed. "Cassy, looking fucking *hot* in your dark, long hair." He gave my hair an aggressive tug, pulling me forward. "Is that even your real name?"

A rush of nausea hit my throat again.

"Burn in fucking hell, asshole," I said, but my threat came out weak and shaky.

Devon laughed and grabbed my knee. "It's a shame your chest is getting smaller, though. Those big tits were sexy on you."

I jerked my leg away from the grip he had on it and looked at Sarah.

"Sarah, wake up," I cried while ignoring his rough hand, which landed on my knee again. Slowly, my blurred gaze looked up, locking with his. "Look, scumbag," I managed to mumble out through a shaky breath. "I don't think you realize what you've gotten yourself into. If I were you, I'd think twice before you touch us." My warning sounded pathetic. The room spun again, and all I wanted to do was shut my eyes. But if I did, he would rape us both. I needed to keep his focus on me.

Devon was on me before I could throw out another threat. He shoved at my chest, slamming me hard against the back of the couch, straddled both sides of my thighs, and squeezed his legs together, his erection digging into me. He pinched my hips with his knees so I couldn't move. My hands moved up to blast him away with my powers, but nothing happened.

This isn't going to happen! I need to fight harder without my magic.

Panic rose in my chest, and my stomach felt like a hard rock was pressing against it. Devon needed to have his ass handed to him by Sarah's and my powers combined, but the drugs knocked us down defenseless.

We will not be raped.

"Are you a human?" I asked while Devon placed his hands on my chest and rubbed my body, gliding his hands up and down my breasts. I tried to dig my nails into his wrist to stop him, but he slapped my hand away like I was an annoying fly.

Devon didn't answer me. He simply opened his mouth, and fangs protruded. "Seeing how you disguised your appearance, my only guess is that you're a witch." He glanced over at Sarah. "Or she is."

"Sarah," I said sluggishly, but my eyes stayed on his. "Are you still with me?"

There was no answer from her. She was already fading away.

I tilted my neck, exposing my skin, hoping he'd be tempted to drink instead.

"Why don't you just drink from me," I said. "I know blood is more tempting than sexual pleasure. This is what you really want, right?"

Maybe if I asked, it would entice him, but it was clear he was only interested in one thing, and it wasn't my blood. His hands were now by my thighs, pulling up my dress.

I froze, screaming in my head over and over, but no sound came out. The drugs were in full effect now, rendering me paralyzed.

Anything but this.

My body went completely numb, and my hands dropped to my sides. I closed my eyes and tried to go to another place, but suddenly, Devon's grimy hands left my thighs, and the pressure against my hips was released. When my eyes shot open, I saw Devon shoot across the room with a trail of flames behind him. I turned to the doorway, and Caleb stood there, fire blazing from his fingertips, and his eyes were brighter than I had ever seen them.

At that moment, I thanked God I had forgotten to text him on the hour and that we were safe.

CHAPTER 6

MERCY

"Did you kill him?" I asked as I awoke in Caleb's bed the following day.

When he didn't respond, I looked at him, and an unsettling feeling hit the pit of my stomach. He was seated across the bedroom in a chair facing the open window.

Caleb's hands rested on his face, his elbows on his knees. His shoulders slumped, and his stare was empty and distant when he finally looked at me. The last time I saw Caleb like this was a year ago when I told him we would never be together.

He wouldn't answer, so I pressed another question. "Fine, where's Sarah?" I only needed to hear him speak.

"She slept in the guest bedroom downstairs," he said finally.

Relief washed over me. Sarah was safe. We were both *safe*.

"Is she ... is she okay, at least?" I asked.

He nodded. "I think so, but she's not woken up since I laid her in bed. You'll want to speak with her when she's awake. Don't worry, I slept in Roland's room since he's still out of town," he explained, as if he had been reading my thoughts. He probably assumed I thought we shared a bed together. I wouldn't have cared; we would have just slept. Despite our past, I trusted Caleb with my life.

"Does the coven know where I am?" I asked. "They'll worry since I didn't come home last night."

He nodded and moved in my direction then laid down next to me, creating enough distance so we didn't touch. "Yes, he's dead," he said. "After his body turned to ashes, I swept him outside the back door into the parking lot. Your cover isn't broken. He'll just be a missing person to them."

"To my *father*," I corrected, watching the gloom on his face turn to surprise as his brows raised.

He pursed his lips and blinked. "What are you talking about? Your father?"

Still staring at him, I said, "Alexander is alive."

Caleb's eyes grew wide, tipping his head to the side. "He was there?"

"He wasn't just there. He's the leader of the Black Horse Clan and the owner of the fucking club," I explained. "He never knew it was me, though. Sarah's spell didn't fade until we left the main dance floor. He didn't see me transition back."

"Jesus Christ," he said, letting out a heavy breath. "This changes things a bit, doesn't it?"

"No. I'm not going to let emotions change things. Alexander is a vampire who runs one of the most dangerous vampire clans on the east coast. I won't hesitate if I have to kill him," I said.

Caleb's phone beeped, pulling his attention away from me. I waited as he read an incoming text message, then turned to face me again.

"It's Melissa. She found a fresh tattoo on the inside of Tippy's lip. She thinks the person who killed him did it postmortem. She's sending me the image now."

We waited a minute, and the image came through. Caleb clicked on it, opening it to its full size. The tattoo was of a black horse with red eyes. We looked at each other and back at the image. "A vampire murderer is leaving us a signature. That's a new one for us," I said.

"At least we were right about who's doing this." Caleb closed down his phone screen. "It's obvious that whoever did this wanted us to know he's part of the Black Horse Clan. They're drawing you out," he said. "Let's be one step ahead."

"We always are." My phone rang, but I didn't answer. I didn't even look down to see who it was. "I don't want to train today," I said, not giving Caleb my reason because he didn't need one to understand my need for a break.

He shifted his body to face me, nuzzling his neck into the pillow. "I wanted to kill every fucking vampire in that club last night after I saw what that piece of shit was going to do." He shut his eyes tightly, and when he opened them back up, the amber in his eyes was brighter, more vibrant.

"I know." I placed my hand on his cheek, but as soon as I touched his skin, he shifted to turn away from me and sat up on the bed.

Awesome. I really hurt him this time.

He slid off the mattress and looked down at me, but my head still rested on the pillow.

"I have a few errands to run today," he said. "Stay as long as you need. I drove you back in my car last night, but I had Sarah's car towed here."

"I'll leave her the keys and order a ride to take me home," I said.

He nodded but wouldn't look at me again. My heart ached as he walked away. It killed me to see Caleb in this much pain. As I heard the front door shut, my mind immediately drifted to the day I left him alone in front of my house. Everyone had been waiting for me inside.

After I took away my feelings for him, Caleb fell to his knees, his skin digging into the gravel, but he didn't move. I didn't feel the need to comfort him or tell him it would be okay. For him, it would never be okay. Nothing I said would have mattered.

My phone rang again, pulling me out of my memory, and this time, I looked down. It was Dorian.

Dorian!

Why the hell is he calling me? We'd agreed he'd never call me, only text messages.

"Hello?" I said, my voice shaky.

"Mercy, it's Noah."

My heart rate sped up, and butterflies roiled through my stomach.

"Hey, what's going on? Why are you calling from Dorian's phone?" I asked, panicked.

"Dorian's fine. He needs you, though. Can you get to Three Brother's Tavern after sundown?"

"Of course, I'll meet him."

Noah snickered on the other line.

"What?" I asked.

"Dorian's just really excited to see you."

I rolled my eyes. "Bye, Noah. Tell him I'll be there at six."

I hung up and headed for the shower. After getting ready, I texted Laurie to let her know I'd swing by tomorrow afternoon to help with a few household items and take Cami out.

As I exited the mansion, I glanced at Sarah, who slept peacefully in the downstairs bedroom. She was stronger than most, but I knew she'd need some time to process what had happened and had almost happened at the club.

I sent her a text to call me when she woke up.

—ell—

When I entered Lily's Café, I spotted Bradley sitting at a table toward the back with a book in his hand.

"Hey," I called. "What's going on?"

Bradley placed the book on the table and looked over at Lily, who had just finished helping a customer. "After she locks up the shop, we'll head to Salem Harbor."

I looked through him as the realization registered with me. We had spread my mother's ashes over Salem Harbor. I looked down at my phone and eyed the date on my clock.

Ah, shit.

Bradley's eyes widened, and he placed his hands in his lap. "I'm so sorry. I thought that was why you were here."

I shook my head. "I understand why Lily didn't tell me," I said. "It's fine."

Lily interrupted us. "Hey, Mercy. What brings you here? We were just heading out to do some shopping."

Right.

"I'm coming with you to Salem," I said, cutting her off from continuing her lie.

Her eyes went wide, and she gave Bradley an accusatory glare. He looked down as if she scared him. It's not his fault she was keeping this from me.

I killed my mom a year ago today. I missed her, regardless of what she did to me. Being there where we laid her ashes would be hard, and I understood why Lily didn't want me to go, but I hated that I wasn't given a choice.

"I'm sorry," she said. "I honestly didn't think you'd want to go."

I stood and walked to the cash register, and Lily followed. When I turned around to face her, I asked, "Do you blame me for her death, Lily?"

She gasped, "No. God, no. You did what you had to do. I know you blame yourself for what happened. You could barely stand the last time we were there when we put her ashes in the harbor. I didn't think you could handle it, especially with everything going on right now with you and the coven."

I secured my purse over my shoulder and flashed her a warm smile. "Well, I want to go."

When she smiled back, Bradley, watching us from across the café, walked toward us and handed Lily her keys.

As hard as this was going to be, we'd get through it together.

⸺⁓⁓⸺

We picked up Joel on the way, who looked surprised to see me in the car, but I flashed him a smile, hoping it would help everyone relax and stop being so goddamn weird around me.

Once we reached Salem Harbor, we hurried over to the lighthouse, where we sprinkled her ashes and sat on the rocks.

For the next hour, we talked about her life before she started changing into someone we didn't recognize. Because Bradley was with us, we had to tread lightly when we spoke about my mom. For all he knew, she had a mental illness and died of a brain tumor. We weren't far off from the truth, just omitted a few details.

"I wish I had known her," Bradley added.

"You would have liked her. She was a huge fan of Star Trek," I said, giggling quietly.

"I like Star *Wars*," he said, sounding offended, and everyone barked out a laugh. Everyone except for Bradley. I laughed so hard that tears welled up in my eyes. I wasn't sure if the tears were from grief or happiness, but either way, the sudden change in my mood was what I needed to relax and not care about anything else.

"You're such a nerd, sweetie, but I love you," Lily said, squeezing his hand. He finally joined in on the laughter, but I could tell there was a slight discomfort beneath it all.

"Well, they *are* different," Bradley said, and this only made us chuckle harder.

I tapered off my laugh, stood up, wiped the tears from my eyes, and strode toward the water. I placed my hand on the surface, my fingers lingering above the water, and swished around. "We'll be back in a year," I said to the wind.

Joel and Lily suggested we grab a drink or two before heading back. Bradley didn't drink much, so he volunteered to drive us home.

"We should have teleported," I suggested once I had downed my third cocktail. I kept my voice low, and in a joking manner in case Bradley overheard.

"True," Joel agreed. He and Lily snickered. They were about four beers in and drunk as a couple of skunks.

"We should probably get going, guys," Bradley suggested. "We're going to hit traffic."

We all agreed, closed our tab, and headed toward the parking lot.

As we neared the car, it dawned on me that I had to meet Dorian in less than two hours. "Hey, Bradley. Can you drop me off at Three Brother's Tavern? I'll get a driver home after that."

I flashed Lily a tiny smile when she turned to me. "Dorian wants to meet tonight."

Lily smirked. "Really?" she said as if it amused her.

I shot her my best fake smile back. "It's nothing. He only wants to talk."

"Uh, huh," Lily mumbled, narrowing her eyes at me.

I rolled my eyes. "Dorian hasn't seen me in a year, and I'm about to show up buzzed as hell."

"Buzzed? Oh, honey. You're drunk," Lily teased.

"I have two hours to sober up," I said. "So, we should get going at least."

As I climbed into the car, my eyes darted to a restaurant on the other side of the street. I was tipsy at this point, closer to drunk, but I could have sworn I saw Maurice.

Maurice!

My stomach lurched, and I tapped Lily on the shoulder. "Lily, it's Maurice," I said as I pointed to a man sitting at a table with another woman inside the restaurant. I shook my head, squinting my eyes again.

Was I just being paranoid?

"There's no way he's still in Salem," Lily said, pulling my attention toward her. "You all agreed that his threat was empty, and he'd be long gone by now."

I looked in that direction again, but the man I thought was Maurice was gone. The sun shined brightly outside, so, rationally, I knew it wasn't him. He'd have burned up even if he were inside a building. He was on the west coast, hiding like a rat.

My eyes were blurred at this point. I had to be seeing things. When my rational thoughts outweighed the idea that my greatest enemy was fifty feet away, I shook it out and convinced myself I was imagining things, and I didn't see anything.

CHAPTER 7

MERCY

I entered the tavern and spotted Dorian sitting in the back corner booth. I wasn't as drunk as I had been, but I was sure he'd still see it on my face.

Dorian's head was down, and his fingers lightly tapped the table. As I approached, I noticed he looked slightly different from the last time we had seen each other a year ago. His hair was a few inches longer, almost to the bottom of his ears. He wasn't wearing all black like he always did. Today, he wore a red T-shirt and blue jeans, with a leather jacket zipped up to his chest. I would never pin Dorian as a vampire, but maybe that was his intention. He looked so handsome, and my heart began to thump against my ribs the closer I got to the table.

As I sat down and barely missed the seat, I caught myself and slid down into the booth. Heat flushed up my neck into my scalp.

Great.

I hoped to God he didn't feel my embarrassment, but I knew it was written all over my blushed cheeks.

Dorian chuckled under his breath. "Mercy, have you been drinking?" he asked.

I huffed. "No." Then I fidgeted with my fingers under the table. "I had a few drinks a couple of hours ago, but I'm fine." He opened his mouth to speak again, but I cut him off. "Is everything okay? Why did you have Noah call?"

"You asked me not to call you myself." His deep, soothing voice reminded me of some of the little things I missed about him. Dorian's lips pinched together as if trying to hold back a laugh.

I kicked him hard under the table, and he winced. "That's not funny. I thought something bad happened to you."

"Did you worry about me?" he asked, as if genuinely curious. "Can you even feel concerned for others?" I didn't think he meant for those words to come off so harshly, but it hurt nonetheless, especially from Dorian. A year ago, when I'd first performed the spell, I didn't give him that much of an explanation when I told him what I had done.

"Just because my romantic feelings are gone doesn't mean I'm void of feeling empathy," I explained. "I'm not a robot, Dorian. I'll always care about you."

That was deep. Too deep for us right now. It had to be the liquor talking, because, though I genuinely cared about Dorian and Caleb, I avoided telling them that. I didn't want them to get the wrong impression and think there was any way to win me back. Especially since I couldn't give either of them my entire heart.

Dorian regarded me silently right before a slight smile pulled at his lips. That was precisely why I should not have said that. He was pleased with my words, though I tried to make sure he understood there was no hope for us.

"Why am I here? And where have you and Noah been living?"

He ignored my questions and waved down a server. Once she came to our table, she handed Dorian a menu.

"She'll be ordering," he told her, handing the menu over to me.

I looked up at her. "Just a coffee, please." I handed her back the menu.

She huffed, clearly annoyed. "Are you sure? We've got a lot to choose from. We've got burgers, salads, and we serve breakfast all day—"

"Just coffee," I said. "Please."

She squinted, snatched the menu from my hands, and walked off toward the kitchen.

"I heard about what happened in East Greenwich," Dorian said.

I studied him for a few seconds before I asked, "How did you know about that?"

"Sarah called me. She felt you and your coven would need all the help you could get," Dorian explained. "Don't get mad at her."

"I'm not mad," I said. "I just didn't realize the two of you talked."

"We don't, really. Not like you think. Sarah and I knew each other the entire time she was in the lair, so she checks in now and then. We were friends, too."

It never crossed my mind that, though she was a prisoner, she had made friends while inside, even with those deemed as enemies.

I wondered how much she had told him. I still hadn't spoken to Sarah since she woke up earlier. She'd only sent a quick text telling me she was okay.

"You think it's that clan in Providence?" Dorian asked, changing the subject. He probably sensed how uncomfortable the conversation was making me feel. Also, how much did she tell him about what was going on?

I nodded. "Caleb suspects, anyway. The killer tattooed a black horse on the inside of the victim's lip. It's the clan's logo. We've learned that they moved here a year ago from New Orleans. They'd been quiet since they came here, but the murder happened just a few weeks after the club opened. We all know that when vampires are up to shady shit, they create a secured lair." Since I wasn't sure how much Sarah had told him, this could be a surprise. "The leader is—" I shifted in my seat.

"Is?" he repeated.

"Alexander Winchester," I confessed.

Dorian's eyes went wide. "Well, I didn't see that one coming."

"Yeah, none of us did."

"Then let me help you. For all the clan knows, I'm on the vampires' side. I can help get information."

I shook my head. There was no way Dorian needed to get involved. He had already sacrificed himself by helping me get out of Maurice's lair a year ago and almost got himself killed. I wasn't going to have his life on my hands again.

"Absolutely not," I said. "It's too dangerous. We already had an incident last night, so we need to regroup and decide what to do next."

"What incident?" he asked, the pitch of his voice rising a notch.

Fuck. I shouldn't have said that. I didn't need Dorian worrying about me, too.

"Nothing," I snapped. "We have it handled. Sarah shouldn't have called you."

"Then let Noah help," he suggested. "He's a shapeshifter. He can be the eyes and ears you need when it's difficult to get into the darker places."

That was one refreshing thing about Dorian. He didn't argue with me like Caleb did every fucking second. Dorian didn't question me when I made a decision about something. He respected it. But he was also right about having Noah help us. Having as many supernatural beings on our side as possible would give us the upper hand.

I considered his words. "I'll think about it," I said as I climbed out of the booth. Dorian moved next to me so swiftly that my hair blew to the side. "Show off." I smiled.

He placed his hands under my jawline. I felt a chill on the back of my arms from the coldness of his fingers. The more his touch lingered on my skin, the more my body responded to it. The nerves between my legs went wild, causing my stomach to twist and my body to feel aroused by his very presence. His scent caused my head to spin.

"Why do you have me text you?" he whispered. "If you feel nothing, why do you care so much if I'm okay?" He brushed my cheek with the back of his fingers and slid his hands to the back of my neck, gripping tightly to keep my head from turning from his gaze. I stopped him from inching closer to me by pressing my hand to his chest, creating a gap between us. His hand dropped to his side, and he flinched.

"Goodbye, Dorian."

He reached out, gripping my elbow to stop me. "Wait, you're not driving, are you?" he asked.

"No, of course not," I said. "I'm going to call a driver."

He shook his head. "No. I'll drive you."

I wanted to leave, clear my head after our conversation, and wait until my body finally snapped out of the nonsense I felt when I was close to him. However, Dorian was being a gentleman, and I couldn't argue with that.

⁓

We drove in silence to my place, and before I stepped out, I turned to Dorian.

"Thank you," I said. "And not just for the ride, but for everything."

He bit his bottom lip and placed his hand on mine. "Call me if you need us," he said. "I'm *not* texting you anymore. I'm in your life whether you like it or not." A playful smile pulled at his lips. "Noah and I live near Goddard Park."

My eyes went wide. "You moved here?" I asked, surprised.

"We've been living here since Tatyana rescued us."

He had been living less than ten minutes from me this entire fucking year, and I hadn't a clue. I never saw him in town, so he must have gone out of his way to hide from me. Dorian was respecting my wishes, but still, that hurt to know.

I nodded and exited the car, watching him drive away until he turned the corner at the end of the street. Dorian was back in my life, and I wasn't sure what to think of it. Did I want this? Sure, I was happy to see him today, but I didn't know what that meant.

CHAPTER 8

MERCY

"They found another body," Leah told me as I climbed out of the shower, pulling my robe tight around my waist.

"What?"

"In East Greenwich again, right in the middle of Main Street. It happened last night when you were out with Dorian. We didn't find out until this morning," she explained.

I grabbed my phone from the nightstand, and there weren't any missed calls or texts from Caleb. "Does Caleb know?"

"He's the one who told me." She looked uncomfortable, avoiding eye contact. "He left early this morning to meet with Melissa." Leah looked up when I scrunched up my face, and her shoulders slumped. "Sorry. I thought you knew until I realized you were taking a shower instead of joining him at the morgue."

Waving my hand in the air, I said. "Caleb's been doing that a lot lately. I don't fucking care anymore." It was a lie, of course. I hated being left in the dark. "Thanks for letting me know, at least."

I quickly got dressed, jumped in my car, and headed to Lily's.

Once I reached a stoplight, I grabbed my cell and pulled up Sarah's number.

> **Me:** *Hey, I know we didn't get to chat on the phone yesterday. I'm heading to Lily's, then the morgue, to see what information we have about this new body found on Main. Are you doing okay?*

The light turned green, so I put my phone down, but I heard a message come in a minute later.

Once I reached another light, I looked down.

> **Sarah:** *I'm still shaken up, but I'll be fine. Please thank Caleb for me for helping us that night. Let me know what you find out.*

I sucked in a breath, relieved that Sarah was okay, and then dialed Lily, who picked up on the first ring.

"Mercy," she said, almost sounding out of breath. "Did you hear what happened? There's been another murder."

"I know," I said. "I'm almost to your house, and then I'm heading to the morgue to meet Caleb. Are you even home?"

"Yeah, we just got back. Bradley and I were on our way to the post office this morning, and they had blocked off Main Street. We jumped out and walked over to a police officer on the scene, and it was just like last time, except the body had already been taken away. They were taking pictures and trying to clear the street of pedestrians lurking around," Lily explained.

"Who was the victim?" I asked, my stomach twisting in knots, praying it wasn't someone I knew.

"Miss Darla," she answered, sadness coating her words.

I instantly felt sick to my stomach. Miss Darla was a widow whose husband had died five years ago. She mostly kept to herself and would never utter a cruel word to anyone. Whoever was doing this was a sick son of a bitch. They were picking people at random. Miss Darla and Tippy had no connection to each other whatsoever. They may have waved at each other in the marketplace, but that was it.

"Mercy?" Lily asked. "Are you still there?"

My attention snapped back to the call. "Yeah. Sorry. I feel a little left in the dark this morning."

"I thought you knew, especially after I saw Caleb. He said you've had a hard couple of days."

I heard Bradley speaking in the background.

"What's he saying?" I asked.

"Oh, just that you'd think a place like East Greenwich would be a safe haven for everyone who lives here." Lily chuckled. "Bradley thinks I should buy a gun."

I smiled at the idea of Lily with a handgun. Lily only needed the magic at her fingertips to protect herself, but we didn't need to tell Bradley about that.

⸏⸏⸏

When I arrived at the morgue, Caleb and Melissa still hadn't responded to the text I'd sent them both to open the door for me. I saw Caleb's car hidden near the back alley, so I assumed the cameras were already down. I placed my hand on the latch, using my powers to unlock it. I opened the back door and tiptoed as quietly as I could before reaching the autopsy suite.

Caleb sat against Melissa's desk, and they snickered about something. I stopped moving toward them when he placed his hand on hers, stroking his thumb over her fingers. She smiled and blushed as his lips found the crease of her neck, and his hand moved and slid up her thigh.

I'm not going to watch this show.

Steadying my breath, I scurried around the corner behind the wall. Though my feelings no longer existed, and I knew they were dating, fucking, or whatever the hell their relationship was, I hadn't witnessed it with my own eyes. Ezra just had a loud mouth and couldn't keep a secret.

Seeing Caleb with someone who wasn't me was different and confusing. It felt awkward to walk in on it. But I couldn't stand in the hall like this, or I'd get caught, which would be painfully worse.

Once I cleared my throat, Caleb quickly retracted his hand from her exposed thigh.

"Hey, sorry I'm late for the party." I glared at him, narrowing my eyes. "Hey, Melissa. Same killer?"

Melissa adjusted her shirt and climbed down from the counter, moving over to the steel table. "Yep." She pointed to Miss Darla's neck. "Right there are the same two marks Ryan Harrison had." She slipped on a pair of gloves and parted Miss Darla's lips. "Same tattoo of a black horse, too."

I over-exaggerated my glare at Caleb since he didn't even tell me he was coming here when I awoke this morning. "Looks like I need to go back to the club."

"Fuck that!" Caleb snapped.

My body tensed. I understood Caleb was scared something awful would happen to me again, but this was my call, and I wasn't going to be left in the dark because of one shitty night.

Melissa looked down, averting her eyes from us. She covered Miss Darla's face by zipping up the yellow bag and stepped back. "I need to go enter a few notes into the computer; give me like five minutes."

She hurried out, leaving Caleb and me ready to argue again.

"You're not giving me orders to stay home!" I barked back.

"The hell I am."

"This is about the coven," I reminded him. "Someone is doing this to get to us, and you can't just take over and leave me out of it."

The stubbornness of my own voice made me cringe, but Caleb was so infuriating sometimes; he brought it out of me. And I despised him for it.

"Oh, yes, I will," he threatened.

I felt an intense energy building up inside me. My magic was surging with my temper. I couldn't control it; I couldn't suppress it.

I slammed my hand onto the metal table next to me, and the energy that left me exploded through the room. It caused every piece of glass to shatter around us and metal objects to rattle violently.

Oh my God, what was that?!

The green energy leaving my fingertips blasted a second time without my control, shooting Miss Darla's table across the room and almost knocking her body off the table. I quickly backed up, holding my trembling hands against my chest to help keep my powers concealed.

"Holy shit. What the hell was that?" Caleb gasped.

Melissa quickly ran in and looked around. "You guys need to go. Now. My boss is going to fire me if he sees this!"

I looked at Caleb, who stood there with flared nostrils and cold eyes.

As I averted my eyes from him, I saw the mess in the room and instantly felt sick. This was the first time I'd lost my temper with someone who wasn't an enemy. I had no control over my powers in this state.

"Shit, Melissa. I'm so sorry," I apologized. "I'll clean this up right now."

"No," she said. "Just get out. This is why I hesitated to help you all in the first place." She pointed to the door. "Please leave."

As Caleb stared at me in disbelief, I backed up, catching a glimpse of myself in the reflection of a cabinet's broken glass pane. I didn't recognize the woman that destroyed an office with just the tips of her fingers. I breathed in shakily as I backed toward the door and ran outside to my car.

CHAPTER 9

MERCY

Cami was far from healed, but she was still the most consistent person in my life, and I needed a dose of normalcy right now.

When I walked through the door, I saw Cami sitting crossed-legged next to her mom on the couch, fiddling with her phone.

"Hey, Laurie," I called out.

When she looked up, I noticed Laurie's eyes were bloodshot and glistened with newly shed tears. "Keep the blinds closed, please; I have a headache this morning," Laurie said. "The fucking neighbor's dog wouldn't stop barking all night. There's not a damn pill I could take to shut off the noise."

I wished so badly I could help Cami's mom, but there was only so much I could do at this point.

"How about I take Cami out of the house for a bit, let you rest," I suggested.

She answered by waving her hand in the air and turned over, her face disappearing into the couch cushion.

"Cami, come on. Let's go," I said, holding out my hand.

Cami gripped her cell, placing it into her pocket when she stood up, then kissed her mom on the cheek. She had no emotion on her face; she just stared at me, waiting for the next command.

Their home was the most suffocating place I had ever been, even compared to the vampire lair they had held me hostage in this last year. Her mom kept the house disgustingly filthy, and I was the only one in their life who gave a shit to help them.

With Cami's condition, she was never able to return to college and couldn't work. Laurie sunk deeper into her alcoholism and lost her job shortly after Cami came home from the hospital. After that, I came there twice a week to sort through their mail, write and forge checks, and do some light cleaning to ensure the two of them could function. This was my obligation. I was the reason this happened to her. It was my responsibility now to make sure they were okay.

Lily's Café was only a few blocks from Cami's home, so we went there before I helped manage the house. It was the only way I could get Cami to go outside.

"I'll go get us some food," I said as we sat in the outside eating area.

Cami sat there, staring blankly out at Main Street, watching each car pass by the café.

After placing a quick order, I hurried back outside, but Cami wasn't sitting at our table.

Shit.

My heart raced as I looked around. "Cami?" I shouted, looking up and down both ends of the street.

This isn't good.

Cami was unstable. She never left the house without me; now, I had lost her. I ran down the road and poked my head into every open shop.

"Cami?" I called as I looked inside a pizza shop. I crossed the street to the other side and started with the shops directly across from the cafe.

I looked over by the post office then scanned the street, and there was Cami, standing in the middle of the road with her arms outstretched.

Oh my God.

The post office was the first building on Main Street, near the front entrance to all the shops on that side. The street peaked, then declined until it hit the post office. If someone were tearing down the road, they wouldn't see her until it was too late.

"Cami, get out of the road!" I shouted, waving my hands, but she wouldn't move or look my way.

I hurried as fast as I could, but not fast enough. A black pickup truck appeared at the top of the street, speeding down in Cami's direction. They couldn't see her. It would be impossible to slow down and avoid hitting Cami head-on.

"Get the fuck out of the road!" I yelled again.

I didn't have time.

I stopped running and pulled my hands out to the side, thrusting them forward while releasing my powers at the truck. The green light hit the vehicle like a head-on collision, causing it to fly up into the air. The truck missed Cami by only a few feet. I used my other hand to throw it to the right and into a light pole, slowing it down before it collided, easing up on impact.

Cami stood still, not even a flinch. She just looked over at the damaged truck and then at me.

Once the truck was no longer moving, I ran toward her as fast as I could and pulled her out of the road. I led her over to the post office, near some tall hedges, out of sight.

Cami had tears in her eyes, but her face stayed emotionless. "I just want this nightmare to end. Please make it stop."

My heart shattered at the absolute desperation in her voice. She was so broken, so lost in the shadow that swallowed her. Several people were coming out of the stores to see what had happened. An older man exited the truck and didn't appear to have any visible injuries. He was just a little disoriented, probably wondering what the hell had just happened.

I pulled Cami into my arms, gripping her shoulders tightly. She felt like a rag doll in my arms, as if she weren't really there. Her mind was somewhere else. Somewhere dark and haunting. I wished I could see what was happening to her. I wished my healing powers could heal her mind, but they couldn't. I tried. Even when I repeatedly failed to heal her, I kept trying.

What is happening?

I couldn't keep Cami in that house without someone watching her twenty-four-seven. Not now. She was way worse than when we first brought her home. Laurie was too far into her own issues to take up the task.

What did Kylan's sick and twisted mind do to her? Caleb had been possessed for only fifteen minutes, and he was an immortal witch. Even he mentioned he felt off for several weeks after that happened. But Cami was a fragile human that had been corrupted by darkness for days. I didn't know how to fix her.

"Alright, let's get you home," I told her. I grabbed her hand and pulled her down the sidewalk back to the car, getting her away from the growing crowd.

I have to admit her to Raven's Mental Institution. We don't have a choice.

CHAPTER 10

MERCY

I waited on Caleb's bed with my hands clasped together while he showered. My mind couldn't stop thinking about what had happened with Cami. I kept replaying the moment on the road over and over.

Leah and I had called Raven's to have her admitted. She wasn't a supernatural being, but her mental state had been caused by one. If any place could help her, it would be there. With Leah's connections, they were able to make an exception and had a room ready for Cami.

I let Laurie know I would still visit her house and help take care of it, so she was okay with her daughter leaving. Laurie may have been intoxicated most of the time, but she was coherent enough to understand that her daughter needed help. After I told her what had happened on Main Street, she cried in my arms and begged me to get Cami some help.

Since I was the reason that this had happened to her, Leah and her family were going to be covering the cost, and we'd be sending her there tomorrow morning.

I turned my attention toward Caleb's bathroom door as it opened. When Caleb emerged, steam from the shower billowed into the bedroom. There was only a towel around his waist as he moved to the dresser to pick out his pajama bottoms.

As I watched the water bead on his perfect body, I swallowed, averting my eyes for a moment, then looked up again at him. I hated it when these feelings of lust took over when I needed to think of him as only part of my coven to avoid distractions.

My body was weak; there was no doubt about that. I may not be in love with Caleb, but I wouldn't hesitate to think about him when I touched myself.

"Sorry about what happened this morning," I said, breaking away from this uncomfortable feeling, or truthfully, the lust-filled arousal.

Caleb wouldn't look at me as he sifted through his top dresser for a shirt.

"I don't know what happened," I continued, though I didn't deserve an apology. The truth was, I really should have been begging for Melissa's forgiveness. My actions could have gotten her fired, and she had been helping us for a year at significant risk to her livelihood.

After he pulled a white T-shirt over his head, he said, "I get it. You're used to running things within the coven. But *as* a coven, we're also supposed to look after each other. Your dad is the leader of that clan, which complicates things. You can't be involved in this anymore."

Caleb was right, but I couldn't care less. Someone from my father's clan was killing people *because* of me. At least, that's what we assumed. I refused to believe my own father was a murderer.

He and Roland trained us to protect people, not harm them. Vampire or not, he knew right from wrong. Hell, every one of those bloodsuckers did.

On the other hand, we believed by now that every vampire alive knew I was reborn. If that was common knowledge among them, why wouldn't he come looking for me? It would be a strange way to get my attention, but I couldn't rule it out completely.

I had a sinking feeling that another body would turn up again if I didn't go to Alexander in my own flesh. He was my father; maybe he would just tell me if it was him or if he knew who was doing it. This felt like a familiar pattern from last year after I escaped from Maurice. Back then, when bodies turned up in East Greenwich, it was always to draw me out. The vampires feared I was on a rampage to slaughter them all, so they tried to outsmart me. They thought they could capture and bury me alive if they saw me coming. It rarely worked, and I'd still end up killing the vampires. Once the coven and wolf pack agreed to a treaty with them, the body count dropped to zero. Whoever did this didn't get the memo, or something else was at play.

"Fine. I won't be a part of this case," I lied, hoping to hide my deception.

This is bullshit.

Caleb grabbed his boxers and flannel pants, pulled them from under the towel, then dropped the towel once he was fully dressed. That time, he watched me ... watch him. A smile pulled on the side of his mouth, so I looked away.

Stop it. He's enjoying this.

"You'll still be informed of what's going on, but I can't have you going back to that club," Caleb explained.

"Yeah, I get it," I said too quickly.

"You're going to go there anyway, aren't you?" he asked, calling me out.

Arguing with him was pointless. "We'll talk about this later," I said.

I stood and stepped to walk past him, but he moved into my path, blocking me from the door. As he looked down at me, my heart pounded against my chest. He wasn't only looking down at me; he was staring and examining every detail of my face.

"Move," I demanded. "I don't want to use my magic on you, but I will."

He laughed out loud. "Oh, Mercy. I have the rest of the coven backing me on this. We can use our magic to keep you here if we want." Caleb leaned in until his lips touched my ear. "I'll tie you to the fucking bed if I have to."

I gulped and put my hands up. A warning. My powers slowly slinked up my arms and to my fingertips, lighting up the tips above my nails. "Alexander is my *father*. He won't hurt me."

Caleb straightened his back, and his eyes drew to my hands. Then he slowly stepped forward, ignoring my warning.

Such a fool.

"No, Mercy. That's where you're wrong. Alexander *was* your father. Not only is he *not* a part of your life in this century, but he turned into a blood-sucking monster. That alone will likely change how he feels about his little girl."

"It never changed with Roland or Abigail when it came to their love for you, did it?"

"They never ran a murderous vampire clan," he said, raising his hand to touch me.

I moved back and warned, "Don't." The light still lingered on my fingers. Now Caleb was pissing me off. While clenching my jaw, I felt the energy build up inside as my anger escalated. "You need to step away from me. Now."

He didn't move or listen. In fact, he stepped closer.

The feeling going through my body was just as it had been in the autopsy suite. I'd always been able to control my powers and turn them off if I wanted, even before my Awakening, but I couldn't anymore.

What is happening?

My frustration only built as I lifted my hands to shove him away. Instead, the energy left my fingertips and flung Caleb across the room and out of my path. The energy still lingered above my fingers as I realized what had just happened. Now on the floor, he looked up at me in disbelief. His mouth fell open, and he shook his head at me.

What the fuck did I just do?

I didn't speak. I didn't apologize. I only ran.

CHAPTER 11

CALEB

"Pick up, dammit," I cursed. "Why is Mercy ignoring me?"

"She's ignoring all of us, Caleb. What the hell happened yesterday with you two?" Leah moved to my right and sat beside me, placing her hand on my shoulder. I brushed it away and stood up. "Okay, tough guy. You don't need to be an asshole. We're all trying to help figure this out. I'm not saying it's your fault she ran away, but something *did* happen."

Yeah, it was my fault. I tried to stop Mercy from leaving. I had learned from her in the past year to never stop her from doing something she had set her mind to.

She wasn't the same girl she had been a year ago. Too many people were hurt last year, and Mercy blamed herself. She told me that after the dust settled last year, she would do whatever it took to keep the ones she loved safe. Her stubborn nature was so fucking sexy and infuriating at the same time.

Simon joined us at the kitchen island and placed his plate of eggs down, turning to Leah. "Did you get Cami admitted?" he asked her.

Leah nodded. "Yeah, I got her all checked in," she said. "I have the best doctors at the facility working with her."

"Good," Ezra said as he joined us for breakfast. "Now we need to focus on getting Mercy back. You know she went back to that club, right?"

I gripped my cell phone and slammed my fist on the table. I winced at the stinging pain and outstretched my hand, feeling the muscles cramp up. I should have chased after her when she ran out of my room, but I let her go, and this morning she was gone.

Fuck!

"Caleb!" Leah yelped. "Calm the hell down. We don't know where she went." She glared at Ezra. "We don't know that she went there for *sure*, Ezra."

So help me, God, if she went into that fucking club without backup, I'm going to drag her ass out by her hair. That girl makes me insane.

We needed to get down there now, but if she were going under an unfamiliar face again, I couldn't risk exposing her idiotic plan and getting her hurt. We had to come up with something better than rolling in there, powers blazing.

"Is Sarah missing, too?" Leah asked. "We need to know if we are looking for Mercy's face or another."

I shook my head. "I don't know," I said. "I'll call Sarah when we're done here."

Still chewing his food, Simon said, "Well, we know Mercy's not dead. We can all still feel her connected to us."

"She can't die anyway, you idiot," Ezra said.

"Stop. You're acting like toddlers. Go to your rooms," Leah scolded playfully, and the two snickered at her joke. I didn't think it was funny.

None of this was funny.

I have to find her.

I leaned over Bradley's shoulder, looking at his computer while he typed.

"Can't you just hack into her cell phone server?" I asked. "I only need to access her GPS."

When Joel put that spell on her that shielded her blood from vampire senses, it also blocked him from casting any kind of location spell on her. Her complete presence was off the map to the supernatural world. We knew it was dangerous, but we couldn't risk her being found by our enemy.

"Caleb, can I talk to you outside for a minute?" Lily asked, standing patiently in the corner of her office, watching us work.

I let out a frustrated sigh and followed her out. I wasn't mad at her, just at the situation. Lily seemed uneasy about us involving Bradley. For all he knew, this was just a typical missing person situation, and we knew Bradley would return to being in the dark once we located her.

"Bradley won't know anything," I promised. "I only need Mercy's location, and I'll leave," I explained when we stepped out onto her front porch.

Lily shook her head and fiddled with the bottom of her shirt. "The truth is, Caleb, I ... *want* to tell him."

I should have seen this coming. Lily and Bradley had been dating for a while now. It was only a matter of time before she wanted him to know the real her.

"Look. You're an adult. It's not up to me to give you permission. The only thing I ask is that you leave as much of it out as you can. He doesn't need to know *everything*. Maybe leave out the part about the Chosen Ones."

She nodded. "Of course."

When we rejoined Bradley, he looked at me with a massive grin on his face that reached his eyes. "Found her."

My heart rate picked up. "Where?"

Bradley cleared his throat. "Okay, so Mercy's GPS was turned off, but I hacked into her phone and turned it back on. Once I did that, it showed her last location about two hours ago." He pointed to his computer. "The pin marks the corner of Parker and Addison Lane in downtown Providence," he explained.

"Just as I thought." Bradley and Lily looked at me with confusion. "She's at the club," I explained.

"The Black Horse?" Lily asked, panic rising in her voice. "Do you think she was taken this time?"

I shook my head. "No, she went on her own."

I cursed under my breath. This was getting too dangerous.

Lily paced the kitchen and looked up at Bradley. "Honey, can you give Caleb and me another minute?"

He nodded and walked out to the front porch. Once Bradley stepped outside and shut the door, my hands flew up. "That girl needs a fucking GPS device injected into her arm."

Lily smiled and shook her head at me.

"I'm not kidding, Lily. Whether she's sacrificing herself to a clan of vampires or going under a different face, she didn't really think this one through. I've heard the rumors about this clan. They won't show her mercy." I huffed. "We need Joel. Can you call him and have him meet us at Joe's Bar and Grill? I don't know what she's up to, but we aren't repeating what happened last year."

My fury kept me from filtering my mouth. What was she thinking? I taught Mercy everything she needed to know when it came to fighting. She could knock a two hundred and fifteen pound me across a room with one hard kick. She also knew her powers better than I did at her age. She learned quickly, and all in a year. But I couldn't shut off my feelings for her or my instinct to always protect her.

Bradley poked his head in, wiping the sweat from his nose and readjusting his glasses. "Everything okay? Should I call the police about Mercy?"

"No, babe. Everything's fine. I'll call you later, though. We're meeting my brother for coffee to discuss what to do about the Mercy situation. I'll see you tonight for dinner," Lily replied in an assuring tone.

Bradley smirked and entered the kitchen to kiss Lily goodbye. He didn't look at me. Instead, he waved his hand in the air and walked out to his car.

⁓ℓℓ⁓

Sarah informed us she was not with Mercy, which meant she went there in her own face.

It was right before six when we met Joel and Derek at Joe's Bar and Grill. Derek was getting beers for us while Joel drummed his fingers on the table, trying to muster up his thoughts. "We know she wasn't taken," Joel said, "but do you honestly believe Alexander would hurt her? She might be reckless sometimes, but she isn't stupid. Let's give her a little credit here. Maybe she has a plan."

Joel looked up and saw my doubtful expression. I didn't believe she had a plan but gestured for him to share his theory anyway.

He continued, "Do you think she walked up to her father and said, 'Hi, I'm your long-lost, reincarnated daughter. Nice to see you again?'"

I finally was able to laugh, because that did sound exactly like something Mercy would do.

My phone vibrated on my hip. "Excuse me." I moved away, reached into my pocket, and looked down at my phone.

Melissa: *There's been another body brought in. Same as last. Marks on the neck and the tattoo. His name is Ned Parker. It's right outside my jurisdiction, but as we've done in the past, I was able to get the body transferred here. Police said he was a homeless man they'd spotted a few times near Goddard Park.*

I placed my phone in my back pocket and walked back to the table. "I'm heading to Providence to get her. Another body turned up near East Greenwich. I can't just sit here and wait for her to return."

Lily shifted in her seat and turned to Joel. "We'll go with you." She gathered her things while Joel stood and kissed Derek on the lips, telling him to head home without him.

We climbed into my car, leaving Lily's in the parking lot, and drove to The Black Horse.

When we arrived at the club, all the shades were closed, and the door was locked. I wasn't sure if the clan lived here full-time or not, but we figured we might have to break in to find out. I couldn't hear any music or voices through the thick metal door.

Lily moved around me, placed her hand on the door lock, and we heard a click.

Once we entered, we noticed that the top floor was empty, so we assumed they were down in the club beneath us. We headed to the back and down the stairs until we reached the door to the underground club. It was unlocked, so we walked right in. In the corner of the room, sitting on a bench, was a vampire. When he spotted us, he immediately stood to his feet and gestured toward the back as if he were expecting us.

"We were wondering how long it would take you to get here," the man said. "They're in the back."

I already had my hand out, ready to ignite a fireball if I had to, but I didn't feel threatened by him. I lowered my hand and looked back at Lily and Joel—their hands thrumming with power like mine were.

"I think we're okay," I said, and they both lowered their hands.

We slowly entered, and Mercy was sitting next to her father. They both turned their heads toward us.

"I'm sorry, Caleb. I knew you'd try to stop me, but I had to come," Mercy said before we fully entered the room. "As you can see, I'm safe with my father."

Are you fucking kidding me right now? She's sorry?

"Caleb, nice to see you again after all these years," Alexander said while standing up and approaching me with caution. The fucker knew I had no emotions for him, as Mercy did. I wouldn't hesitate to end him. "I'm not going to hurt you or her. Relax." His voice was eerily calm.

"I've just come here for Mercy," I said, biting down on the inside of my cheek.

Alexander flashed a slight smile at me and looked at his daughter. "Do you want to leave with them?"

Mercy shook her head. "Not right now," she said. "I appreciate that you're checking on me, guys, but as I said, I'm safe."

Was she really dismissing us? Just like that?

Mercy sat next to a man who hadn't seen her in centuries, and she already trusted him. Alexander could have been killing innocent humans to get to her for all she knew. He ran a dangerous vampire clan, for fuck's sake. I didn't doubt for a second that he would snap the neck of an innocent victim without hesitation.

No. Mercy's not staying here.

"Mercy," I started, attempting to keep my tone as controlled as possible. "Get your ass off that chair and leave with us. Now." My voice came off as more authoritative than I had intended it to be. I didn't want to upset or boss her around, but it was clear Alexander had manipulated her, and she wasn't thinking straight.

Mercy stood and walked up to me. "I'm not leaving."

I shook my head. "What's happened to you? You have a coven and a family who love you."

I glanced over my shoulder at Alexander, who wore a stupid grin on his face, then turned back to her.

"If you weren't over here playing house with vampires, you would have noticed that the body count hasn't stopped rising. We need you. A homeless man turned up dead in Goddard Park. It was the same as the others. Bite marks and a tattoo of *your* fucking club." I turned to Alexander again, seeing if he'd react to my accusation.

He didn't; he only shook his head, walked up to me, and held out his wrist. "Feel that?"

I grabbed his wrist, placing my fingers near the vein.

Heartbeat.

I let go of his wrist, glancing at Mercy, then back at him. "What the hell?"

She placed her hand on my arm. "Alexander isn't the one killing people. I fed him my blood a few hours ago. He doesn't want to be a vampire. He never has. For years, he ran this clan to keep this group of vampires under control. My father doesn't kill people, but he hasn't always been in control of those in the clan who did. He's going to give it all up to help us."

Joel and Lily exchanged a glance, then looked back at Alexander.

"I'm Mercy's uncle, and this is her aunt, Lily." Joel reached out his hand. They shook before Alexander turned back to Mercy, wrapping his fingers around her arm. My body stiffened when he touched her.

"We may be divided by the two different lives Mercy has lived, but we are *all* family," Alexander said. "I would never hurt my daughter. I knew she was alive, but I wasn't ready to face her yet. I'm glad she came to me, and I'm also sorry about what happened at my club the other night. I would never have left anyone with Devon if I had known he would do something like that."

I grunted out a snarl and looked away.

Mercy must have noticed my annoyance because she walked up to me and placed her hand on my chest, hoping it would help me relax. "My father is a powerful witch. You know this. We could use his magic," Mercy said, and my shoulders relaxed the more she touched me. Not because of what she said but because she still hadn't removed her hand from my chest, and her touch always helped me calm down. When my eyes met her gaze, she continued. "He's agreed to help us find out who is killing in East Greenwich." She turned and smiled at her father. "Alexander has the ability to read minds."

Alexander's smile made me feel uneasy, but I listened as he said, "Which is why having me help is crucial. If someone from my clan did this, I'd know by reading their thoughts."

I wondered if that would work. Would the vampires really allow a witch to get that close to them? His clan would know right away he wasn't a vampire anymore. They'd slaughter him before he drew breath in their presence.

The vampire who greeted us at the door entered the room. Alexander waved him over. "Thomas, are you ready for my daughter's gift?"

"I'm ready," he said.

He walked up to her and grabbed her wrist. She closed her eyes, and his teeth reached for her skin.

"The fuck!" I screamed.

"Caleb, it's okay," she said, holding up her hand to stop me from intervening.

The vampire bit down, and Mercy winced but relaxed as Thomas drank from her. He sucked her blood for about ten seconds and let go. He scrunched up his nose and looked like he was about to throw up.

"Try to hold it in," she said. The man blinked a few times and took a heavy breath.

"Wow." Thomas looked at her, and a tear formed in the corner of his eye, slowly dripping down his cheek. "Seven hundred and sixty-five years," he said. "That's how long I've been undead. I thought I'd never be free from my bloodlust."

"Do you feel it?" she asked him.

He nodded with a smile, pressing a hand to his chest.

"I don't know where your soul has been. I only know that whatever my blood can do, it somehow brings it back," Mercy explained.

"Thank you," he said as he turned to us. "I don't know how to explain this feeling. It feels like a stream of warm water entered my body while igniting every emotion like love, desire, and empathy that was taken from me." He looked up at Mercy. "Good luck to you, child."

Thomas walked out but had his hands in front of him, moving his fingers around. It was just like we had witnessed several times since Mercy's Awakening. It was a newly turned human from a vampire, shocked at the sudden change in their body and feeling the blood rushing through their veins again. It was a surreal moment, and no matter how much I hated seeing them touch her and bite down into her flesh, it was a beautiful moment for everyone to witness what she could do.

Mercy smiled with pride and turned to her father. "Roland is human, too, Father. With the two of you returning to your powers, we can all be a family again and work together." She turned away from Alexander and walked up to me. "I'm sorry for using my magic on you yesterday. I lost control ... again. I'm also sorry I left without letting anyone know where I was going." She wrapped her fingers around mine and squeezed. "I haven't abandoned the coven, Caleb. But I knew you wouldn't let me come here alone. I had to be alone for him to hear me out. I'm safe with him and plan to stay with him for a little while."

"Out of the fucking question," I snarled.

"This isn't up to you!" she snapped.

"Why would you stay with him?"

"He's going to teach me how to control my powers. I don't know what's going on with me, but whenever I get upset, I lose all control. My father knows more about my powers than everyone here combined. I need *his* help. And I need you to be safe."

I knew she was losing control, but if anyone could help her, we could. I felt fucking helpless. "I won't be able to focus knowing you're here. With Alexander being human now, shouldn't you be leaving this lair as soon as you can?"

"My father has a home in Newport. That's where we'll be crashing from now on. It's close to Abigail's mansion, and I'll gladly give you the address. We're heading there after my father gathers his personal belongings at the club." She gently placed her hand on my arm. "See what you can find out about the homeless man's body. Once I have more control over what is happening to me, I'll come back."

Joel had his arms folded and walked up to Alexander. "And who will run this place after you leave? Won't they wonder what happened to you and go on a killing spree? I've heard the stories of what your clan does to their victims."

"Don't believe everything you hear. These clan members haven't always been on their best behavior, true, but I've seen worse from the other groups. I'll help you find out who from the clan is responsible for the deaths in your hometown, but I'm not going to worry about who's taking over. I'll keep Mercy safe. I swear to you."

His promise meant shit to me. I didn't trust him. I didn't like any of this, but I had no control over her. As much as I tried, I never had.

The hardest part about all this was that she didn't *need* me. I needed her, but she would never need me other than to balance our coven. She could take care of herself. Her powers were stronger than mine.

I walked up to Mercy and placed the tip of my fingers under her chin. She looked directly into my eyes. My heart was aching, but I had to let her go. Centuries of love and heartache came crashing down on me all at once. There was only one way this would end, and it wasn't with her in my arms again.

"I'm letting you go," I said, my heart feeling as if someone had ripped it out of my chest.

"Thank you," she said. "As I said, I'll be safe with my father."

I shook my head. "No, I mean, I'm letting you *go.*" Her face went still as I slowly inched forward, and when I saw she wasn't resisting, I pressed my lips to hers. The kiss was tender and short, and then I released her. "You were right about taking your feelings away. I wish I could do that for myself with you. But I don't have the power to do it."

Her face was still unmoved as I walked away, Joel and Lily following behind me. I didn't know if anyone really knew what to say at that moment. All I knew was that I was letting my heart move on for the first time since she and I were barely adults in a life that ended hundreds of years ago.

CHAPTER 12

MERCY

The door shut behind him as they left me standing there with my father's gaze on my back.

I touched my lips and turned to him, who waited for me to say something, but I had no words.

The only feeling I felt was relief. There was no heartbreak or loss. Sure, I felt slightly guilty that Caleb would be hurting much more now. I didn't find pleasure in being the source of someone's pain, but what did he expect me to do? I'm not in love with him, and I hated that it hurt him as much as it did.

This was good. Caleb could finally move on and be happy. Maybe find love with someone else.

"Are you okay?" my father asked.

"I felt nothing when he told me that," I explained. "What the hell does that say about me?"

"It says you're fulfilling the mission for which you were created," he said. "You don't owe Caleb a damn thing."

I shook my head. "Why did Tatyana create me this way? Why did I ever have to do that stupid spell if all I am is an element? Why not just make me be this way from the start, with no feelings, remorse, or humanity"—a small tear formed at the corner of my eye—"if I'm *just* an element?"

My father reached out and placed his hand on my shoulder. "Oh, Mercy," he said. "You're more than *just* an element."

I looked down at my feet as a tear trickled down my cheek.

"What do you remember from your life before you died?" he asked as I wiped my cheek.

"I don't remember everything. Just flashes and visions," I said. "Memories of my time training with the coven before the age of thirteen, and when we tracked down the clan that had killed Caleb's mother, turned Roland, and had taken you. My last memory seemed to take place a year before I died." I let out a sigh. "There's still a large part of my memory that's blank."

He slid closer to me, touching the top of my hand and gripping his fingers around mine. "Mercy, our families were close. We always had been. Your mother, Mary, and I were blessed to represent centuries of witches who had the power to heal others by using the element of Spirit. We couldn't heal ourselves as you could, but if we used spells to pull that universal element, the essence of Spirit was our strength.

"When Tatyana came to Earth, she shared with us about the growing vampire race. We wouldn't be able to defeat them without taking the elements in themselves, putting them directly here on Earth. The angel would need to take those elements and put them into a human body—not just inside a witch who could use them, but to transform that element into a life force—the five families tied to those elements would be able to fight together and destroy the vampires she had created by mistake.

"She told me that the element of Spirit that *our* bloodline would bring into the world would be the key element in reuniting a vampire with their soul."

My eyes widened. "You knew all along what my blood could do?"

He nodded. "Roland and I were the only ones Tatyana told. We kept it a secret to protect you, but then a vampire attacked you in a clearing outside the village one night. He turned human after biting you, but you didn't realize what was happening to him. His clan showed up right as the sun's light shone into the clearing. The vampires hid to protect themselves from the light, but the affected vampire never moved from where he stood. You thought your blood gave vampires the ability to walk in the day when the vampire stayed there, soaking in the sun, shocked at what was happening to him. He took off before you could question him.

"It wasn't just you that believed it, but also his clan who witnessed it. I'm sure the vampire who turned human was too afraid to face them if they knew, so he ran, and their clan told everyone what they had witnessed. The rumor had begun that the element of Spirit would allow a vampire to walk in the daylight without bursting into flames. It became a prophecy among the clans."

I shook my head. "I wondered how that rumor started."

"The element of Spirit was everything perfect in this world. When you died, you took that element with you. It was as if your death had drained the world of that power."

I frowned, clenching my father's hand. It was my fault. I had given myself up to the mob and allowed them to kill me all those years ago. I made the sacrifice for love over duty to my family ... my coven.

My father must have seen the pain on my face, because he gripped my hand tighter, and a warm smile pulled at his lips.

"Tatyana also told us you would fall in love in your past life. How could you not? You represented the soul. *You* have a soul, my sweet daughter. What is a soul without the power to love? You are not *just* an element."

More tears formed in my eyes. I couldn't hold it back anymore but allowed myself to cry and feel the growing pain tugging at my chest.

"Did she see who I'd be with?" I asked. "Did she see Caleb and me fall in love?

He nodded.

"And Dorian? Was he part of that plan?"

He nodded again and released my hand.

"Just because she foresaw it doesn't mean it *had* to happen," he explained. "You choose your own path, Mercy."

This feeling I had with my father, whom I barely remembered, was familiar and comforting. I had only vague memories of him from my past life and none of my birth father in this life. Alexander was the closest I had to a father, and I felt safe and close to him at that moment, as if my memories of him never went away. A quick glance at the clock told me it was five in the evening.

"We should get going," I said. "We probably don't want to be here when the rest of your clan shows up after dark." As we were about to walk out the door, I turned to my father and asked, "Have you ever killed anyone?"

I wasn't sure if it was a stupid question. Alexander promised he wasn't the one killing those in East Greenwich, but was he like Dorian? A vampire who had done everything he could to keep himself from drinking from humans? It was their nature to do it; to them, it wasn't wrong.

"Yes," he admitted.

My heart sank. "Oh," was all I could say.

"Look, you lose much of your humanity when your soul is taken from you. Some more than others. I met a woman, and we thought we were in love," Alexander said.

My jaw dropped. My father had killed someone he cared about.

"She told me I could drink from her, so I did, but I couldn't stop for some reason. I've always been able to stop, but not with her. By the time I could will myself to let go, she was on the brink of death. What I didn't know was that she also was married. Her husband came home at that moment, so I laid her down and ran out of the house. Before I fled, I watched through the window as she slipped away in his arms."

"Oh my God. I'm so sorry."

Alexander shook his head. "She was able to speak with him right before she passed. I hoped whatever they said to each other brought him comfort and peace before she died. I've carried that guilt for over eight years."

I grabbed his hand and squeezed. "You have your soul back now," I reminded him. "You're a different person. Live the life you should have always had before they took it from you."

He smiled back, and those were our last words before we left the club and drove to his place in Newport. My plan was to hide out there until I was ready to face Caleb and the rest of the coven again. My father and I had a lot to catch up on, too, and I needed to get a grip on my powers. I wasn't sure what was happening to me, but it was scary, and I didn't want to lose control anymore, especially with those I cared for.

CHAPTER 13

CALEB

I hadn't seen much of Melissa in the last three weeks since Mercy went to stay with her father. I didn't know how to reach out to her aside from a couple of text messages. I was avoiding her, and I knew it hurt.

Tonight, there was desperation in Melissa's voice as she stood at the doorstep, asking me to have her stay over and let me hold her until morning. She knew I was still upset over Mercy's choice to distance herself from the coven, and I was letting it affect my and Melissa's relationship.

I didn't want that.

That wasn't what either of us wanted. Instead, we fucked out the anger and frustration we both had felt since Mercy had destroyed her office. I admit I didn't defend Melissa when it happened; my only concern was ensuring Mercy was okay. Naturally, Melissa blamed me for that, but it wasn't as if I had condoned Mercy's behavior, either.

Despite our lack of sleep, we started the morning early, as she had to stop in the office to work for a few hours, and I needed to train with the coven.

When she entered the kitchen, she eyed the coffee I had brewed and poured herself a mug.

Melissa carried a notebook and reading glasses, putting them on to review the notes in front of her.

"The homeless man, Ned," she started, "had been dead for over twenty-four hours before they found his body. This means Ned was killed before Alexander became human again, Caleb. Mercy's father could have done it. We haven't had a body bitten by a vampire come in since."

The timing *was* too perfect, and now Mercy was alone with her father at his place. I tried to shake the thought and hoped we weren't wrong to let her go and be out of reach of me and the coven. But then again, he did live here in Newport. I could swing by in the morning and secretly check on them.

Maybe even convince her to get the fuck out of there.

I placed my hand under Melissa's arm and stroked the top of her skin while she put the notebook down, removed her glasses, and bit her bottom lip. Melissa's wanton gaze pierced me like a needle, and I could feel desire bubbling in my chest.

Melissa and I have talked off and on for the last few months, and though I knew Mercy wouldn't give her heart to me, a part of me felt like I was cheating on her. I held back with Melissa, never fully giving her everything I should have. Up until now, it was only sex, but she and I both wanted more.

Melissa was stunning with her golden-brown eyes that matched her tight curls that fell to the center of her back. It's what drew me to her in the first place. Her hair was like exquisite bronze caught in firelight. Almost every inch of her skin was covered with ink, from vibrant green vines to dragons, starting at the tip of her shoulder and reaching down to her wrist in a perfect sleeve. When Melissa wore her work outfit, no trace of the beautiful art was seen, but when she was undressed, her body was a living-inked masterpiece.

Looks aside, she was the only other person I could talk to about anything outside of the coven, and I didn't feel like I had to calm her down from the fear my life would potentially bring her.

The one thing I couldn't tell her was that I still felt something for Mercy, and I couldn't promise it would go away anytime soon. I wouldn't tell her about what happened three weeks ago at The Black Horse. Absolutely not. I felt guilty about it, but Mercy hadn't called me since I told her I was letting her go, not even a fucking text. It was what I wanted, so I had to lie in that bed.

According to Leah, who *had* heard from her, she was still staying at Alexander's place here in Newport.

Did the farewell kiss freak her out?

Fuck.

"What are we doing?" Melissa's voice pulled me out of my thoughts.

"What?"

"This," she said. "What is *this* between us?"

Great, I didn't even know what this was. "You know I care about you. Let's start there."

Melissa frowned and moved over to the side of the table, standing closer to me. "All our relationship is, is just sex," she said, instant guilt slamming me in the chest. "Caleb, I like you. I want to go on an *actual* date." She smiled and placed her hand over mine. I reciprocated and grabbed her hand, rubbing my thumb over her skin.

"How about dinner tonight at La Masseria?" I asked, because I did want that. Sex was fantastic between Melissa and me, and every time I was with her, the more I desired to get to know her outside of the bedsheets.

"What about your coven?" she asked. "You're usually with them on the weekends."

I pulled from our touch and ran my hands through my hair. "I'm only training with the coven this afternoon, but we'll be done early. I can pick you up at six."

Melissa didn't have to persuade me. I wanted to take her out. God, I really did. I'd wanted to ask her out for a long time but didn't want to face the coven's judgments or ruin what I thought would or could have happened with Mercy and me. I wasted my time on someone who would never love me back when I had this gorgeous woman in front of me who already cared.

I'm moving the fuck on.

— ✺ —

While driving to Melissa's, my phone beeped, and I glanced at it quickly at a red light. Mercy's name appeared on the screen.

It was about damn time.

> **Mercy:** *Someone broke into Alexander's home last night. It's not safe for me here anymore. I'm coming home.*

She always did have the worst fucking timing.

Melissa opened the door wearing a lacy green dress that reached right above her knees. She had styled her hair in a braid wrapped around her shoulder and smiled as soon as she saw me standing there with a single red rose in my hand.

"Such a gentleman," she said, taking the rose from me. "This was sweet. Thank you."

I wore a sleek black suit and gray tie, and I'd shaved off the beard I had been growing for the last three weeks as I nervously waited for Mercy to check in with me. I cleared my thoughts and focused on the beautiful woman at the doorstep instead. She took my hand as I held it out.

Later that evening, after a few glasses of wine and La Masseria's delicious spaghetti marinara, Melissa excused herself to the ladies' room. I took the opportunity to respond to Mercy.

> **Me:** *What exactly happened last night?*

She responded almost immediately, as if she had typed it all out, waiting for me to respond first.

> **Mercy:** *We woke up to broken glass near the balcony window. The room is three stories high with no window or rooftop to connect to where the window sits, so either someone had thrown a rock through the window, or we're dealing with something supernatural. You'd have to be Spiderman to scale that wall.*

Melissa was rounding the corner, so I typed up my last text to her for the night.

> **Me:** *Stay at the mansion tonight. There's a house key under the blue vase by the front door. I'll turn off the alarm with my phone. Come in and make yourself at home. I'll be back by nine.*

I shut my phone down and glanced up at Melissa, who had rejoined me at the table.

"Everything okay?" she asked.

I let her know what was happening with Mercy, and given Melissa's kind nature, she showed genuine concern. Still, when I mentioned Mercy would be staying with me tonight because of it, her body language changed instantly. Her shoulders slumped, and she bit her bottom lip. She didn't whine or share her thoughts, but I knew she wanted to say something.

The rest of the evening, I gave Melissa my full attention, but my thoughts kept returning to the fact that I would see Mercy for the first time in three weeks. Yes, I was moving on, but since her Awakening, this was the longest we had gone without seeing each other.

Mercy's safety had always been my number one concern. I didn't know if this ruled out Alexander as the killer in East Greenwich for sure, but her father turning human again was undoubtedly a game changer unless, as Melissa had pointed out, he killed the last victim before he changed. But if that were the case, what was his motive? If it were to draw Mercy out, he had her within his grasp now. Was it to pull her back to him so he could return as a witch? It's not like she'd refuse a vampire who wanted to be a human again.

One thing was for certain. Whoever it was had known Mercy was at his house, and they were coming after her.

The lights were dim in the family room when I entered.

Mercy had helped herself to the fireplace, and sitting next to her on the table was a cup of hot cocoa. She must have just made it, as I eyed the steam hovering over the mug. I could smell the cocoa as I neared her lying on the couch. Her eyes were closed, and I could see that she had fallen asleep while waiting for me to come back.

"Mercy." I gave her a gentle nudge. She opened her eyes and looked up at my wall clock.

"Hey, sorry. I was having a hard time sleeping, so I thought a warm cup of hot chocolate would help me sleep," she said, rubbing her eyes.

"It's okay." I watched her yawn and stretch her legs, still coming out of her slumber.

"Truthfully, this house is a bit large and haunting to be upstairs alone."

I smiled. "Yeah, it can be kind of creepy."

I grabbed the blanket that had slithered off the couch and pulled it over Mercy. I sat with her, and she snuggled closer to me, laying her head on my chest. My fingers stroked her arm, trying not to push too hard on her boundaries. I tested the waters by kissing her on top of the head. Her response was only looking up with a warm smile.

Thank God.

This right here, this was perfect. I knew where her heart was at this point, and I was okay with it. But fuck, I couldn't lose her as a friend.

Maybe she kept her distance this entire time, knowing I still loved her, but now that I had told her I was moving on, she was comfortable with me touching her.

"How was your date?" she asked, her eyes sizing me up. "You don't ever dress up like this."

I only smiled at her. Mercy loved to call me out, but I wasn't ready to tell her who I had been with.

Not yet.

"Tell me what happened," I asked, ignoring her question.

She pushed herself up so she was sitting upright and sighed. "We had just returned from visiting a few of my father's old clan members. They respected him, so they welcomed us with no trouble. No one knows who would do this. They have kicked a few members out of the clan in the last decade for being traitors, so the only conclusion he thought of was that they're trying to frame him. The other theory is that it might be a vampire who joined them last year whom I have a history with."

My eyebrows rose a notch. "Dorian?"

"No. Dorian would *never* do this. He's not a member of the Black Horse Clan, either."

I huffed, realizing she was right, but I still hated the guy. "Then who?"

She swallowed before saying, "Maurice."

My blood instantly boiled, and my hand clenched into a fist. If Maurice were after Mercy, he would torture her to make her pay for bringing down everything he created.

"He joined that clan?" I asked incredulously.

"In February, right after the treaty. They were civil with each other until Maurice found out that Alexander was my father. He became enraged and told Alexander he wanted to kill me and wouldn't stop until he found a way. Then he took off, and they hadn't seen him since. My guess is that he's trying to frame my father and then use me in my broken state to torture or kill me." She shifted in her seat. "I know we don't have the dagger, but the fear that Maurice would find it is always in the back of my mind. Ever since he threatened he would."

I looked away, trying not to make eye contact with her. I knew the truth would eventually come out, but I didn't want to ruin this moment with her.

Mercy's eyes narrowed, and her brows creased. I knew that look well.

"What is it?" she asked.

Shit.

I can't hide this from her. "Mercy, I have to tell you something."

Mercy's body seemed to scoot further from me as if she were avoiding our touch, knowing I would say something to piss her off.

"Two weeks ago, I realized that, though Joel is a gifted witch, he isn't as strong as us. If a mind-reading witch were to get to him, they'd be able to read his mind to find the dagger, which would put us in danger."

She squeezed her eyes shut as if annoyed by my words. "You moved it because you thought my father would use his power on Joel and go after the dagger," she said. "What the fuck, Caleb?"

Mercy quickly stood and paced back and forth. I didn't try to calm her down. She deserved to be upset with me, so I let her be angry. I betrayed her and the rest of the coven by moving the dagger without talking about it first and not telling them after I did.

"How many times do I have to tell you that my father isn't trying to kill me? Do you really think I'd be standing if he were? I just spent three weeks alone with him, and all he wanted to do was get to know me and what my reborn life had been like these last twenty-two years. Remember, the former version of myself has been dead for over three hundred years. I'm a little different now."

I now stood and hoped my words would help her relax. "It has nothing to do with your father and everything to do with Joel. We are the only ones who should know the location of the dagger. I didn't even tell Simon where I was going to put it after he helped me get it back."

Mercy held a hand up as if she were about to push me back. "Simon helped you?"

I let out a low grunt of frustration. Fighting with Mercy again wasn't on my agenda tonight.

"Look," I said, keeping my voice as calm as I could manage it. "I was a fool to have Joel be the one to hide it in the first place. Once I realized it would be too dangerous, I had Joel teleport Simon and me to the Santa Barbara Mission. It was in a secure safe inside the walls."

Her body tensed. "And that is exactly where it needs to return."

"No. Everyone, by now, knows about the fucking dagger. We need to protect it. They can't read our minds without us fighting back with our powers. They'd be damn fools to try."

She stopped pacing and looked back at me. It was as if the wheels were turning, but she couldn't find the words. My eyes darted to her hands, which were balled into fists.

"Well, where the hell did you hide it?" Her hand came up again. "And don't lie to me. You're telling me where it is."

"Upstairs," I answered honestly.

"Just *upstairs*?" Both hands flew up that time. "That sounds safe."

I frowned. "It's in a secured safe in my bedroom, under the floorboards," I told her.

"You think that's safe enough? Here? Of all places? That sounds incredibly stupid."

I shrugged. "I'm the only one who knows the code," I said but was met with Mercy averting her eyes from me, as if she was holding back her rage and irritation.

Yeah, I knew it wasn't the wisest place to hide the only magical weapon that could kill us, but protected spells don't last. Using a coded safe was the best thing we could do now.

"Fine, whatever. I should get to bed," Mercy said. "I'm meeting Lily in the morning, and then I need to check on Laurie and take care of a few things in their home. I should probably stop by Raven's, too. I haven't been to visit Cami since Leah admitted her."

I flashed her a warm smile and told her I needed to get to bed myself, but when I turned toward the stairs, Mercy grabbed my hand.

"Wait," she called out. "The other day at the club, when you said what you said, did you mean it?"

I nodded.

"Then ... thank you."

"You're welcome," I said, pausing for a moment before adding, "Happy belated birthday."

She released my hand and headed upstairs without discussing more about what had happened.

I crawled into my bed and tried to shut my mind off to get the first good night's sleep in the past three weeks.

I can do this. I can let Mercy go.

CHAPTER 14

MERCY

I wrapped my hair into a messy bun and walked into the kitchen, where Caleb was making breakfast.

"Coffee?" Caleb asked, pouring me a full mug and placing it in front of me.

"Do you even have to ask?" I teased, grabbing the mug and savoring the warmth on my palms. "Thank you." I took a sip and looked up at him. Caleb moved back to the stove to finish cooking what looked like scrambled eggs with veggie sausage and a side of hash.

I giggled at how domestic he looked in the kitchen and the fact that he was willing to eat a vegetarian breakfast with me. Caleb wore plaid pajama bottoms which hung loosely from his hips and a red tank. His hair was tousled in such a way that I thought he looked like an angry cockatiel. I had to bite my lip to keep from outright laughing.

He turned, placed a generous portion of eggs on my plate, and turned back around to grab himself some.

After we ate in complete silence, my phone buzzed next to me. I looked down and saw a text from Dorian. Caleb eyed my phone as I opened the message. His mouth formed a straight line, and he glanced down at his food. He seemed bothered.

Of course, he is.

I sent a text to Sarah, letting her know I was coming back to East Greenwich today. We had kept in touch the last few weeks by texting. I wanted to check in with her often and make sure she was doing okay. What happened at the club had freaked her out, but she was ready to join me back in crime-solving mode whenever I needed her again. Sarah was a resilient witch, and I respected her strength.

I peered up at Caleb, who now stood next to me.

"Dorian and Noah are following Maurice for us. Dorian tracked him down a few days ago," I explained. I waited for a response.

Nothing.

I cleared my throat and took a few more bites of breakfast. I couldn't handle the silence anymore. "They're helping us, Caleb. I think I may have spotted Maurice a few weeks back in Salem, but I wasn't sure. For one thing, this was during the daytime, which makes no sense, so Maurice very well could be using a witch to help him during the day. Either way, it's confirmed that he didn't leave for the west coast as the rumors indicated. He was here, or rather, he *is* here. Having Dorian and Noah on our team and helping us track him is a good thing."

Caleb let out a subtle grunt while still chewing his last bite and walked over to the sink, placed his dish inside, and turned on the water to rinse it clean.

"I don't like him," he confessed as he turned around. "I never have. But I'm thankful he's willing to protect you and track Maurice for us."

I was sure that it took a lot of humility to admit, and that wasn't something that came easy for Caleb.

I studied his unreadable expression for a few seconds and asked, "So, you won't mind if I have dinner with him tonight?"

His eyes widened, but he kept his cool. "Of course not."

My shoulders relaxed.

That was a lie, but at least we aren't arguing over it.

I had to change the subject, or this was going to lead to awkwardness, and I was too tired for that. "Was your date with Melissa last night?" I asked, watching his mouth curve into a smile.

"I guess Simon couldn't keep his mouth shut," he said as his smile grew. "We had a great time. I like her ... a lot, actually. She's sweet."

Sweet? He clearly avoided saying "beautiful." She was, without a doubt, beautiful. Caleb needed to understand that I didn't care anymore. He could be with whoever made him happy. As long as it wasn't me.

"That's great," I said before taking a few more sips of my coffee. "Mind if I use your shower to get ready? I don't need the twenty questions at my house with the coven. I'll call them to let them know I'm back in town, but I have too many things to catch up on now that I'm home."

"Of course. Clean towels are in the hallway closet. Roland gets back from his trip today, and I'll let him know about the possibility that this murderer could be Maurice."

I nodded, placing my mug down. "When do Abigail and Desiree get back from Hawaii?"

"*If* they come back." He smirked. "It's been a while since they've been in the sun."

I smiled at that thought. Abigail and Desiree were the first vampires who stepped up to be changed back into their human forms. They weren't just human again; they had their powers back, which they had always yearned to have again. They never loved what they were, just like Dorian, though I couldn't see him changing his mind any time soon.

Caleb pulled me out of my thoughts by walking up to me and placing his hand on my fingers. He didn't grab my hand, but his touch lingered on my skin ever so delicately. "Have fun on your date with Dorian tonight."

He smiled and walked away. I could have explained that Dorian and I weren't dating, but I knew it was pointless. Caleb had only said that to get under my skin.

I visited Lily for an hour, then stopped by Laurie and Cami's place to take care of the household chores. Laurie was in the upstairs bedroom, sleeping off what looked like a rough night. I didn't want to wake her, so I quickly wrapped up the chores and quietly locked up. I finished the rest of the day by getting groceries for the house since I had been gone for three weeks, and met with Joel for a light lunch before I took off again to meet Dorian.

"Are you going to order food?" our waitress asked. She was the same one from the last time we dined, her tone appearing irritated.

"Water and your Cobb salad. No ham, please," I said.

"And I'll just have a beer, thank you," Dorian added.

The waitress broke into a satisfied smile and left us to put in our order.

It was nice seeing Dorian again. I missed his company.

"Glad you're eating this time," he teased.

"You're one to talk," I said. "How *are* you surviving these days without the clan's supply?"

He looked away as if ashamed to tell me.

"You don't have to hide anything from me. I won't judge you unless you're killing people." I half-smiled, and he didn't reciprocate.

"Noah, actually."

My mouth gaped open.

"He's strong enough to have me drink from him when I need to feed."

From the first time I met Dorian, he never liked what he was. In the seventeenth century, we didn't have blood banks like we do today, and no one in their right mind would willingly give vampires their blood. I was too afraid the coven would find out, so I never offered him mine. Which was oddly a good thing because if I did, he would have turned human and wouldn't be sitting in front of me now. Dorian had to take blood against people's will back then. Still, he was weirdly polite about it, always apologized, and practically starved himself until he absolutely needed to feed to survive.

After being rescued from Maurice's clan, and before we went our separate ways, he explained how Maurice would let him drink the drained blood from the victims who were hooked up to the harvesting tank. Maurice would have kicked him out for not blending in with the other clan members, but as a compromise, Dorian offered his services to be one of his bodyguards in exchange for him never having to pierce the skin of another victim. He had also chosen not to own a human or witch and did his best to stay as invisible as possible.

"How does that work exactly?" I asked, genuinely curious. "Noah isn't human."

"On the contrary, Noah's DNA *is* human. He was born a shapeshifter, yes, but when a shifter changes, their DNA changes. As long as I drink from him while he's in human form, I can survive on his blood," he explained. Dorian looked at our waitress as she set our drinks on the table.

"Your salad will be right out," she said, smiling at Dorian. He smirked in her direction but immediately shifted his gaze back to me.

"How are you?" he asked.

His question took me aback. *How was I?* I didn't even know how to answer that question without lying or breaking down. I thought after everything I had been through since I found out my purpose here, I would be a lot stronger, but I wasn't so sure. The truth was, after finding out about my father from my past life being alive, Caleb finally letting me go, and now having Dorian back in my life after an entire year, not to mention someone targeting innocents to get to me ... I was overwhelmed.

"Always fine," I answered flatly.

He narrowed his eyes at me and creased his brows. "Are you?"

"Look, Dorian," I said, swallowing nervously. There was no way I'd explain to him that though the spell worked a year ago, he still lingered in my thoughts and between my legs whenever I was lonely. "Let's just stick to business."

"Business?" he asked in a tone that revealed his confusion with my sudden formality.

I can't fucking do this.

"I just need to know about Maurice," I explained as I grabbed my salad bowl from the waitress the second she handed it to me. "Thank you."

I dug my fork into my lettuce and took a bite as Dorian watched me. "He was last seen on Derby Street. He met with a few of the men I recognize from the old clan."

"Could you hear anything they were saying? Like, maybe why he's back in Massachusetts?" I asked after swallowing my bite.

"No, we didn't want to get too close, just in case they were listening, too."

I took another bite of my salad as a bell over the restaurant doors chimed behind me. I turned around and spotted Noah walking in, in all his massive, muscular glory. He had a powerful presence about him, that was for certain. Quite a few of the female patrons took notice of him as he walked to our table.

"Is Mercy all filled in?" he asked Dorian, taking a seat next to him.

Dorian just nodded and tapped his fingers against the laminate table.

"Hi, Noah. Nice to see you, too," I said.

Noah smirked at my remark and leaned back.

"How can we assist your coven?" Noah asked, holding his hands out and bowing.

I rolled my eyes and said, "If you could keep watching Maurice and report back to Caleb or me, I'd appreciate that." I looked over at Dorian. "Do you have Caleb's number? You don't always have to call me."

He snickered under his breath. "I'll just call you."

Noah shook his head at us and chuckled again. "Let's go," he said, picking up his cell from the table. "I spotted Maurice about fifteen minutes ago in Salem."

"You fly fast," I said, remembering Noah in his eagle form the night he'd snatched me and taken me to the lair.

"I guess you would know," Noah replied teasingly. I scrunched up my face at him. He had a flair for sarcasm and annoying the hell out of me.

I didn't hate the guy for kidnapping me last year. He was just doing his job back then, and it was me who had sacrificed myself in the first place. He was always kind to me in the lair and was Dorian's best friend. So, if Dorian trusted him, so did I.

Dorian reached out and placed his icy fingers over mine. "I'll call you later." He slid out toward the edge of the booth until he and Noah stood next to me and looked down. "You look stunning today, by the way."

Those were the words Dorian left me with, and I won't lie, those sweet words coming from his lips sounded nice.

CHAPTER 15

MERCY

I was no stranger to being followed. That was how this all began in the first place; it became a familiar sensation. My skin prickled at the surface while my heart pounded heavily against my chest. Once again, my life was tethered by a rope, threatening me with death, and I was left unable to see the predator until it was too late. But things were different now.

I'm ready this time.

The leaves weren't crackling beneath their feet, though. They were careful. Whoever was in the woods this time knew what they were doing. Maybe it was my Spirit senses and gifts that Tatyana had given me when I was born that allowed me to detect even the slightest of threats. Or it was just my human instinct.

I hurried into my house and secured the lock behind me, activating a secondary shield spell as well. According to her last text, Leah and the guys were out getting burgers and milkshakes. Unless they decided at the last minute to go somewhere else, I would be alone until ten tonight. I could have called Caleb, but did I really need him?

I locked all the windows and placed the box I had found on the doorstep on my kitchen counter. I stared at it for what felt like fifteen minutes before I grabbed a knife from the drawer and sliced through the tape.

After pulling up the flaps, I immediately stepped back.

Well, I didn't expect this.

Inside the box was a tightly sealed glass mason jar of what appeared to be blood. Folded around the jar with a rubber band was a small note.

I've seen my share of blood, but this was different. I was being threatened in some sick fuck's game. This was a message.

I should probably call Caleb now.

I rang his phone, but he didn't pick up.

Okay, I guess I'm calling Dorian.

He, luckily, did pick up. I explained what I had seen to Dorian, and he agreed to come over to help me. When he arrived at my house twenty minutes later, my nerves had calmed enough to where I had finally stopped pacing the floor.

"I haven't touched anything." I gestured to the box and looked up to meet his eyes. "Is this human blood?"

My curiosity was piqued, wondering if he could smell it through a sealed mason jar.

Dorian shook his head. "It's sealed airtight," he explained. "I'll need to open it."

"No. Don't," I said. "What about fingerprints?"

"For one," he started with a slight grin adorning his face, "if someone went to this length to send this to you, I guarantee they were wise enough to wear gloves. I'd be careful about my own fingerprints, but you and I know we aren't giving this over to the police."

Okay, he was right. This was a situation only *we* could handle. I walked over to the mason jar, grabbed the lid, gripped it tightly, and turned it until the sealed lid popped up, releasing the air inside. The pungent aroma of copper and iron filled my senses, and nausea flooded my stomach. I looked up at Dorian as his fangs protruded and his eyes turned as red as the liquid inside the jar. He clapped his hand over his nose and mouth and backed up, composing himself, letting out the breath he had been holding in.

"Yeah, that's blood," he affirmed.

"Is this human blood?" I asked.

He nodded.

I quickly grabbed the lid and sealed it back up. I quickly turned on the vent below the microwave to get the smell out of the kitchen. Perhaps just the scent alone would drive Dorian into a frenzy, and I wasn't going to be responsible for having to beat the shit out of him to protect myself. Since I came back into his life, it was apparent that he had changed somehow; he was always on edge. It didn't help that my blood was like liquid gold to vampires since my Awakening, tempting them with a delicious scent until it turned them human again when they'd lose control and drink from me. I watched carefully as Dorian shuddered. Whatever blood lust had claimed him finally released its hold.

I placed the jar back on the counter and pulled the note from under it.

St. Mary's Cemetery. 9 P.M. Come alone.

I looked up at Dorian. "This may be the only way to find out who's doing this. I know it's crazy, but I have to go."

"You don't have to explain this to me," Dorian said. "I'm not telling you not to go, but I am coming with you. Don't worry. I'm good at staying hidden."

My mouth pulled up at the side into a smirk, remembering how he and Noah had somehow gone undetected for the last year, as he lived only a few miles from me.

I nodded and eyed the clock. It was eight-thirty.

"We need to go, then," I said.

I didn't have a plan. All I hoped for was that whoever this asshole was wouldn't be a coward tonight and that they would show themselves so I could take them the fuck out.

⁓·ℓℓℓ·⁓

We drove to Saint Mary's Cemetery and parked a few blocks down the road. Dorian hid behind a large grove of trees as I cast my eyes around the grounds. No intuitive abilities were screaming at me—I didn't see or sense anyone.

"Come out, you fucking coward!" I screamed, holding my hands out while energy hovered slightly over my fingertips.

Though I didn't see any movement between the tombs or the trees behind them, I did spot an object a few hundred yards away. It was difficult to see exactly what it was because it was too dark outside, and the cemetery wasn't lit up by the streetlights. I approached a massive cement crypt with trepidation. As I neared it, my heart began to beat faster than ever before when I could clearly see what it was.

Not *it*, but who it was.

A rush of adrenaline shot down my spine, immobilizing me—spinning my head in circles. I had to pace my breathing to slow down my pulse as the aching pain in my chest grew.

No ... No! It can't be.

"Dorian?!" I yelled, but he was already speeding toward me. I felt the breeze from his movements fan my skin before he stopped by my side, staring at the body with me.

"Oh, fuck," Dorian said.

"Is it really her?" I asked, turning to look at him. "I don't understand. Where are her wings?"

"She's fallen," he explained, keeping his eyes locked on her lifeless body.

What does that mean—fallen?

I turned back to the crypt. Tatyana, the angel who had created me and my coven, was sprawled across the concrete lid on her back. She was dead.

Tatyana looked like an ordinary human because her wings were missing. Not cut off, but as if they were never there to begin with. Her eyes bulged open in shock, frozen in time. Her pale face was now bloodied, as if someone had struck her repeatedly with their fist. A look of pure horror was painted across her face—the last thing the killer saw—would now be forever embedded in my own mind.

A sword pierced through her stomach, and congealing blood dripped down the cement crypt onto the cemetery grounds.

"Who could do this?" I whispered.

My legs buckled underneath me, causing me to collapse to the ground. As much as I tried, I couldn't hold in the vomit that rose in my throat. After I stopped throwing up, I wiped my lips with my sleeve and then placed my hands on the grass. My nails dug deep into the soil while gritting my teeth, willing myself not to faint. I felt Dorian's hand on my shoulders, and I squeezed my eyes shut as his touch attempted to soothe me. After a few minutes, I turned to face him and held my hand out so he could pull me to my feet.

Someone had slaughtered my creator. Why was she even here? And what the fuck happened to her wings?

CHAPTER 16

MERCY

The coven surrounded me as my hands trembled around a hot mug of tea. Leah rubbed my arm, attempting to soothe me, but I couldn't relax. I couldn't get the image out of my mind of Tatyana's body impaled by that sword, lying in a pool of her own blood that painted the grass beneath her.

"She's in shock," I heard Dorian tell them, but I looked up toward Caleb.

They can't see me like this. Pull yourself together.

"Tatyana's dead," I stated for the twentieth time.

"We know," I heard Caleb say as he sat beside me. "We're all in shock with you."

"How did this happen?" I asked, still not understanding what I had seen. Angels couldn't die. They were immortal.

I looked over at Dorian, who had his arms crossed over his chest. "She's fallen."

"Yeah, you said that earlier. What the hell does that mean?" I asked.

"When Tatyana rescued Noah and me from Maurice's lair," Dorian said, "she told me she couldn't return to Earth again. That was her only chance to meet you face-to-face since she created the five of you, and to make things right. The angel was only allowed to create the Chosen Ones, not help you beyond that. She explained that if she were ever to return, she'd have to sacrifice her wings by becoming mortal. Hence, a fallen angel."

I looked at Caleb and the rest of the coven. "But why would she do that? Why was she even here?" Dorian shrugged, so I looked over at Caleb. "Why would she sacrifice her wings?"

"I don't know, either," Caleb said. "If Tatyana went so far as to sacrifice her immortality, she must have been desperate to reach you."

My hands gripped into fists as the only obvious explanation hit me. "Maurice. It must be Maurice." I looked up. "She took down his clan to rescue everyone and took everything from him. Maybe she came to warn us about what he's been doing, and he killed Tatyana to stop her." I turned to Caleb again. "It *has* to be him."

Caleb placed his hand on mine and gripped it tightly. "Then we'll find the piece of shit and put a stake through his heart."

The rest of the coven had been silent up until now. They joined Caleb, agreeing that Maurice was the prime suspect in the murders in East Greenwich and of Tatyana. However, Ezra mentioned a good point. It could be two completely different killers. A vampire hadn't killed Tatyana. It was death by sword, not by a bite.

The fury in the room from the coven gave me hope. I wasn't alone in my anger and desperation to find Maurice and make him pay for what he was doing. All of what he had done to Tatyana, to the innocent victims in East Greenwich. It had to end now.

"What do you want to do?" Caleb asked me, his voice deep yet calm.

"I want to *talk* to Maurice. We can't kill him just yet," I said, knowing they would never be okay with that. "Believe me, killing Maurice is our top priority, but he has answers he cannot confess when he's a pile of dust."

"No." This time, Leah stepped up. "No way. It's too dangerous, and you know it."

"I'll go with her," Dorian said, stepping near me. "I know Maurice and every single one of you knows I'd give my life to protect her."

"And you betrayed him," Caleb reminded him. "He'll kill you without a single thought of remorse." When Caleb saw Dorian by my side and me not backing down, he added, "So, the three of us will go."

That wasn't exactly what I wanted. Caleb and Dorian despised each other, and we had yet to work as a team for any cause. I wasn't ready for it.

"What do you want us to do?" Simon asked, moving toward Ezra and Leah.

"I'd love to kick a vampire's ass right about now. It's been painfully too long," Ezra suggested, pulling his lips into a wicked grin.

"No one is kicking anyone's ass, not yet," I said. "I just need to talk to Maurice and find out what he wants. My blood is of no use to him. He doesn't want to be human. Do you think he'd honestly risk his life over us taking down his lair? He knows we can't be killed unless ..." I paused, looking up at Caleb. "Caleb, when was the last time you checked on the dagger?"

"The dagger?" Leah barked. "I thought Joel teleported it somewhere we weren't supposed to know about?"

Caleb turned to her. "Simon and I teleported to its location and retrieved it to protect Joel. He isn't strong enough to defend himself against a witch trying to read his mind. I have it hidden in Abigail's mansion."

Simon looked down and tried not to make eye contact with Leah and Ezra.

Leah gasped out in surprise, and Ezra threw his hands up.

"The fuck is wrong with you two?" Ezra said. "That would've been nice to be included in that decision when our fucking lives depend on whether our enemies find it." His tone was full of both anger and panic. He then turned to Simon. "I expected something like this from Caleb but not from you, man. You put us all at risk."

Simon shrugged.

"Enough!" I yelled. I was too exhausted for this shit. "Caleb, we need to go check on the dagger. Now. Simon, you and the others need to run surveillance and gather as much information as you can about what happened to Tatyana. Follow up on Ezra's theory of a potential second killer."

The guys were still adamant about me going to see Maurice, so it looked like Caleb, Dorian, and I were going on a little trip together after we made sure the dagger was where Caleb had put it.

⸺︰ﷅﻬ⸺

We climbed into Caleb's car and went to the mansion, heading up to the second floor and into Caleb's bedroom. He lifted the floorboard, opened the safe, and cracked open the lid.

All we did was stare for a long moment. It felt as if all the air had left my lungs, yet I managed to speak.

"Caleb, how could this happen? You said this would be more secure, that there were security spells on top of the safe's lock. How did someone get into the mansion in the first place?" I asked him while keeping my eyes on the empty safe before us.

His mouth gaped open.

"Caleb?" I repeated his name, watching him blink several times before turning to face me.

"Only a witch could have opened this," Caleb finally answered.

"We're such fools," I added. When I felt a cool touch, I looked down to see Dorian's hand wrapped around mine, gripping it firmly.

"Maurice will never lay a hand on you again," Dorian said. "I'll kill him myself if I have to."

Caleb narrowed his eyes to where I held Dorian's hand, but I didn't care. I was furious at Caleb for being so careless about hiding the dagger without going through the coven first. I should have moved it somewhere safer the moment I found out it was *only* in a safe in the mansion.

"Let's go," I said to them both before we headed out of the mansion and drove toward Salem, where Noah had just reported having seen Maurice.

CHAPTER 17

MERCY

This new lair was vastly different from the gothic mansion Maurice had lived in. It almost looked normal. Almost too normal. There was no security gate or sentries guarding the door. There were no signs of movement from within the building.

Something was off.

Noah reported he had spotted Maurice coming in and out of this two-story Victorian-style home several times a week since he started to trail him. We guessed this was his new home.

I could already feel my powers spark beneath my skin, but I had to take a few deep breaths to conceal it so I didn't lose control. My father taught me how to subdue my powers whenever I'd get too angry during the few weeks that I stayed with him. We found that whenever my emotions took over, so did my magic. The result would be massive bursts of destructive energy. We believed it was due to me not being able to gradually get used to them over the course of twenty-two years, which is why witches didn't get all their powers at once. It was too overwhelming. In the last year, I had not only learned what I was, but I'd gained all my magic *and* my mother's all at once. I thought I had control, but it was evident that I didn't.

"We should just knock," I suggested. Dorian and Caleb looked at me like I was crazy. "If he feels threatened, he'll attack us without a second thought."

They must have known I was right because they didn't argue with me.

Slowly, we walked up to the door and knocked.

The feeling of butterflies fluttered in my stomach when Kyoko opened the door. She was pretty loyal. I had to give her that.

"Mercy," Kyoko said, calling me by my given name. "We weren't expecting you at our doorstep at this hour of the night. Maurice will be thrilled to see you again. However, it will have to wait until morning. He's finishing his midnight snack—a beautiful redhead-ed woman we've kept locked behind our doors to buy some time until you found us. It helps Maurice fill a void." Her eyes darkened as she glared into mine. "To be honest, I'm a bit surprised how long it's taken you."

I didn't want to give her the impression that her words would faze or upset me, so I stayed silent, staring her down. Kyoko straightened out her pencil skirt and fidgeted with her fingers for a few seconds before we heard footsteps coming toward us. It was clear that I made her nervous, which gave me great satisfaction.

Kyoko's eyes landed on Dorian, and she licked her lips. "Dori-an, looking sexy as ever," she added right before Maurice stepped between us, causing Kyoko to step back. My stomach churned, but I had to remind myself to be strong. The only thoughts going through my mind were the memories of every God-awful thing he had done to me a year ago.

Dorian grabbed my right hand, and Caleb gripped my left, attempting to push me back, but I kept my feet planted on the doormat, refusing to cower to my enemy.

"Well," Maurice said, his voice unnervingly calm, "come on in, you three." His eyes never left mine. A sinister smile flitted across his lips as I walked past him, and it felt like a hard lump was pressing against my throat.

Dorian and Caleb stayed close to me while we entered the home. It felt like I had two bodyguards glued to my hips that I didn't need. I wondered if the protection was for me or for Maurice and Kyoko. They knew I was on the verge of ripping their fucking heads off.

Kyoko rested her back against the wall by the fireplace while Maurice adjusted his silk, collared shirt and glared at me as if he wanted to devour every part of my soul. My magic stirred.

Relax, Mercy, or you're going to lose control.

"The dagger," I said, keeping my voice level. "Where the hell did you hide it?"

Maurice chuckled and turned to Kyoko. "Did you take their precious little dagger?"

Kyoko shook her head and smirked. "Of course not."

As much as I wanted answers, the two of them made my skin crawl. Their behavior was odd, and it only made me more nervous about being there. I learned a few things in the brief time I spent around Maurice. He was smart, calculated, and five steps ahead of me.

Maurice didn't move closer to us, though I could see in his eyes he was ready to strike. He wouldn't while I had Caleb and Dorian on each side of me, still caging me in. I wanted to kill this son of a bitch, but I needed answers.

"Cut the bullshit, Maurice. Where is it?" Caleb asked.

Maurice chuckled again and then subtly licked his upper lips, his eyes growing darker. "If I had the dagger, I'd be plunging it straight into the covens' chests.

I wasn't sure how to respond to that.

It wasn't the death threat. That was expected coming from him, but was he telling the truth? Maurice may be a murderous asshole, but he never hid who he was.

Could it be someone else? Maurice was too narcissistic not to admit how "badass" he was for being one step ahead of us.

"The killings in East Greenwich?" I started again. "Is *that* you?"

Maurice shook his head. "No. I don't need to kill human scum to get to you. I've been watching you ever since you left my lair, you know." He took a step closer, and Caleb and Dorian gripped my arms, trying to push me back again. "If I wanted you dead, I'd come for you."

My stomach fluttered again. I didn't want to be afraid of Maurice, but I was.

"Tatyana?" I asked. "What about her?"

Maurice stood there, non-responsive, and then a slow grin formed on his face. "Oh, yes. That one *was* me."

I pounced on him like a lion after a gazelle, a vicious scream tearing from my throat. Green energy flew not just from my fingertips but from my entire body. Maurice plummeted to the ground as I tackled him. I heard a commotion behind me, but I ignored it, focused only on the smug bastard beneath me. I used my superhuman strength and punched him straight in the face, drawing blood from his lip. As I used my powers to pin him to the ground, I slammed my fist harder and harder. I wanted to kill the piece of shit and rip his head off with my bare hands. I could have easily killed him right then and there if I wanted to, but I needed to know why. Why did he kill her?

Strong arms wrapped around my waist, hoisting me off him.

"No!" I screamed, kicking my legs in the air. "I'm not fucking finished, Dorian. Put me down!"

I looked back at Caleb while still wrapped in Dorian's grasp. He had Kyoko in a firm chokehold. I knew it wouldn't be enough to subdue her for long unless we plunged a stake through her heart, but it was enough to keep her still ... for now.

Maurice stood in front of us, panting, his face covered in blood, while Dorian slowly put me back down on the ground.

"Why?" I asked. "Why did you kill her?" Adrenaline still coursed through my veins, and I was shaking with rage.

Maurice chuckled and glared at me with red eyes blazing. "I'd been following you for months, little witch. Months! Every second, I thought about retaking you. Oh, if you only knew what I had planned for us. Just when I was finally within reach, that fucking angel got in my way. Tatyana destroyed everything I had built. To my surprise, her wings were gone. I don't know why she was there, but I wasn't going to let her reach you. She had to pay for what she did, and I couldn't wait to watch your face as you looked at her, covered in blood. Oh, the satisfaction of watching you cry over her death tonight. It made me fucking hard."

My anger raged. "I hate you!"

"Likewise ... Akasha," he barked back with a sharp grin; it seemed as if he was enjoying our banter.

I cringed at the sound of the name he'd insisted on using a year ago. I hated that name and loathed the sound of it coming from his lips. I raised my left hand and snapped my fingers. Green cords of light shot from the floor and wrapped around Maurice's legs, yanking him to his knees and holding him in place. I relished in the look of indignation Maurice made.

"Keep him on the ground," Dorian ordered. "I'm going to look around for the dagger."

Caleb remained, gripping Kyoko's arms and keeping her in place.

Maurice didn't take his eyes off me. The wounds from my bloodied fist had already healed, and Maurice wiped off his own blood with the bottom of his shirt.

Dorian came in a few minutes later, shaking his head. "I don't see it anywhere, but it doesn't mean it's not here."

"What about the girl Kyoko mentioned?" I asked. "Is she okay?"

Dorian shook his head. "She's injured, but she'll live. I helped her slip out through the back door."

The side of Maurice's lips turned up. "Always ruining my fun," Maurice said. "The three of you can get the fuck out of my house now. I don't have your dagger. As I said, I would have used it to kill the coven already." He glared back at me. "But not you, Mercy." His head cocked to the right. "I have other plans for you ... for *us.*"

I tensed. *What the fuck does that mean?*

Caleb released Kyoko but shoved her hard, causing her small frame to fly forward. His boot slammed next to her, a threat if she were to move.

I stepped toward Maurice, kicking him in the face one more time with the toe of my boot. He was held on his knees, giving me all the power. If I weren't ready to kill him, I'd make him suffer just a little longer.

The bastard was up to something, and knowing Maurice, he wouldn't be working alone. Yes, he was smart, but he always had an army of followers ready to do his bidding.

"I have a stake," Caleb said, gesturing to his hip with his eyes. "You can use it on them right now. End it."

After he handed it over, I wrapped my fingers around the grip. "Not yet," I said. "Not until we find out what they're hiding from us." I turned to Maurice. "What are you not telling me?

Maurice stayed silent, all but a challenger's smile playing over his lips.

Fine.

I walked over to face Kyoko, her eyes widening. "Drink from my wrist or die, Kyoko," I ordered.

Her eyes grew even wider, and she looked at Maurice as if she hoped he would save her, but he wouldn't move to her rescue. His eyes, however, were crimson red, and he threatened me by showing his fangs.

"Answer, Kyoko, or I'll decide for you," I threatened.

"I'd rather die than be a pathetic human," she said, sizing me up.

I stepped closer to her, and she didn't move. However, Maurice did. I had loosened the magic holding him down, anticipating he would charge. He bolted toward me with lightning speed, but Caleb lifted his hands and blasted a flame at him, hitting Maurice hard against the chest. Dorian rushed to his side, keeping him down with the palm of his hand, and I re-tightened the cords.

"I'm sorry, but you and Maurice are too dangerous when you work together. But don't worry, Maurice will be joining you very soon in whatever dark hell you guys go to."

"Oh, Mercy," she hissed, "if you only knew your fate. You think this is over, but it's just the beginning."

A shiver slithered down my spine. The threat was real. I knew it in my gut; the duo had something planned.

"Goodbye, Kyoko. I hope there's peace for you in the afterlife, allowing you to be reunited with your parents again," I whispered as I plunged the stake into her chest.

Maurice hissed with such viciousness behind me while trying to stand, but Dorian kicked him in the face so hard he blacked out. We knew it wouldn't be long before he regained consciousness, so I undid the binding magic, and we left as soon as I picked up the stake and handed it back to Caleb.

"Let's get the fuck out of here," I said.

CHAPTER 18

MERCY

Caleb had left to meet up with Melissa once we got back to my house. He was worried about her, especially now that we had pissed off Maurice enough that he would start going after the ones we cared about. I called Lily, Joel, and Riley to let them know the latest information and to be on guard.

Dorian and I stood outside my place when he dropped me off. The rest of the coven waited for me inside. "Can we talk for a minute?" he asked.

I nodded.

"I know this is terrible timing, but there's an art gallery show on Friday that I think you'd enjoy. You've mentioned a couple of times about Joel and Derek's art pieces in New York. I figured, if they're living in East Greenwich now, this would be a great opportunity for them to make some contacts." He let out a small laugh under his breath. "The art pieces might be a bit different from theirs, but they might enjoy it."

My forehead creased. "You want to meet my uncles?" I asked.

It's not as if that would surprise me. Dorian wasn't as pushy as Caleb was about reversing the spell, but Dorian was at least trying to be friends. Friends meet each other's families. I needed to not read into it. It's not as if he was taking me on a date. Maybe having my family there would make it less awkward.

"When have you ever wanted to get to know Joel and Derek?" I asked, but he only frowned. "Dorian, what's going on?"

He looked away, then back at me. "I needed a hobby when you left me," he confessed.

"This is *your* event?" I asked, surprised. Dorian had never mentioned any hobbies he had in this life.

I smiled. "I'd love to go."

It had been a while since I had done anything for myself outside of training with the coven. With everything going on—the murders, the dagger missing, and Maurice threatening us—the timing wasn't the best. Still, I was going to lose my goddamn mind if I didn't do anything fun.

Dorian and I arrived at the gallery event around seven in the evening. A server walked by with a serving tray of wine, and I grabbed one before she could pass me.

I felt more nervous tonight than I had in a while. Maybe the wine would help me relax a bit. My mind couldn't shake the thought that Maurice was going to strike after what I did to Kyoko. What I had learned from the clan when I stayed in the lair was that Kyoko and Maurice were best friends. He saw her like a sister, and now, I had just taken away the last of his family.

There was also that feeling we all shared that he was up to something, and whatever the plan was, it was about to hit us straight on.

"I don't find pleasure in telling you what to do," Dorian said, "but I know alcohol can cripple your powers, so maybe only one drink? Just in case." The coolness from his breath near my skin created goosebumps on my neck.

What the hell?

"I just need to relax," I confessed. I was unsure if the nervous feeling was because Maurice could break down these doors at any moment or because I was with Dorian tonight. Someone I loved eons ago. I had to remind myself that if it was the latter, it was just physical attraction.

It has to be.

"Are you nervous about something?" Dorian teased with a slight smirk that pulled at the side of his mouth.

I resisted the urge to roll my eyes, not wanting to entertain his assumptions, and looked around the gallery. My mouth gaped open as I saw the paintings around me. They were breathtaking ... and familiar.

I padded across the gallery toward a painting of a woman's face, colored in dark amber, green, and yellow. It was a face that reflected my own. I turned toward the others, which were all from our old village in Salem. He had painted images of ancient buildings from my visions. There were paintings of children in Puritan clothing playing in a grassy field filled with vibrant purple daisies.

They were all so beautiful but also sad. Dorian had created a world that was no longer mine, no longer ours. But why?

I turned to him. "Why did you paint these?"

He had a slight smile that didn't reach his eyes before taking a sip of the white wine from his glass. "It was the last time I was truly happy—when I had you as mine."

How do I respond to this?

"See, Joel, why are we not opening a gallery here? Look how many guests have shown up," I heard Derek ask. I felt instant relief that they were here.

"True," Joel replied. "I wasn't sure how long we'd be here to even think about opening another gallery. We'll have to look into it later." Joel picked up a champagne glass from the tray as the same server walked by.

"Grab two," I said to him.

Joel raised an eyebrow.

"I don't blame you for worrying about me, but I kind of need this tonight," I confessed. "After what we did to Kyoko ..."

"You know you had to," Joel said. "We all know you didn't have a choice."

"Tell that to the psychopath who'll be coming for my blood now," I said.

Joel rolled his eyes. "More reason to not drink." He grabbed my half-empty glass and placed it next to me on a marble console table against the wall. Then he placed his hand on the curve of Derek's lower back, escorting him to the wall near the back that was covered with Dorian's art.

Dorian reached for my hand and intertwined his fingers with mine. "Come on," he said. "I want you to meet a few new friends of mine."

* * *

After the party had ended around eleven, Dorian grabbed my jacket from the coat closet and locked the gallery up.

I heard a text come through as I climbed into his car. Lily and Bradley wanted to host a breakfast tomorrow morning at her place with just the family. They had something to share with us.

Before I exited the car, Dorian leaned in, kissing me gently on the cheek.

I looked at him in surprise. "What was that for?" I asked, feeling my cheeks blush.

He sucked on his bottom lip, looking away as if trying to avoid my eyes.

"I know it's been strange lately between us," he said, but his eyes turned back to meet mine, "but having you there tonight meant everything to me." That adorable smile I committed to memory years ago flashed across his face, showing his teeth.

"Well, how did you do tonight?" I asked. "Did you sell any paintings?"

He smiled. "I sold about eight and grabbed a few business cards, but honestly, I don't do it for the money. Just having the paintings there for people to look at and for me to see them on display is all that matters."

I placed my hand on his and tilted my head. "I'm sorry you feel like you can't be happy anymore."

He turned his palm up and squeezed my hand. "I *am* happy."

I hope so.

"Night, Dorian," I said, kissing him back on the cheek. The moment my lips touched his cold skin, my stomach pleasantly jumped. It was as if I couldn't tear my face away from him, losing his scent and the feeling my body experienced by being near him. "Thank you for inviting me. I ... I enjoy seeing this side of you."

I leaned back, placing my hand on the door handle and watching his gaze that wouldn't leave mine.

CHAPTER 19

CALEB

Melissa's hands trembled as I reached out and caressed them with my fingertips, hoping to steady her aim. "Now pull it back and let go," I instructed.

She steadied the bow, then released it. The arrow flew toward the target and hit the tree a few inches from the center. "Yes! Was that good? I think it was good. I mean, for a rookie, right?"

Fuck, she's so adorable.

"That was hot," I said playfully. "We can practice out here any time you'd like. I know you hate guns, so learning archery is a great alternative."

Melissa laughed. "Are you trying to turn me into a superhero?" she asked. "I'm not like your coven."

I brushed the curls from her face. "You might not have magic; being armed is the best alternative. Right now, with Maurice on the loose, we can't risk it."

"I carry a can of mace," she said. "I mean, honestly, you think I'm going to carry a bow and arrow every time I walk alone?"

I chuckled. It was silly. Melissa needed something practical she'd always have with her, but watching her shoot an arrow toward a tree was the highlight of my morning. She looked so sexy doing it.

"How about this? I'll show you how to throw a knife and not miss the center of their eyes. You can keep a dagger in your purse instead."

She nodded. "That's more like it. You can teach me during our next session, Sensei," she teased, bringing her palms together and bowing.

I leaned in, placed my hands around her neck, and pulled her to me. Her lips met mine, passionately and seductively. She was driving me crazy, and I fucking loved it.

Melissa's hand lingered on the back of my head, threading her fingers into my long hair. My cock twitched as she gave my scalp a squeeze.

Fuck.

I wanted to get her back to my place and spend a few hours worshiping her body, but I had to train with the coven.

"Caleb, I ..." Melissa cut off her sentence, biting her bottom lip. I didn't know what she wanted to say to me, but she looked like she was battling something in her mind. "I have to get back to the office."

No, that wasn't what she wanted to say, but I didn't press her.

"You also have your training, right?" she asked.

I nodded. "Yeah, the coven's on their way. It's easier for us to practice the magic part of our defense outside the basement. Just in case it gets out of hand." I laughed, and she shook her head at me.

"You guys are crazy," she said as she leaned in to plant a kiss on my lips one last time.

ele

Shortly after Melissa left, the rest of the coven showed up in the forest behind Scalloptown Park, except for Mercy. She had something planned at her aunt's house this morning.

"I like this spot. It's more secluded than where we've trained before," Leah said as she neared the clearing.

I had cleared an area of forest debris and stood at the center before Leah, Simon, and Ezra walked over.

After joining hands, we formed a circle, closed our eyes, and chanted a spell we had been working on for the past six months. I felt my powers flow through me and amplify, and when we opened our eyes, they were all glowing a bright shade of color representing our elements. Breaking the circle, we positioned ourselves in a fighting stance.

"We're going to be testing out new attack spells on each other. When something becomes too much, you need to give the signal for the caster to drop the magic. Otherwise, we'll keep going," I instructed, cracking my neck in preparation, and I nodded at Leah to begin.

Leah lifted her hands and pulled the water from the surrounding soil. It had rained earlier, so she could extract enough to form a large orb of water in her palms.

"Alright, you can use me, Leah. Go for it," Ezra said, just seconds before Leah threw the water ball at him and encased his head, drowning him with her powers.

"Fuck!" he mouthed, stumbling back.

Ezra pulled his hands up to his neck and gasped for air. After a few seconds of struggling, Ezra gave the submission signal, waving his hand in the air with three fingers flushed together. She released the water back down to the earth, and Ezra coughed up the remaining liquid that had entered his lungs. "Holy shit, Leah." He coughed some more. "Can we trade powers for the day? That spell worked great!" he asked. "I feel like your powers have gotten a lot stronger, too. That was fucking badass."

Leah winked at Ezra before Simon stepped forward.

"This might hurt a little, guys," he warned. "You all might want to start running."

Simon lifted his hands, and a gentle draft tickled my neck. The force of the breeze increased, and the leaves around us blew violently like a hurricane passing by. It wrapped around the coven like a tornado, and Leah had to brace herself on the ground, clinging to the trunk of a tree to keep from flying away. As the wind encircled the coven, I felt my breath leave my lungs, and I could no longer gasp for air. I became lightheaded, and Ezra's hand raised, signaling it was enough. Carefully, Simon lowered his hands while we all gasped for air again, pulling it back into our lungs so we could breathe.

Ezra turned to me. "I'm ... next," he said, still trying to catch his breath, but his wild eyes were filled with a hunger which I was familiar.

We were so fucked.

Leah and Simon exchanged glances before Leah readjusted her grip on the tree, and Simon hunkered down by a fallen log. I took a few steps back, ready to make a run for it if Ezra decided to split the earth open beneath my feet.

Ezra shook his head. "Yeah, that's not going to save you, ass-holes," he taunted, raising his hands, and I heard the roots ripping from the trees around us as he pulled branches in our direction. He threw his hands out, and forest debris flew toward Simon, grabbing him by the foot and pulling him away from the large log he held on to. Ezra directed the earth to move away from him, the log now slipping from Simon's hands. A branch from the log wrapped around his wrist and, with the debris tether, stretched his body until he could no longer move.

Leah bolted to my right, which wasn't the best choice of action. Ezra used his powers to pull the soil up from the ground, creating a hole that Leah fell into.

I pulled my arms out to the sides. Fireballs appeared at my fin-gertips, and I threw them toward Ezra, but he had powered up the leaves on the ground in front of him to create a wall for protection. The fireball slammed into it and torched the leaves instead. Ezra slammed his hand into the dirt, sending a wave of soil toward me, ready to encase me in an earthen tomb.

I held up a hand for everything to stop. Ezra scrunched up his face before releasing the power. He obviously didn't want it to end while he had the upper hand on us. After the earth settled, he walked to Leah to help her out of the hole.

"Okay, I think this was the most fun we have had in a while," Leah said as she gripped Ezra's hand. "We need to do this more often, Caleb."

Simon brushed off the twigs and leaves sticking to his sweater. "The sparring is fun and all, but there's nothing like using our powers," Simon added.

"I know. But it's the same shit I've been telling Mercy since she went through her Awakening," I said. "There may be a situation where our powers are taken from us like they were with Mercy when she was held captive in the lair. By all of us improving our fighting skills with our hands, not magic, it may be the only thing that can save us."

"Yeah, we get it, but this was much more fun." Ezra beamed. "Admit it."

I looked up at the sky, and gray clouds were forming overhead. "Shit. A storm is supposed to roll in today. We can keep practicing or head out."

"Let's keep training," Leah answered for everyone.

Simon and Ezra both agreed.

We trained for another hour, but we headed back when the storm became too fierce. With Ezra's power, he controlled the elements of the earth, which also meant he could control the weather. Still, we vowed to let nature take its course and only use our magic if it was necessary or when we were training.

CHAPTER 20

MERCY

It was early, and I mean early. I eyed the clock as I neared Lily's home, which read eight in the morning.

On a Saturday.

I had barely fallen asleep around two in the morning, and the coffee had stirred me awake.

Why the hell do people do this?

I walked in and found Lily in the kitchen, cooking our breakfast. Bradley sat at the table and smiled at me the moment we locked eyes. Joel was watching the morning news in the living room, but I didn't see Derek anywhere.

"Where's Derek?" I asked as I joined him on the couch.

Joel turned to face me. "I bought a ticket for him last night to fly back to New York early this morning."

I cocked an eyebrow. "Everything okay?"

He nodded. "Mercy, this shit that's going on with Maurice and the killings; we both realized our place is here, where we can protect you. Well, me. I won't put Derek in the crossfire. But he could at least head back home, meet with our real estate agent, and find us a place closer to you two."

"Wait, are you moving here permanently?" I asked, my voice rising.

Joel smiled and turned off the TV, directing his attention back to me. "We are. We're going to list our home in two weeks," he said. "Derek's going to get the house ready for showings this weekend."

I beamed, "That's amazing news!" I looked over at Lily in the kitchen. "Is that why everyone is meeting here? To tell me that?"

He shook his head. "No, the news is something Lily wants to share with us. I still don't even know."

"Breakfast is ready, guys," Lily called from the kitchen.

Lily had made pancakes with chocolate and fruit toppings, and I didn't waste a minute before diving in, forking the edge of my pancake, not adding any toppings yet.

"Alright, what's the big news you wanted to share?" I asked, my mouth stuffed.

She looked at Bradley, who flashed a massive grin, then held out her hand. A shiny diamond ring almost blinded me. The buttery pancake turned to a bland paste on my tongue, and I swallowed hard.

I looked over, and Joel looked just as surprised as I was.

"Oh, congratulations, guys," I said, hoping she couldn't hear the hesitancy in my tone. I was happy for them, I really was, but fuck, we barely knew him, and what did that mean for our secret? Joel had never intended to tell Derek about being a witch, but one day, he had walked in on Joel performing a spell when Joel wasn't expecting him home. They had already been married for a few years but had dated since they were in high school. We loved Derek. We trusted him; to this day, he's told no one, and he accepted that part of our lives.

But Bradley? I wasn't sure.

Maybe Bradley was like that, too, but I'd been so busy with this newfound discovery of who I was that I hadn't been able to get to know him as I should have by now.

"Thank you," Lily said, but her beaming smile turned into a frown.

Okay, she noticed the tone in my voice.

Bradley squeezed her hand when he noticed her behavior change. "We aren't getting married right away, Mercy," he added. "We're setting the wedding date for next spring. It will give us all more time to get to know each other and plan the wedding the way Lily had dreamed about since she was a kid."

What the hell? Since when?

Lily never dreamed about getting married. She hated the idea of marriage being a contract with a piece of paper. Lily didn't want or need those items to prove how committed she was to the person she was with.

Then again, a lot had changed in the last four years. Maybe Lily had, too.

We all became quiet during the meal, eating in silence except to ask for the syrup or bowls of toppings. Afterward, we cleaned the dishes, and Bradley and Joel stepped into the family room to watch a game on the TV. Lily had brewed fresh coffee, and after pouring a cup, I leaned against the counter, eyeing her.

"Does he know about us?" I asked. "Or do you plan to tell him?"

Lily placed the last plate in the dishwasher and turned to face me. She leaned her back against the counter and wrapped her arms around her waist. "I want to tell him. I even brought it up to Caleb the other day. It won't be easy to keep quiet about the fact that you and Joel aren't witches, and yet I am. We're from the same bloodline. Not that people who don't know about us would put something like that together, but he would. Bradley's sharp."

I nodded. "I get it. You can tell Bradley I'm a witch, but I don't speak for Joel. I think telling him about the whole vampire thing may be a bit overwhelming, though."

She chuckled. "Yeah, Bradley may not take that so well."

I smiled. "Tell him but know that it could put his life in danger the more he knows."

"I thought about that," she said. "The whole 'keeping a secret from your loved ones to keep them safe.'" She looked down and bit her lower lip. "But it didn't keep Cami safe."

Jesus, Lily. That stung.

Not that Lily blamed me, though I sure blamed myself. The difference was Cami didn't know about us, and yet she had been taken over by the darkest of evil. I failed to protect her by being so ignorant.

I started thinking about Cami being locked away inside the Asylum, all alone and terrified about what was happening to her. There was no way for her to escape her nightmare.

"I should go visit her today," I sighed, feeling guilt stab at my heart.

"If you'd like, I'll go with you," Lily suggested.

I shook my head. "No, it's fine." I leaned into the family room. "Congrats again, Bradley." His eyes stayed glued to the TV. "Joel, I'm heading to Salem to see Cami. I'll catch up with you later."

They both waved a hand to send me off, which was good enough.

Mr. Kriser handed me my badge and escorted me to the same area where my mom had died in my arms. A rush of emotions hit me as I neared that door that led into the room that changed my entire life.

My mom didn't just die in there; I killed her. I don't know how long after someone died that their spirit lingered in or above them, but I felt my mom watching me cry. I would never get that feeling out of my mind.

I probably should have gone through therapy after what happened, but I went from losing my mom, to my Awakening, to bringing down Maurice's lair, to having to train daily to be this vampire hunter that I was destined to be. I couldn't mourn like ordinary people. There was nothing I could even do to heal my mind. I had to live in a fucking nightmare, no matter how hard it was for me.

Mercy doesn't get a choice.

"This might be harder than I thought," I admitted as he gestured for me to enter the room.

He looked at the cracked-open door and back at me. "I can see if the break room is available."

I shook my head. "No, I ... I can do this. Sorry." I stared at the door intently. "Just give me a minute."

I shut my eyes and took a deep breath, hoping it would calm my nerves. After a few slow breaths, it worked. My body relaxed, but it wasn't only this room that made me nervous. This hospital suppressed our powers. I still had them, of course, but there was the shield that protected the staff from the creatures behind these walls from using magic, including me. This was the first time in a year I felt normal. It was both refreshing and terrifying.

When I entered the room, I spotted Cami lounging on a couch with her legs tucked under her. I watched her flip through the pages of a smutty romance book. That was progress. Cami loved reading before the possession.

"Hey, Cami. What's the newest smutty book you're reading?" I asked as I sat down next to her. "Oooh, he's hot." The shirtless guy on the cover held a woman's ass straddling him on a chair. When I looked over at the book's text, I noticed the letters were upside down. The sleeve from the book had been placed the wrong way. She wasn't reading it at all. Cami kept her eyes glued to the book and even flipped a page, scanning the words from top to bottom.

What the fuck?

"Mercy," Doctor Harrison said as he entered the rec room. He was the therapist that had been treating my mom. Leah had assigned him to Cami's case as he was a witch who would sometimes perform an exorcism or a spell to help those who had been taken hold by dark entities. The kind of power that would make you do something you normally wouldn't.

Leah had explained that they referred to him as a Witch Doctor. He could not only connect with someone's spirit if they were still alive but could communicate with spirits who had passed on after this life and wanted to speak with the living. The only spirits he couldn't connect with were vampires.

He had asked me several times in the past if I wanted to reach out to my mother after she died, but I refused. My mom must have hated me for what I did to her. The shame was too much to bear from what I had done, and I couldn't face the repercussions of a pissed-off ghost.

I stood to my feet, shook his hand, and looked at Cami again. "I'll be right back," I said.

Cami ignored me, still staring at the upside-down book as if she were deeply engrossed in the story.

"She's been like that since she arrived," Doctor Harrison explained as we entered the hall.

"She hasn't spoken to you?"

He shook his head. "Not a word."

This was disturbing. Cami at least spoke to me occasionally. It was always brief, but she still used her voice. Maybe she was scared and didn't trust anyone here. What if she was shutting down?

Doctor Harrison escorted me into his office and gestured for me to sit. He grabbed a folder and a recording device.

"When she first came here," he started, "I felt her energy, even inside these walls."

I held up my hand. "Wait, are you allowed to share this with me?"

It was a silly question. This wasn't a typical facility, and her mom wasn't in her right mind to make decisions for her. However, there was still the issue of doctor-patient confidentiality.

"I know what you're thinking," he continued. "I *can* share Cami's medical diagnosis with you. Laurie signed a consent form to allow us to speak with you on Cami's behalf."

I was happy to learn this. The more I knew, the more I could help her. *If* I could help her. I nodded for him to continue.

"The energy was not that of a normal human being who has experienced an evil possession. This was something I hadn't seen before.

He pressed play on the audio device in front of him. I heard Doctor Harrison ask Cami a few questions about how she was feeling, then Cami screamed. She cried out so loudly that Doctor Harrison fumbled with the device to turn it down. "Sorry," he said.

The scream faded, and she began mumbling gibberish. The words made no sense as if she were speaking in tongues.

"What is she saying?" I asked, leaning forward to listen better.

He shook his head. "Nothing I've ever heard." He turned off the recording device and opened the binder in front of him. "I performed a spell to reach her mind. I needed to see what *she's* seeing." He placed the notebook back down. "Mercy ... Cami is gone."

I must not have heard the doctor correctly. "I don't understand."

"When I performed the spell, I saw through her eyes, but not what she's seeing in this world. I saw much deeper than that," he explained. My stomach dropped so far down that it felt as if it hit the floor. I could only imagine the worst—the nightmares that kept her up at night.

"Tell me," I said.

He cupped his hands together and leaned back in his chair. "Cami's seeing Hell, or as we witches call it, the Underworld."

Those words stunned me into silence. I couldn't breathe for a second until the doctor said my name, pulling me back to him.

"Mercy, when Kylan's ghost entered her body, she saw every memory he had. Kylan may have lived on Earth, but he had access to the Dark Underworld, where only the evilest creatures ever go. He came and went between both worlds for centuries. I don't think it's the same type of Hell you read about in the Bible. This is something else. When Kylan died, he left a part of himself, still dwelling and torturing her. The entity inside Cami is *killing* her. It's been feeding off her life force, and when she went into the street in an attempt to kill herself, that last bit of her was destroyed. Her mind is gone, so it's not as if she can come out of this."

Tears welled in my eyes, and I let out a hard sob.

"I'm sorry," I said. "I'm still not quite understanding what you're implying. Cami's gone? Kylan is where?"

My mind moved a million miles per hour.

I thought after she awoke from her spell, she'd be okay. Maybe she'd feel off for a bit, but she would come out of it. She had to. We all needed to hear Cami talk about a new guy she had met or how excited she was to have only one more year before she could move out of Rhode Island.

But what he was telling me was that one of my best friends was dead and somehow still walking around like she'd been turned into a fucking zombie. And Kylan was what, still possessing her?

Doctor Harrison grabbed a tissue from a box on the table and handed it to me, but I simply rubbed my eyes and put on a brave face.

"Do I need to kill her to set her free?" I asked. My question came out cold and emotionless, but I didn't feel that way. I was torn up inside, but I couldn't let him see me that way. Doctor Harrison was a witch who relied on me to protect them. I was their Spirit conduit, their anchor.

I wouldn't show weakness.

He nodded. "I believe you don't have a choice. Her mind is gone, her body is weak, and her spirit is trapped. It's the only way to set her free so her soul can move on to whatever life is after this. Kylan never left, and the only way to free Cami is to kill the body." He winced at his own words before straightening his back and continuing. "Kylan was never like the vampires he created. He had a demonic spirit, whereas vampires have none. You may have killed his body, but his spirit is still attached. He still possesses her, Mercy."

I placed my palm on the table between us and tapped my fingers against the glass. "Can we perform an exorcism to get Kylan out of Cami and save what's left of her?" I asked.

He shook his head. "Even if we did an exorcism to remove Kylan's spirit, her mind is already gone. Her spirit was barely holding on before she came to the hospital. Kylan's extraordinary power has permanently stored each of his memories in her mind until she could no longer fight it. She'll always be in that *hell*."

I stood up abruptly, turning to the wall to hide the rage on my face. The one that said the hospital would most likely have to admit me too if they saw what brutal acts of violence I had planned for that monster once we exorcised him.

"Alright," I said, turning around to face him. "I'm going to need you to lower the shield so I can use my magic."

He shook his head. "I can't allow that for the safety of my staff, but there is another way. A room where you can use your powers as freely as you wish."

I nodded and walked toward the door. "Well, let's get on with it."

The doctor's brows pulled together, watching me act like a fucking robot to mask my feelings. Didn't I have to be that way in order to kill my friend?

No. Cami is already gone, I had to remind myself. Kylan killed her. I was only setting what was left of her soul free.

I walked down a long corridor that led to this other room while the doctor went to get Cami. Once entering the room, I immediately felt my powers flood through me. The relief hit me, but then that peace was overshadowed by pain. The magic that brought me to life would now be used to take Cami's.

While I waited, I cast my eyes around the room. Aside from pungent herbs and books lining the walls, everything about the space seemed simple and ordinary. Other than a heavy metal chair with shackles at the center under the skyline.

Oh, dear God. This must be where they do exorcisms.

Doctor Harrison entered the room, Cami's arm linked with his and directed her to the chair.

"Please don't shackle her," I said, holding up a hand. "I understand what I must do, but tying her down until she takes her last breath is barbaric."

A giggle escaped from Cami, drawing my attention to look her in the eyes—the eyes that showed a darkness I hadn't seen before.

I took a few steps toward Cami as her head turned slightly to the right, and a strange grin spread along her lips. The corners of her mouth stretched so far they reached the top of her cheekbones, and her bottom lip ripped in half.

Oh, fuck.

This wasn't Cami we were staring at.

She giggled again. "Fuck you, you bitch! You fucking whore."

The voice coming from Cami's lips was deep and masculine. Then, her head fell back, the bones of her neck pressing against the skin of her throat as if the entity inside her was attempting to break it. Streams of blood from Cami's torn mouth dripped down her chin and splashed onto her bony chest and the floor.

Shit. Shit. Shit.

Once her head came back up, her eyes meeting mine again, I said, "Do you really want to play this game with me, Kylan?" My voice cracked, but I remained in control, my hand out with my power crackling at the ready. "Perhaps you forgot what happened the last time we came face to face. I melted yours right off. Shall I do that again?"

"Oh, goody!" That same creepy voice, which didn't sound anything like my friend, sent a chill up my spine. Cami clapped her hands and still wore that stretched-out grin. More blood dripped down her chin, soaking her clothes.

She looked up at the doctor, and her face changed again, but that time, her lips formed a flat line, and her eyes narrowed, her light brows tilting inward.

Was this Cami or Kylan looking at him now? The face she wore was one I didn't recognize.

The doctor approached her, but he didn't get far. Her hand reached out, and without touching him, she flicked her wrist, and his neck snapped. I gasped as his body collapsed to the floor.

"Fuck!" I cursed, my hand still held out in front of me. "Cami, don't!"

Her hand came up again, and she grabbed my throat and squeezed so tight I thought she'd crush my bones. I slammed my hand into Cami's chest and blasted her with my magic across the room, but she hopped up the moment she hit the floor. She turned to face the wall, digging her fingers into the drywall ... then climbed.

Oh, hell no.

Cami's small limbs climbed like a bony spider straight out of a horror film, scaling the wall and gripping it with the tips of her fingers as her body contorted in an unnatural position that made my skin crawl.

Soon, she was above me, and her neck twisted until she met my gaze, and she giggled again like a little child, but the tone of her voice was low and utterly demonic. I raised my right hand, trembling slightly from the nightmare unfolding before me, aiming an energy pulse for Cami.

She quickly darted toward the skyline and slammed her fist against it, shattering the glass, and jumped out through the small hole.

What. The. Hell. Was. That?

CHAPTER 21

CALEB

I sat on the edge of Mercy's mattress, gripping the note that had her name scrawled on it. It had been waiting for her, tucked right under the doormat.

"I spoke with Leah," Ezra said when he entered the room. "Mercy was supposed to visit Cami at the hospital today. We're going to call in to check on her."

I looked down at the note's message when Simon came into the room to join us. "Let's open it," Simon said. "It's not like it's a love note from a secret admirer. We know who it's from."

Mercy wasn't here, and this involved all of us. Addressed to her or not, I opened it.

I have the dagger.

The letter wasn't signed. They left no instructions as to what they wanted. Nothing.

"What the hell am I supposed to do with this information?" I asked them.

"Whoever wrote that only wants to fuck with us," Ezra said. "Seriously, if the creep has the dagger, why don't they just come after us?"

Was this an empty threat? Or was this person stupid enough to come after the coven?

Maurice was the obvious choice, though I found it strange he wouldn't admit he was the killer when we cornered him. It wasn't as if he was afraid of us.

Leah rushed into the room, panic reflecting in her eyes. "Raven's just called. Cami escaped the hospital when Mercy showed up."

"What?" I asked.

I looked at Simon and Ezra right as my phone beeped at my hip. It was Mercy.

> **Mercy:** *Cami's possessed by Kylan's spirit. Her mind is gone, and we can't bring her back. She escaped Raven's twenty minutes ago. We have to kill her. Keep watch. I'm going to stay with Riley for a few days. Call or text if you need me, but I won't be coming home tonight.*

I didn't tell her about the note. As much as she needed to come home right now, she also needed to work out whatever was going through her head before she could face whoever was targeting us, and we knew something or someone was coming.

"I'll call Joel and Lily," I said. "Everyone needs to pay attention to their surroundings from here on out. Someone has that dagger,

and all it takes is one stupid move from any of us, and we're gone."
I ran my hand through my hair. "Fuck!"

How did everything go bad so quickly? Between whoever has the dagger, Maurice's threat, and now Cami, the coven and I were in a very dire situation.

I informed Lily and Joel of the latest developments and sent a few text messages to Riley, but he hadn't responded. I trusted him to be alone with Mercy, but I needed to make sure he'd report to me when she wouldn't. Mercy being away from the coven again wasn't the best idea, but she needed her best friend.

CHAPTER 22

MERCY

Riley's hand rested on my shoulder as he took a seat on the bench next to me. The last time we were at Goddard Park together was the day they had released me from the hospital. The day Caleb came back into my life.

"Is Cami really gone?" he asked, and I answered with a silent nod. A tear formed in the corner of my eye and slowly trickled down my cheek.

Riley grabbed my hand and squeezed it. "There's nothing left of her," I said.

Now Riley's eyes watered, but he choked back his sobs. "Then you have to do it. You need to set her free."

I rested my head on Riley's shoulder and closed my eyes. His hand touched the top of my head, and he rubbed my hair like he was comforting a sick child. Riley was what I needed right now. With him, I wasn't afraid to show the weakest and most vulnerable parts of who I was. He was my best friend and the one person who would listen to me without judgment.

We sat out there for what felt like hours. The wind picked up, and the breeze tickled my skin. He rubbed my arm gently, warming it up, then kissed me on the top of the head. Riley understood the pain I felt, because he felt it, too.

"Does the coven know where you are?" he asked. "Caleb's been reaching out to me every five minutes."

I nodded, leaning back on the bench, and continued to stare at the cove. "They know I'm fine; that's all that matters."

"You're not fine, and there's no shame in that," he said. "None of us feel okay about any of this."

My eyes stayed glued to the water. "I don't care anymore, Riley." The sun beamed down on my cheeks, warming them as we continued to sit on the bench, staring out at the cove.

I may have gained the knowledge of who I was in my past life and my purpose on Earth, but I was still lost. I had gotten my powers back, and this was supposed to be the new me, but why did it feel like I was drowning? I lost a huge part of who I was, and it all started the night my mom thought she had the right to snuff out my life.

Who am I, really?

I stood and walked to the edge where the grass met the water and cried harder than I had in years. My hand rested on the scar my mom left me, another reminder that I had to be strong. I had to be strong for Cami.

I threw my head back and let every ounce of frustration and pain out in a bellowing, blood-curdling cry. Maybe, just maybe, the rest of those goddamn angels up there who let Tatyana fall would get their shit together and send someone else. She failed. I failed. This world was going to fucking burn, and they were going to let it happen.

My chest ached, and I found it hard to breathe. I was gasping for air. I slowly sucked in a breath, and when I released the air from my lungs, I rubbed the heel of my palm against my chest.

I felt the power inside me build, wild and uncontrolled, and I didn't care if a hiker or someone in their boat saw me or my power.

Then ... I screamed again. Raw with rage, hatred, and despair. My scream carried it all.

The cry that left my lips caused my chest to ache. I clutched my hands together, keeping them secure, but the energy was too much for me to hold back. My arms flew out, and my powers surged out of my fingertips, blasting across the park on each side of me. I heard trees timbering over and the water crashing in heavy waves under the force of my magic. The impact was so powerful that it sounded like thunder crashing from above us.

I relaxed just enough to pull back my power, gaining control of my emotions. I slowly turned around to face Riley, who stood behind me in his beautiful wolf form. Once we met each other's gaze, his head flew up, and his snout pointed to the sky. His howl echoed through the woods around us, and the hairs on the back of my neck stood straight. It was a howl of pain, love, life, and of death. Death of the wonderful woman we once knew. The death of Cami.

It was the most beautiful sound I had ever heard.

I neared him slowly, and he bowed his head, so I dropped to my knees to be on his level, pressed my forehead to his, and let out the remaining breath I had held in. "Thank you, Riley," I whispered. "Thank you."

CHAPTER 23

CALEB

The text from Riley had come through only moments before eight o'clock at night. He had witnessed Mercy's break when the walls she had built up to protect herself came crumbling down, shattering around her like broken glass in a place where she'd always felt safe.

It pained me that I couldn't be the one to hold her in that moment of hopelessness, but Riley was the better man. The one who always made her feel grounded.

She'll never be the same once it happens.

Even when Mercy took the life of vampires, she never felt good about it. Yes, it was her duty, but not all missions came with the reward of victory. Most came with pain of regret, haunted by the image of what you had done.

Mercy was going to kill Cami, and it was gutting me inside that she'd have to carry that weight for eternity.

I heard a knock on the door, and I knew it was Melissa. I tried to calm my breathing, to pretend I was all right, but I couldn't. The knock came again, louder that time.

"Caleb," Melissa called through the thickness of the mansion doors. "It's me."

I tried to answer, but nothing came out. I felt paralyzed. My mind was whirling, and my body wouldn't cooperate.

When she was met with silence, the doorknob turned, and she walked in, strolling to the couch once she spotted me. Her soft, feminine hand reached out, taking her index finger to lift my chin up and look into my eyes.

"I've been so worried about you," she said.

Nothing I could say would make this situation any better; no words of encouragement to let her know I was okay. I wasn't okay.

"Talk to me," she said, her voice the tone of warm honey.

"I'm sorry," I said, as my face contorted. "I'm all sorts of fucked up right now."

"We'll figure it out," she said. "If you've taught me anything since we've met, it's that even when you're utterly broken, you and the coven always find a way to bring each other peace through your powers. I know I don't have some magical bond with you as they do, but please let me do that for you by just being here."

I shrugged. "Or maybe I want to feel this way," I said. "The agony prepares me for the harder shit."

Melissa smirked and sat beside me, placing her hand on mine.

I turned to face her, but I knew she saw no hope in my expression. "Are you sure you're ready for all this?" I asked. "Dating an elemental witch comes with the possibility that I'd have to kill." I watched her flinch, but she kept her expression poised. "And not just vampires."

Melissa's expression fell. "I think maybe I'll pour us a glass of wine. Yeah?"

I smiled for the first time since the call. I needed something stronger than wine.

After she poured two glasses, we walked into the library. It was the one place I could decompress. The smell of the leather and paper was like a soothing caress on my turmoiled mind and burning guilt.

"There are so many books," Melissa said, running her hand over the dusty shelves in the mansion's library. "Have you read all of these?"

"Most of them," I replied.

"Most of them?" She gasped. "Seriously, there are easily over four-hundred books on these shelves."

I took a sip of wine. "I had these brought down from my place in Salem. I kept a few books I had read throughout the years, but because I was constantly moving around, I had to donate most of them. I didn't have the space in Salem, and these shelves were empty. Abigail said I could keep them here, and so I started rebuilding my collection."

"That's generous. They're taking up the entire room." She scanned the shelves, trailing her fingers along the wood and wiping off the dust from her fingers when she reached the end. "You really have seen a lot, haven't you?"

Melissa was attempting to distract me, and it was working. Talking about this space gave me a small amount of peace. Reading has always been my outlet, from the seventeenth century until now.

I nodded. "Yeah, but it also has been lonely." My confession sounded so damn pathetic. "When you know you have all the time in the world, you waste it. You also keep to yourself, because you'll only watch those you love die."

The words slipped before I could stop them. Melissa's face grew somber, but she didn't look away. "Then what are you doing with *me*?" she asked. "Your coven and father are the only constants in your life. I can see why you're drawn to them instead of those from the outside world."

How do I respond to that?

I didn't have the answer, not one she'd like. I wish I did. I'd tell Melissa that I wanted her now. I wanted her tomorrow; it didn't matter if she grew old, and I didn't. It wouldn't matter if I watched her die at forty, sixty, or a hundred years old. I wanted to be with her. But it also meant she had to live with my demons. She'd have to understand that even if my heart entirely moved on from Mercy, she would always be in my life.

We'd have to make the most of her life before she grew old, and I'd have to watch her slip away.

"You know I care about you," I said. "But having a relationship with me also means you have to take the bad, and there's a lot of fucking bad."

"Yeah, I know," she said unapologetically, placing her hand on my cheek. "I know, and I don't care."

My hand brushed against hers at her side, and she stepped forward, closing the gap between us.

"So, why are we inside a library?" she asked. "You're about to head into a war zone with your coven, and I have to sit back and watch for the possibility that you won't be here when I return."

Her words gave me pause.

My feelings for Melissa weren't a lie. I cared for her more than she probably believed. I needed time to figure shit out, that's all. To sort through my feelings. I needed time to be okay with Mercy's choice to remove me from her life and the consequences of that choice.

As if Melissa could read my thoughts, she said, "Mercy's not here. I am. I'm here because I care about you. Even knowing you still love her."

I attempted to mask my shame, but I knew it showed.

"I understand you need time, and maybe it makes me desperate because I've been lonely for so long. But it wasn't until I met you that I finally believed I had a second chance at love. Perhaps you do, too, but you must let Mercy be loved by another, because eternity is a long time to be alone."

There was another pause between us. I could feel her breath on my face. And for a moment, I forgot about everything else. I forgot about Mercy and all the complicated emotions swirling around in my brain. I took a step forward, my hands sliding around her back. She kept her eyes on me as I pulled her in, our lips meeting in a kiss. The sweet, warm embrace I needed. Everything my body craved.

Our mouths were hungry for each other as Melissa pressed her body against mine, and I could feel her heat. My hands went to her ass, and I squeezed while her moans hummed against my mouth.

In a moment of clarity, I pushed her away and took a step back. I didn't want to use her. I didn't want to feel like I was taking advantage of her.

God, I'm such an ass.

We stared at each other for what felt like an eternity. I wanted Melissa but didn't want to feel like she was just a conquest. It wasn't in my nature to use women like this. But after a moment, she put her hand on my chest and leaned in to kiss me again.

Melissa had to know. There was no world in which she didn't understand that I was still hoping Mercy would tell Dorian she didn't love him as she loved me, but that would make me a giant fucking asshole. Then I'd have to admit that Mercy didn't want me, no matter how much I loved her.

This little movement between Melissa and me must have indicated that she didn't care either. She wanted this as badly as I did, even if it meant she had to be second string to Mercy. At least for now.

I wanted to touch her, but I also wanted to push her away. I couldn't do both, so I surrendered to the kiss.

Her hand went to my crotch, rubbing me under my jeans, and my cock twitched. She slightly pulled back and looked into my amber eyes. Whatever she must have seen there made her smile.

"I think it's pretty clear we both want and need each other tonight," she whispered.

Melissa didn't have to beg. It wasn't as if this was our first time.

I took her hand and followed her up the stairs, down the long hall, and into my bedroom. We were unable to keep our hands off each other; item after item, our clothing ended up on the floor, and we were in my bed, under the sheets.

Something inside me broke free. All my resistance fell away like autumn leaves blowing in the wind. The beast inside my head took over, and I grabbed her forearms gently, lifting her away from my body and flipping her onto her back.

I climbed over her, my hands roaming to her breasts and squeezing. My fingers toyed with her pert nipples, her back arching underneath me at the sensation. Melissa's legs wrapped around my waist, and I could feel her heat on my hip bone. I slipped inside her all at once, and she cried out my name, her head falling back.

She was so fucking tight. So wet. So warm. My head spun as I pushed myself into her over and over again; the force of my thrusts forced her into the mattress. I ground my hips into the sweet heat, and she arched her back, her body writhing underneath mine. My lips slipped down her neck, traveling over her shoulder and collarbone—eager to mark her as mine in every way there was.

The full moon shone through the window, casting a white glow all over the room. Her skin was almost glowing, as if an inner light was radiating from within. Her tattoos stood out like negative space against her skin, decorating the temple of her body like stained glass.

"Oh God," she cried out again. The sound of her moans hummed like the sweetest melody, curated for my ears only.

Her inner walls clenched around my cock, the most exquisite torture I'd ever experienced. I didn't want it to end. I dug my fingernails into her back and then squeezed her ass. She was moaning so loudly that I felt the entire bed rumble underneath me, only urging me to fuck her harder until I could barely contain myself.

"Fuck! Caleb!" she moaned as she climaxed, her body trembling beneath me. Her pussy clenched around me, firm and violent, as if it wanted to prevent me from ever abandoning her. Her juices gushed out, soaking my cock and balls.

"Fuck ..." A moan broke free from my own lips as I shook on top of her. I felt my orgasm approaching, and I didn't fight it. I picked up my pace, hitting that spot inside of her over and over again, chasing my own peak ... But she beat me to it, coming all over my cock once again with a loud moan that seemed to suck out all air from her lungs, leaving her breathless. Her sharp nails raked down my back, leaving red lines in their wake. I captured her wrists and threw them above her head on the pillow, pinning her in place as I ground into her repeatedly. Melissa's body writhed beneath me, her legs clamped tight behind my thighs, pulling me in as deep as she possibly could. I gritted my teeth and squeezed my eyes closed so tightly that it hurt. Then, with a ferocious growl, I found my release.

The world exploded around me in a burst of color and heat. I growled, my head falling back. I was barely conscious as I let out a throaty moan and then collapsed on top of her, panting and gasping for breath. We were both covered in sweat. It dripped from my face, ran in rivulets down my back, and soaked the sheets beneath us.

I rolled over on my side and rested my head on my palm. Melissa turned on her side, popping her hands over her head while I brushed her curly hair out of her face.

"I think I am falling in love with you," she said. It was all but a whisper, but I had no response to her confession. Instead, I grabbed her by the waist, pulling her to me in a possessive hold. We lay there together for a few minutes. I could feel her heart beating through her body, her chest rising and falling with each steady breath until our eyes grew heavy, and we fell asleep in each other's arms.

Broken glass echoed from the first floor, jolting me awake. I sat bolt upright and looked over at Melissa, who was sound asleep. We crashed immediately after sex, and I realized I had forgotten to set the house alarm. Someone was inside the house.

I leaped out of bed, ran out of the room, and locked the bedroom door behind me. I quickly cast a shield spell over the door and hurried downstairs, looking through every corner and room on the main level. Once I entered the library, I saw shards of glass on the ground below the window.

I stumbled forward but managed to stay on my feet. Right then, a jolt went through my body. It concentrated around my scalp, causing a moment of vertigo, and my mind spun in circles.

Once I gained my vision again, I looked up, staring at the intruder who wore all black from head to toe, with no recognizable features. But the shape of his broad shoulders and thick, long legs told me it was a man. He wore a mask, gloves, and, in one of his hands, a dagger.

Our dagger.

I lifted my hands, and flames appeared. He charged toward me, but I moved left and slammed my elbow on the bridge of his back, a coil of flame wrapping around my forearm, burning a hole through the black shirt. The intruder fell hard on his knees and dropped the dagger.

While he kneeled on the wooden floor, I swept it up, but something burned my hand, and I quickly dropped it.

What the hell was that?

The dagger had been laced with magic, and I couldn't touch it. Whatever attacker this was, they were working with a witch.

Fucking Maurice.

"Get up, Maurice. I know it's you. Have you come for another ass beating?" He stood, and I mustered up the flames in both my hands. "You're not going to win this fight," I threatened, then blasted the flames toward him, but he lifted his hands, and the fire vaporized before it touched him.

What the fuck? He can use magic?

He looked at me one last time and bolted out the door.

No!

I chased after him as fast as I could, but he had disappeared into the forest behind the property.

"Are you fucking kidding me?!" I shouted into the night.

I rushed back into the library and searched the floor for the dagger, but it had gone with him.

Fuck! Fuck! Fuck!

I had him. I fucking had him! I eyed my office desk, placed my hands firmly on the top, and slid them across, tossing everything onto the floor. I kneeled and placed my hands on my head. "I'm going to kill that son of a bitch."

I looked up at the clock on the library wall; it was three in the morning. I hurried upstairs to check on Melissa. After dissipating the shield, I unlocked the bedroom door and peered into the room. Melissa hadn't heard the confrontation downstairs and was still sound asleep. I grabbed my phone and called the coven, then tried Mercy, but she didn't pick up, so instead, I sent her a text message about what had happened. I no longer cared if she was still broken up about everything; she needed to get her shit together and help us with this.

Me: *The killer broke in tonight. It's not Maurice unless he is using one of his witches. They*

> *used magic! Be ready. They have the dagger. I couldn't touch it, though. It's laced with some kind of repelling spell. I'll be over at your place in the morning. Mercy, you need to be at the house. Stay on guard and lock every door and window.*

I shut my phone down and lay next to Melissa, watching her chest rise and fall, and prayed our drama would never reach her and damage her like it had so many people we cared about. I couldn't go back to sleep, not knowing that whoever had broken in could come back. But if they did, I'd be ready to take them out.

CHAPTER 24

MERCY

The newly formed pack was still small, living on the north side of campus at Brown. They recruited Aaron and Hannah a few months ago; everything was so new to them still.

"I'm sorry the nightmare is circling back around. How can we help?" Amber asked, tipping her beer up for a drink.

"Thanks," I said, placing my hands on the kitchen island and taking in the surroundings of their new place. I hadn't been to their apartment before. "Honestly, I haven't quite figured out that part yet," I admitted. The newly born werewolves, Aaron and Hannah, watched me, their intense gaze never faltering. It was as if they were ready for instructions, but I didn't run their pack. It wasn't up to me what they decided to do. That responsibility wasn't what I needed.

I sighed and wiped my mouth with a napkin, leaning back into the chair. "Maurice is coming back for revenge. We know he killed the angel who created me and my coven. We also know a vampire killed at least three people in East Greenwich and has connections to the Black Horse Clan. We feel pretty confident that it's Maurice, but he's only taking credit for the angel. The immortal-slaying dagger is also missing."

I rubbed my eyes. Just saying all of that aloud gave me a headache.

"Then there's Cami," I continued, "who, last year, was possessed by a demon who created the vampire race. He left a part of his soul inside her, and now she's gone. Whatever happened last year destroyed what remained of her. Cami escaped from Raven's yesterday morning, and now I have to track her down and kill her before she hurts someone. I need to set her free."

I waited as all eyes were on me, and Hannah's jaw dropped. Maybe they didn't realize what they were getting into when they asked Amber to turn them into supernatural beings.

"Look, all of this is the coven's responsibility, not yours," I told them. "But if you join us, we will forever be in your debt. Truthfully, we will always be on your side, no matter your choice."

Amber looked down and bit her bottom lip as if contemplating my request. "Mercy, a year ago, when Riley helped me sniff out my pack, I was devastated to have found them the way we did. Their scent still lingers in those woods from what Kylan had done to them," she explained. "Kylan being dead didn't change anything. Witches and werewolves have been bound for the same purpose. To kill vampires."

Amber was right. We weren't divided as witches and werewolves; we were on the same side, in the same fight.

Kylan had planned for months before he tracked me down to take me out. He punished her pack for interfering and protecting me by slaughtering them. Thankfully, when he attacked the pack, Amber was looking for me and wasn't caught in the crossfire. She searched for her family for months, but little did she know they were burned to ash in Salem Woods. With the help of Riley, her newest pack member, they tracked their scent and Kylan's. They had also picked up a human scent, which we assumed he possessed at the time, to carry out the murders because of the curse Tatyana put on him.

"We'll help you take down what's left of Kylan and rid him of this earth for the last time. Just tell us what we need to do. We do this together," Amber said.

Riley smiled at her with pride.

It had taken me a while to accept Riley as a werewolf. I didn't want this life for him, not like it was ever my choice, but seeing how much he had grown and who he had become made me proud. He was happy this way, and that's all I wanted for him.

Riley turned to Aaron and Hannah. "Are the two of you ready for this? It's not just Kylan's spirit we're taking out, it's Maurice, too, and whoever is killing in East Greenwich, that is, if it's not the same person."

Aaron smiled and spoke for the first time. "We're ready to do what Amber and Riley created us for." He grabbed his sister's hand and squeezed. "Tell us what to do, and we'll do it."

I pulled my phone out of my purse, and once it powered on, I opened my texts, and there was a message from Caleb.

Oh, shit.

"I gotta head back. I'll call you later, Riley."

"Everything okay?"

"No. The killer broke into Abigail's home last night and attacked Caleb. He's okay, but he mentioned the attacker had the dagger." I pinched the bridge of my nose. "Fuck!"

"Maurice?" Hannah jumped in, her tone denoting an eagerness for her new role.

"It wouldn't be Maurice himself, but rather one of his witch lackeys. They used magic," I explained.

Riley's mouth dropped. "So did Kylan."

I shook my head. "But he's in Cami's body. The person who attacked Caleb was a man. Yes, he could have left Cami's body to possess another, but why would he? From what I witnessed at Raven's, Cami's body is just as strong to do his bidding."

Riley stood and brought me in for a hug. "We're with you until the end."

CHAPTER 25

MERCY

When I arrived at my house, I spotted Caleb's car in the driveway.

I shouldn't have turned off my phone.

The coven stood around the kitchen table, including Roland, when I walked through the door. The room was completely silent.

"Sorry. My phone died, and I didn't have my charger on me," I lied, feeling unease hit me like a brick as everyone watched me take a seat on the couch. I had walked in on something intense. "Jesus, I told you I'm sorry."

Caleb moved around the table and walked over to me. "Mercy, we got another note."

"*Another* note?" I questioned. "When did you get the *first* note?"

He brushed off my question, only handing me two envelopes. I opened the first one that read, "I have the dagger." I opened the second one, but there was a photo in the envelope instead of a note. Glancing at the photo, I was trying to understand whom I was looking at.

"Oh my God!" I cried. "I don't ..." My thoughts mangled as I choked back a sob.

It was Sarah.

Leah had moved to my side while my eyes stayed on the picture. "I'm so sorry," she said, holding my hand and squeezing it. "Whoever did this is going to pay. I promise you."

I turned the photo around, no longer able to look at her dead body at the bottom of a shallow grave.

There was a note on the back, so I read it out loud.

Now I'll always know your true face.

My stomach lurched as the meaning sunk into my mind. Whoever was doing this knew the power Sarah held.

"Mercy?" Caleb said, pulling my attention away from the envelope in my hand with a picture of my dead friend. "Now may be the time to consider that it's not Maurice."

"What the fuck are you talking about? Of course, it's Maurice. He knew her. He was upset that she had helped me. It's just like his revenge on Tatyana. He's going after everyone who did him wrong a year ago."

"But it was a witch who attacked Caleb last night. Did you not get the text?" Ezra asked, seemingly annoyed by my rant.

Yes, I got the fucking text, but none of this made sense.

"Then Maurice sent a witch to do it," I said. "He's always had witches working with him. Always!"

"We ... have another theory," Simon spoke, barely finishing the sentence. I wasn't going to like this theory, and he knew it.

I looked up at Roland. He crossed his arms over his chest, silently watching me.

"Gee," I said. "You're pretty quiet over there, Roland. I'd like to hear this theory from you." I knew exactly what the coven was thinking, and it was bullshit.

"Okay, fine. I believe it's your father," Roland accused while walking toward me, stopping at my feet, and looking down. He placed one hand on the armrest, leaning forward. "You gave him your blood, and now he's using his magic against us."

I shook my head. "No," I seethed. "He wouldn't do that."

"Yes, actually, he would," Roland snapped. "Alexander knew killing those people would draw you out. He manipulated you into turning him back into the powerful witch he's wanted to be again after all these centuries. And now he's taking out the coven, because he can't stand that you're still more powerful than him."

I jumped to my feet, stepping forward so abruptly that he moved back. "How is that any different from what *you* did to me, you son of a bitch?"

Roland's face went still. "Not going to let that one go, are you?"

"Never!"

God, Roland was such a fucking hypocrite.

"I'm not killing people," Roland said as my shoulders slumped and I stepped away from him.

I shook my head. "And neither is my father."

Leah stood and placed her hand on mine, probably hoping her touch would calm me down. "Look, we don't want it to be Alexander. But think about it. The killings happened when he was a vampire. Then you turned him, and no one is dying anymore from a bite. Now it's suddenly a witch trying to kill the coven. Your father knows where Caleb lives, so of course, he's going to look in our homes first for the dagger. If he had magic, then he could have easily located it. Not to mention, he has the ability to read minds, so he could have gotten the code to the safe from Caleb without him knowing."

I thought about everything she had told me, and I still couldn't believe it. The memories I had of my father were genuine; he loved me. He loved the coven. My mother and father used our elements for good, so why would he try to remove us from this earth when he knows how instrumental we are to the world?

"You told me that if your father were guilty, you'd kill him yourself," Caleb said. "Has that changed?"

Not that I believed it was my father, but yes, I would kill him if he were trying to hurt us. Of course, I would, but I wasn't ready to admit it. Not right now.

"I need to call Joel, so we can locate Sarah's body with a spell and bury her properly," I said, desperately wanting to cry. But I couldn't anymore; the tears wouldn't come. There was only the anguish and the pain burning through me.

Everyone remained silent as I turned toward the door and left the house.

CHAPTER 26

MERCY

It took Joel and I about twenty minutes to find Sarah using a locator spell. She was still there, just like I had seen in the photo, lying on her back, her face looking peaceful. We observed no noticeable laceration marks. He must have broken her neck.

We buried her in the East Greenwich Cemetery, the grave only being marked by a bloom of flowers I had conjured up. It was in honor of our first conversation together in the lair when she told me about her gifts. I had no one to call about her death. Her parents died years ago, and she didn't have anyone else here but us. Before they had taken her to Maurice's lair, she'd escaped an abusive relationship back in California. She came to Salem to hide from her ex-boyfriend, but what she found was an even worse nightmare of captivity.

Her friends back home didn't believe her about the abuse or about her magic. She had no one she could trust. That's probably why, when Troy showed her kindness in the lair, even though he had laid possession of her, she welcomed and wanted it.

Maybe I should find him and let him know.

I spent the rest of the day over at Joel and Derek's rental home. Derek was still in New York, and after Sarah died, Joel texted him that it wasn't safe. He needed to stay there until we found the person responsible.

Was the killer Maurice, my father, or someone else?

Between the time of Sarah's death and now, Lily had shared with Bradley our secret about being witches. It had taken her several hours before she had the courage to open her mouth to speak and reveal that world to him. Of course, like most, she had to prove to him it wasn't a joke. She showed him a simple levitation spell to cement that what she was saying was the truth. He promised to keep her secret and thanked her for being so honest with him. She did leave out the part about vampires and werewolves, because ... one supernatural creature at a time.

We trained over the weekend while planning our next move, which focused on Maurice or my father. I wasn't happy about the coven accusing Alexander, but if I kept an eye on him, perhaps I might be able to prove his innocence.

Riley and Amber trained their new pack members, and Dorian and Noah kept a close watch on Maurice.

I texted my father a few times. I kept it brief and didn't give him any sign that a few members of my coven thought he was a murderer. He would tell me how busy he was, building up his new business since he wasn't bringing in money from the club anymore and the "other businesses" he conducted while a vampire. He never asked to see me or asked if I was okay. I found this to be unusual and a little hurtful. His child from three hundred and thirty years ago was alive again, and he was now avoiding me.

I now felt as if he was, indeed, hiding something. Though not necessarily that he was the killer.

It was eight in the evening, and Joel had just finished clearing the dinner table when my cell phone chimed. He smiled knowingly as he sat beside me, the two of us looking down to see Dorian's name pop up in my text app.

"Go see him," Joel said, pushing my phone toward me. "I have watched the two of you text every night for the last few days. I know you want to see him."

I shook my head. "Trust me, I want to, but I don't want to give him the wrong idea."

Joel sighed and rolled his eyes. "You're being ridiculous. You know that, right?"

I glanced at my phone again. I *was* being ridiculous. I decided that if Dorian wanted to see me, then, okay, I would go. If not, I was having another veggie taco and watching a show on Netflix.

Dorian: *We just got home. Can you swing by?*

"Don't be home too late," Joel teased.

I bit my bottom lip and drummed my fingers against the table. "Okay, fine. You win," I said. "Don't wait up."

CHAPTER 27

MERCY

"Aloha, my beautiful friend," Noah said, kissing me on both cheeks when I entered the home.

"Hey, Noah." I looked past him, seeing Dorian sitting on the edge of the couch, moving his game piece forward. "You're playing Candy Land?"

Dorian's mouth curved at the corner of his lips. "Isn't this a classic game from when you were a kid?"

"Yeah," I said, taking a seat beside him. "It's a game for eight-year-olds, Dorian."

They both laughed. "We can always play it with liquor ... or naked," Noah suggested, flashing me a toothy grin.

My body tensed, just slightly, as Dorian met my eyes. The thought of being in their home tonight created a wild flutter in my stomach. Dorian's scent did something else to me that I couldn't even admit to myself.

God, he smells good.

As if Dorian sensed my hesitancy, he smiled and said, "Thanks for coming tonight. You're okay, right?"

I nodded. "I will be."

After playing Candy Land for over an hour and then switching to cards, Dorian and I caught up on everything we've been doing this last year. I realized I hadn't been relaxed like this in months. Everything had been so consumed by constant drama and chaos that I had forgotten how to have fun. In fact, I hadn't had this much fun since I was a teenager. My mom sort of robbed me of that.

Noah drifted off about halfway through the last round of cards, so we declared Dorian's victory and wrapped up the game. We cleaned up the game pieces, and I entered the kitchen to refill my water. When I turned around, Dorian was standing behind me, and I jumped slightly, startled.

"Sorry," he said. He lifted his hand to my cheek, but I didn't flinch or pull away this time. I let his cold fingers linger there, caressing my skin and trailing down to my neck. A chill from the coolness of his hands and the seductive touch caused a strong awareness of my heartbeat, and the hairs prickled on the backs of my arms.

Noah groaned something unintelligible in his half-asleep state and rolled his entire body toward the back of the couch. It was clear he was down for the rest of the night. The clock read ten in the evening.

"I should probably go."

"I don't want you to leave," he confessed, and butterflies hit my stomach again. It didn't matter that a spell had stripped away my romantic feelings. It was so incredibly sexy the way he looked at me then that I didn't trust myself with him.

It was also nerves. Dorian and I hadn't been together like that in *this* body. I dropped my gaze and twisted my fingers.

A kiss. Maybe just a tiny, innocent kiss.

No, stop, Mercy. You're thinking with lust-filled eyes and not your heart.

I looked back at Dorian, and his grin made me weak in the knees. If I didn't leave now, we were going to do something I would regret in the morning.

"I can make us our last drink?" Dorian said.

"No. I should probably stop," I said softly, avoiding making eye contact. "I need to be able to drive home." It wasn't really that I thought he was trying to get me drunk or anything, more that I just didn't trust myself around him any less than stone-cold sober. Despite the cursed spell, my body was longing for his touch, and I wasn't sure how much of a fight my brain was prepared to put up against the cravings of my flesh.

"A coffee then?" he asked with a hopeful smile.

"Coffee would be perfect, thank you." I grinned back. Dorian's easy, reassuring countenance was infectious.

From the island, I watched him as he leaned against the counter and reached for the coffee jar. I loved following his body movements, how he would turn his head to look at me, and how his lower lip would curve upwards when he tried to hide his smile. When he turned his head back to look at me, I averted my stare, intent on not giving in to the sinister part of me that wanted to fight against the spell's effects.

Caffeine was needed for that. I was still feeling a little dizzy, unable to quite grasp that I was here, in Dorian's house. Flashes of our old life kept running through my mind.

I needed to go home and sleep, to think about what was happening or not happening.

Instead, when I got up and started moving, my feet led me to where he prepared our drinks. I honestly, truly meant to stand by the entryway that led to the front door and say I should be heading out, but my legs betrayed me.

"Maybe this was a bad idea," I said as I leaned against the counter beside him. He seemed surprised and then shook his head.

"Drink your coffee, Mercy, and stop overthinking everything we're doing."

Okay, maybe that was a little un-Dorian-like to order me around, but perhaps that was what I needed. I was making this out to be a bigger deal than it was. I needed to relax and let someone else take care of me for once.

I couldn't even begin to explain my reasoning without making the situation awkward. I was betting against hope that he wouldn't try. I was delaying my exit, nothing more. I needed to clear my head, and this wasn't the place to do it. How could I reason with him so close to me?

"So, how do you like it?" he asked, holding up an empty blue ceramic mug toward me.

The devious part of my brain jumped to attention, and my core buzzed with warm energy. "Excuse me?"

Still pushing buttons on the single-serve coffee maker, he looked up at me from underneath long lashes. The hint of a smile lifted the edge of his mouth. "Your coffee. Do you want creamer, sugar, or milk?" His soothing voice caressed my skin like silk, enough to melt my panties if I'd been wearing any.

I barely managed to keep the whimper out of my voice. "All of the above."

He grinned and reached over to pull me into his arms. I stumbled and fell against him; I took a slow breath and closed my eyes. He smelled incredible, and I couldn't help but place a hand on his chest. His heartbeat was nowhere to be found, but the drumming of my own heart pounded in my chest.

I felt him lean down, and I clenched my jaw, waiting for his lips to touch mine. I knew I shouldn't have wanted this, but I did. Every part of me wanted it.

The kiss never came, but my treacherous heart screamed at me to beg for it.

He licked below my ear instead, exploring every curve of my neck. I shivered at the coolness of that tongue.

Oh. My. God.

And then he nipped the bottom of my neck.

"Dorian ..."

In my past life, he's had a thing for the spot just above my collarbone. He loved the taste of my skin. But in this life ...

"I know," Dorian said softly, his breath wafting over my face as he released my pounding heart. "We can't, can we?"

And then he stepped away.

He left me leaning against the counter, my mind in a fog, as the air between us chilled the parts of my body where his touch had just been.

I turned to him and forced myself to form words. "I don't need to tell you that we have to be careful, right?"

"I'm not going to hurt you," he said firmly. "I may want you, but I would never make you do something you don't want to do. I know this isn't what you want."

This is exactly what I want.

I swallowed hard and nodded, unsure of what to say. It was true that I'd made the difficult choice to remove my feelings for Dorian, but at that moment, I wasn't sure the spell worked anymore. Every cell in my body wanted his hands back on me so he could explore this new body of mine.

I was also certain that once I left, I wouldn't be able to think about anything except Dorian. The coolness of his skin, his soft lips, and the way his hands moved over my body.

He ran a hand through his hair and closed his eyes, the corners crinkling into tight lines. It was as if he was trying to force away his attraction to me. Just the way I'd been hoping to do by not meeting his eyes earlier.

I failed.

As the quiet click of the coffee maker shut off, I raised my hand to his cheek and turned his head toward me.

"I *do* want this," I whispered, wanting Dorian to believe me.

He opened his eyes and stared intently into mine. I smiled, leaning forward to touch my lips to his. He hesitated for only a second, then put his hand on the small of my back and gently pushed me back against the counter until we were flush against each other.

His mouth was as soft as I remembered, and I moaned softly as his tongue pushed past my lips and met mine.

I grabbed hold of him, my hands clutching his broad shoulders, and I pulled him against me, my core throbbing with a sheer need for him.

His hands found their way under my thighs, and he lifted me onto the kitchen counter effortlessly. Dorian spread my legs apart with his strong hands and pushed himself against me.

I couldn't help but moan loudly as Dorian rolled his hips against mine. My hands found the buckle straps of his pants, and I pulled him against me harder. He pushed down into me, and I could feel his erection straining against his pants.

God almighty, I forgot how amazing his cock felt between my legs.

I wanted to feel him. I wanted to feel every inch of Dorian's body. I was still wearing my jeans and cursed the barrier of rough fabric between us. He pulled back and looked down at me.

"This is okay, right?" he asked.

I nodded, a smirk forming on my lips. "What a silly question, Dorian. I'm already wet, so I would venture to say yes."

Did I really say that?

As my cheeks turned pink from my brazen response, I placed my hands on his chest right as he hiked my legs up around his waist in one swift motion. I gripped his shirt to keep from falling.

Before I could register what was going on, we were moving down the hallway toward his bedroom. There was something about the way that he handled me that had me shaken at my core—in the best way possible. So *fucking* hot. His touch was possessive, as if he owned every fragment of my being, yet mindful and careful at the same time.

The door closed behind us, and he pressed me against it, pulling my top over my head in one swift move.

I exhaled softly as his hands found my breasts. His fingers brushed over my skin, toying around the fabric of my bra before he kissed my shoulder, teasing the edge of my strap with his teeth. Leaning back against the door, one hand still clutching his shirt, I ran the other down the length of his torso. Dorian's body shuddered under my touch, and a low growl escaped his lips.

He lifted me again and sat me down on the bed.

"You have no idea how long I've waited for this," he whispered. He reached behind me, undid the hooks, and pulled off my bra, revealing my breasts and pert nipples. When the cool air hit my flesh, I shivered.

"And there goes my bra," I breathed. Dorian balled it up in his hand and tossed it aside, then moved his focus to the button of my jeans. His eyes were admiring and worshiping as they washed over my naked chest.

"If I'm going to see you completely naked, everything must come off," he growled.

With my ass on the edge of the bed, he pulled my pants down over my hips. I lifted them up so he could pull one leg and then the other free. He dropped my jeans on the floor and ran his hands up and down the length of my legs, his eyes never leaving mine.

"I'll be honest with you. If you hesitate, I might change my mind."

It wasn't that I didn't want him, but my conscious self, or maybe it was the spell, was fighting with the other part of my brain, and I was afraid the one that wanted him between my legs wouldn't win.

"Three hundred and thirty years, Mercy. That's how long since I've been inside you." A smile creased his dimples. "I'm not going to hesitate."

"Then take off all your clothes, so I can see you," I said, my arousal evident in my voice.

With a playful smile, he tore his shirt off, then unbuckled his jeans, letting them fall around his ankles. He stepped toward me, his cock hard against his abdomen. I drank in the sight of his naked body. This new-to-me, untouched body—the body that was mine in another life.

The dips and curves, the corded muscle under his skin, the faint freckle on his shoulder. Dorian was utterly beautiful.

"I need to touch you," I whispered and reached for him.

"No," he said and pulled my hands away. "You don't get to touch me. You don't get to guide this. I've dreamed of this for too long, babe. There are many things I want to do to you, Mercy, and you're going to enjoy every single one of them."

I stared at him. *What is he doing?*

"Sit back, put your hands behind your head, and open your legs for me," he ordered. The look in his eyes showed he meant every single word. He wasn't joking around. "And watch."

I bit my bottom lip, trying to hold back my smile. It felt as if it would have been a dangerous move on my end now that he was so intense.

Slowly, I raised my hands to my head and interlaced my fingers. My cheeks burned as I cleared my throat.

"It must be driving you crazy that you're not in control right now, huh?" he asked with a slight chuckle, kneeling in front of me. His lips found my knee, leaving a soft kiss there.

I bit my bottom lip. "I might get used to it." As he demanded, I watched.

He wrapped his hands around my ankles and kissed the inside of my thighs. I gasped and tilted my head back, hoping he'd go further.

As abruptly as he started, he stopped. My entire body protested, my gaze focusing on him again.

"I said watch. If you don't, I *will* stop," he stated, and then he pushed me back until I was lost in the pillows. I spread my legs as he'd commanded, trying to steady myself as he kissed the sensitive skin on the inside of my thighs again. The sight of that alone would have been enough to make me come.

It felt like fucking torture.

The torture that he increased by lingering there, not going any further. I wanted to scream, but I had to keep my hands behind my head.

"Please ..." I couldn't help it. I begged.

Dorian moved his lips up to kiss my stomach, teasing my belly button with his tongue. He reached for my hands, pulling them from behind my head, and then held them at the wrists until I moved them to rest on either side of my head on the bed. I was shaking in utter desire, feeling as if I was going to lose my mind if he didn't give me more.

I watched as he kissed his way up my body, licking between my breasts and over my neck until he finally reached my mouth.

His hand caressed my breast, and I gasped against his lips while he teased my hard nipple with his thumb. His other hand was between my legs, finding just the right spot with his fingers. A circling motion that his fingers moved in echoed somewhere in the far distance of my mind, sending a shudder down my spine. I bit on my lower lip, trying to steady my breathing yet again.

God, I could feel just how soaked I was already.

"Do you remember this?" he whispered in my ear, low and hoarse.

"Dorian!" I called out, clenching around his finger, my toes curling at the sweet sensation.

"Tell me to stop," he said. "Mercy, tell me you want to forget this—that this is what you tried to erase. Tell me *now* that you don't want me to fuck you like this."

I shook my head. "I'm not going to say that, because you know it'll be a lie."

"Then what do you truly want?" Dorian asked as he moved his finger in and out. Still slow, still teasing, as if it was his intention to tease me up to the point of insanity.

As my head spun with pleasure, I closed my eyes. "I want you to take me, just like every memory of us under the stars in that grassy meadow. I want it all to come crashing back. I want it to torture me for being a fool, for needing to forget it."

In one swift motion, he pulled his fingers from inside me and turned me onto my stomach. I let out a small gasp as he pulled my hips up so my ass was in the air. A moment later, he pressed the tip of his cock against my center, prodding playfully.

Was this teasing ever going to end?

"Dorian," I breathed out, desperate to have more of him.

"I'm going to fuck you so deep," he whispered in my ear as he let his cock slip inside me in one slow, deep movement. His hand found my clit, circling around it just the way my body liked. "That you'll remember why you wanted this so often all those lifetimes ago."

He used his other hand to support his weight as he built up a pace, thrusting in and out of me. His cock would slide out of me for a mere second before he'd return it back to its rightful place—in the depths of my throbbing heat. I moaned loudly, pressing back into him. The warmth building inside me was more than I could bear. I felt like I was going to explode and took a deep, sobbing breath.

"Don't hold back," Dorian said. "Feel it."

"I feel you," I gasped, my hands clutching the bedsheets as if it was going to help me anchor myself through the overwhelming sensation.

"Hold on to that feeling as you ride the wave of pleasure," Dorian growled, throwing his hips against me harder now.

"I ... I can't hold on to it. I'm going to come ... Oh God," I cried out, my body shaking. "I'm going to come."

"Feel me, Mercy." He kept a steady rhythm and leaned down to kiss my neck. "Feel me inside you. I want you to feel me in every nook inside your pussy."

I bit my lip as the pressure built. I needed to come, and I needed to come now. My entire body shook violently as it lingered on that edge. It was impossible to think clearly, let alone talk to him right now.

"Fuck, I'm coming," I cried out once again. Dorian gripped my hips, holding me tight against him while he thrust deep inside me, owning every fragment of my being.

My body shook with the force of my release. I moaned and bucked against him, the world around me momentarily becoming a blur. He held me in place while I pulsed around his cock.

I gasped for breath and tried to catch my bearings. Dorian slowly slid out of me and turned me to face him. He wiped the sweat from my brow and kissed it, then ventured lower to my lips.

"Thank you," I said, my voice quiet and hoarse. "I needed that more than I thought."

"I'm not done with you yet," he said as he pressed his hand against my chest and pushed me onto my back. Dorian smiled down at me before his lips collided with mine once again, his tongue sliding against my own, tasting me.

"I'm going to make you come again and again," he said. I bit my lip and nodded before his cock slid back inside. He seemed insatiable for me.

Dorian began thrusting in and out of me again. I squirmed under him, my back arching, hips bucking up to meet every roll of his hips. My pussy was still tender from having just come, yet somehow it yearned for more.

I wrapped my legs around him as he leaned down, his tongue circling around my sensitive nipples. From this angle, each time he slipped back inside of me, he sent electric waves of pleasure that rippled through me.

"More!" I pleaded, clutching his shoulders desperately. I pulled him down on top of my chest, his cool breath on my neck, his length buried deep inside my heat.

"Oh, God," I moaned.

"You're mine," Dorian whispered in my ear. His hand slid between us, his thumb finding my aching bundle of nerves, causing my entire body to tremble. "Always have been, always will be ... Mine," he growled.

His. I wasn't his. I can't be his.

I cried out his name as he pressed against me, and the pressure built again.

"Come for me again, Mercy," he said, his voice strained.

My hips rolled against him, and I held my breath until the heat released inside me. My legs quivered, my toes curling as my body tensed with the force of my own orgasm.

I let out a short scream and trembled, my breathing still out of control as I struggled to wind down. Dorian collapsed completely, his weight pressing into my sensitive breasts.

"God, you're amazing," he whispered against my ear as he kissed me softly. "I love you."

I was unsure if the spell had worked or if I was falling for him all over again. Maybe the spell did what it was supposed to, but I'd underestimated how easy Dorian was to love and how strong our connection had been. I wondered if the spell was not strong enough to hold back what I felt for him.

He didn't give me a chance to respond. Instead, he drove himself inside me even deeper than before. I groaned and bucked into him, the pressure building inside me—threatening to explode once again. I wrapped my arms and legs around him, holding him close while he moved into me, a little slower this time.

I gasped with each thrust, pushing myself into him until I couldn't take it anymore.

"Dorian," I moaned, unable to say anything else. "Dorian." It was as if his name was my own holy grail. The breathless sound of it on my tongue made my heart ache and warm simultaneously.

What was I doing?

He buried his face in my neck and licked my throat. "I've missed this. I've missed everything."

His words were all I needed to push me over the edge. I cried out and held onto him as I came, but he continued fucking me, drawing out my orgasm to the point I didn't know even existed.

"Come with me this time," he ordered, pushing my knees up to my chest and grabbing my hips, holding me tightly against him.

The force of his own release rushed into me as his cock pulsed and throbbed. I let out a cry at the combination of his release and my own. I wrapped my arms around his neck and held him against me, feeling my heart as it beat against his skin. Dorian let out a soft moan into the curve of my neck, kissing the skin with such tenderness that I almost wept.

After a minute of trying to catch my breath, Dorian rolled me onto my side, snuggled close to me, then pulled the covers over us to keep me warm.

"I'm not done with you," he said, his breath still heavy. "I'll never be done with you."

I smiled through the guilt.

Shit.

There was nothing about what we had just done that made me feel regret, but I knew what this meant. I knew what was going to happen in the morning. I was going to hurt him as I walked out the door.

"You're going to sleep?" I asked, my back still facing him. I needed a conversation about anything else.

I felt his smile before he squeezed me tightly against his chest. "Vampires don't *need* sleep, but if we choose to fall asleep, we can." He nuzzled his face into my neck. "Stay with me until morning. Please."

My cheeks flushed again. "Okay." My smile widened. "Goodnight, Dorian."

"Sweet dreams, Mercy," he whispered into my neck, brushing his lips against my hair and kissing the top of my head before I fell asleep.

CHAPTER 28

MERCY

I slipped my clothes back on and crept around the corner of the hallway, hoping I didn't wake Dorian or even Noah, who had crashed on the couch before we had gone to bed.

It was two in the morning, and I honestly didn't think I'd fall asleep. I was going to let Dorian hold me until dawn, but when reality set in about what we did and the consequences, I had to get the hell out of there.

What did it all mean? I didn't know anymore.

"Don't hurt him," Noah said from behind me as I neared the front door. I grimaced and turned around to face him sitting upright on the couch.

"That's what I'm good at, Noah. Haven't you heard?"

"This isn't funny. Dorian loves you."

I rubbed my eyes and walked up to him, realizing I couldn't head out the door without talking first. Not with Noah.

"Okay," I said. "Not that it's any of your business, but none of what we did means anything. I can't let it mean something."

Noah's face hardened, and he huffed. "That's the problem, isn't it?" he said, giving me the most brutal, judgmental stare-down I think I'd ever had from anyone. "Because it means something to him."

I didn't respond to that.

Of course, it did. I'm a fucking idiot and am about to break Dorian's heart all over again.

"Do you love him again?" Noah asked.

"No," I admitted too quickly. "I mean, I love Dorian, but differently. It's strange. There's a part of me that feels for Dorian. I care about him, and I would be devastated if something bad happened to him, but I'm not *in* love."

"You just want to fuck him?" he asked, and I recoiled at those words.

I plopped down on the couch in the living room and set my purse next to me. "Well, that was harsh," I admitted. "I didn't plan this. But last night, that kiss ..."

He cocked his head. "Interesting."

"What the hell is that supposed to mean?" I asked.

He chuckled. "Did that ridiculous spell you cast, prevent you from falling in love again, or did it just take away what you used to have?"

Noah's question caught me off guard. I had to think about it for a second because I didn't know the answer. Did it mean that I could fall *back* in love with either Dorian or Caleb?

I shrugged.

He leaned back against the couch and grinned. "Don't overthink it."

I wasn't overthinking anything, and this conversation was going to frustrate me if I didn't get the hell out of this house. I didn't owe Noah an explanation, especially since I wasn't sure what it all meant myself.

I grabbed my purse and left the house without saying goodbye to Dorian or talking further with Noah about what last night meant or could mean. The coven was waiting for me.

I didn't get far before I heard Dorian's voice behind me. "Where are you going?"

Shit.

I sighed deeply and turned on my heel. "I need to get back to my coven."

He threw his hands up. "Are you kidding me?"

"Please don't do this right now." I held up my hands. "Please, Dorian."

He stopped. He didn't look mad, just hurt. "Alright." Dorian relaxed his shoulders and nodded toward his car. "How about I drive you home?"

"I have my car here," I reminded him. "That's ridiculous."

"I don't want you to leave like this," he said. "It's late, and I just want to make sure you get back to your coven safely."

Those words hit me like a ton of bricks. By the tone of Dorian's voice, I knew I was hurting him. What the hell was wrong with me? He didn't deserve this. He deserved so much better than this.

So much better than *me.*

"Fine," I said. "But what about my car?"

"Don't worry about it," he said. "I'll make sure we get it to you by morning."

"Dorian ..."

"Get in the damn car." A smile edged his lips. "I mean, *please* get in the damn car."

He held out his hand for me to take, walked me to the passenger side, and gestured for me to get in.

Yeah, it was late, and I was too exhausted to fight over it.

After climbing into Dorian's car and a few minutes on the road with neither of us speaking, I broke the silence.

"Okay. I feel something." The words slipped out, and even though I should have stopped them, I didn't regret that confession. "I don't understand it, but I feel something."

Dorian didn't turn to me, but there was a ghost of a smile flitting across his lips.

"I don't regret the spell I did a year ago," I added, "But I don't regret last night either."

A huge grin pulled at his lips, but his smile faded into a concerned, straight line. "Mercy, look."

I turned straight ahead and saw someone lying in the middle of the road. "Stop the car."

Dorian slowed to a stop just in time to see a redheaded woman lying flat on her stomach. It looked like she was unconscious, but I couldn't tell if she was breathing. Dorian grabbed my arm when I tried to exit. "Don't get out."

He quickly locked the doors just as a fist broke through the window next to me. Strong hands gripped my shirt, yanking me out of the car, shards of broken glass slicing my arm on the way. I tried to plant my feet on the ground and use my powers, but the stranger quickly pressed their palms against my temples. I couldn't see who it was. It was dark, there were no streetlights, and their hold kept my head steady. I heard Dorian's voice scream for me in the distance, but all I could focus on was the searing, blinding pain that ripped through my skull, rendering me immobile.

Oh, the fucking pain!

My thoughts mangled, my mind blanked out, and then ... nothing.

⁓ℓℓ⁓

"Oh, thank God, Mercy. You're awake," I heard a man say before kneeling next to the couch where I lay motionless. I flinched at his touch on my arm.

The man was beautiful, with kind eyes, but I didn't recognize him. His skin was smooth and slightly fair, and his eyes were a deep hazel. He grabbed my hand and kissed it gently, his lips creating a ripple of goosebumps along my skin. "I thought I had lost you."

I yanked my hand back and looked at him with one eyebrow raised. "What happened? Who are you?"

His brows furrowed. "You don't remember what happened?" he asked. "Mercy, we were attacked tonight."

Mercy? He kept saying that name, but I didn't recognize it.

I didn't remember anything. I was confused about where I was but, most importantly, *who* I was. I looked down at my hands, examining my skin, then at my shirt. I knew what things were but not how or why they were.

"Do you know who you are?" he asked me, gently running his hand over my head.

That time, I didn't move from his touch; I only shook my head.

"Your name is Mercy, and we were attacked an hour ago in the middle of the road. It was an ambush. I tried everything possible but couldn't get to you in time."

"Attacked?" I asked, but I would have remembered something like that.

"We saw someone lying in the street, and the next instant, someone's fist broke the window of my car and pulled you out. Another person grabbed me; I was pinned down and couldn't move. I couldn't save you. They held your head firmly, and when another car came around the corner, they let you go and took off. They did something to you, and then you passed out."

There was a sudden pounding in my head, and I placed my hand on my forehead, shutting my eyes. "What did they do to me?"

"My guess is that they took your memories. You seem not to remember anything at all," the man explained.

My head pounded again. "I don't understand. How can someone take memories away from another?"

"They must have been a witch."

"A witch?"

The moment that word left my lips, momentary flashes of what I assumed was my life passed through my mind. I saw myself lifting my hands to levitate fallen leaves that surrounded me as I stood in the middle of a grove of trees.

I felt this man's hand on my arm, and his icy touch pulled me from my vision.

His eyes went wide. "You really don't know who you are?" the handsome man asked.

I looked back at him, trying hard to remember more of what I had just seen in that vision, but I still didn't know who *he* was. "Who are *you*?"

He hesitantly grabbed my hand and squeezed. "I'm your boyfriend, sweetheart," he said. "You're the love of my life."

Boyfriend?

"I'm … I'm so sorry I don't remember you," I said. "What's your name?"

A small smile reached his beautiful eyes. "My name is Maurice."

CHAPTER 29

MERCY

I blinked rapidly. *Maurice*. The name did sound familiar.

I searched my thoughts and tried to remember him—to remember *anything*. I knew what a boyfriend was and the concept of a relationship, but people, feelings, and memories weren't there. I had a vague flash of being in a home with my mom, who might have had brown hair. Or was her hair ashy-blonde?

Shit.

I cast my eyes around the room. "What is this place?"

Maurice smiled. "It's our home," he told me. "Look around more. Does anything here look familiar?"

The home didn't trigger any memories, but when I looked back at him, I saw a flash of the two of us holding each other on the beach at night, looking out to the rippling waves of the ocean. His eyes alone sparked a familiarity.

"Wait, I remember something," I beamed. "We were on a beach together at night. I felt your arms around me and your breath on my neck."

His eyes lit up. "This is good. This means you're strong enough to fight whatever they did to you. Come here." Maurice grabbed my hand to pull me up, but my body tensed the moment he touched my skin. The awareness of how cold his hands were, made me feel uneasy. I wasn't sure if it was the coolness that made my body freeze or the fact that this was new and scary to me.

"Mercy, you need to relax. I would never hurt you." He leaned into my space and planted his lips on mine. I froze again, but I let the stranger kiss me for some reason. At least, the man who seemed like a stranger.

Fuck, he was so attractive that I was slightly annoyed that I had no real memories of him. The kiss, though, the kiss sparked a heated arousal in the pit of my stomach, slinking down between my legs.

As Maurice pulled back, more memories invaded my mind of the two of us meeting through a familiar face at a bar. I saw us laughing and holding each other close. Every moment I felt safe with and loved by him.

Maurice's touch was soft and gentle. It felt nice. A little cold but nice. He smiled and squeezed my hand. "I'll go get you some water, okay?"

I answered with a timid smile, but as soon as he left me, I scanned the room again to see if anything in the home would trigger a memory. I eyed the bookshelf in the back corner and looked at the picture frames lining the shelf. He and I were in them, looking happy together. At least, it appeared that way. Seeing myself in photographic memories that I couldn't remember was so bizarre.

"That was our trip to Italy last summer," Maurice explained. His voice echoed behind me, and he joined me at the bookshelf. He handed me the glass of water before saying, "I was born not too far from this shoreline, and you had just met my family for the first time." He watched me out of the corner of his eye. "You'd never been outside the country but always dreamed of visiting Rome."

Maurice placed his hand on my left hip, dragging me toward him. "We can visit again, just you and me." He tightened his grip, leaning toward my cheek and kissing it softly, gliding his lips along my skin. Goosebumps covered my body, and as electric as it felt, I pulled away.

"I'm sorry, I just ..."

"No, shit. I'm the one who should be sorry. You have no memory of me, and I keep putting my hands on you. You're probably so freaked out right now. Everything we do from here on out, we'll take it slowly. I'm sure the memories will soon return."

And with those words, one did.

I looked back at one of the pictures. "A stranger took this right outside a shop where you bought me a mask, right?" I paused as the memory became clearer. "The shop was called Ca' Macana."

The name slipped off my tongue with such ease. The more I remembered, the more I felt comfortable in this home and near Maurice. Hopefulness bloomed inside me, and I could hardly contain my happiness.

My excitement brought a smile to Maurice's lips. It really brightened his features, and he looked even more handsome.

"That was in Venice," he said.

God, I wished so badly I could remember everything.

I glanced around the room again, spotting a pentagram plaque against the wall by the console table near a hallway. "I saw a vision when you first talked about what had happened to me," I said. "I saw myself use magic. It sparked inside me, but I don't know how to use it." I lifted my hands, examining my fingertips. "I'm not afraid, just confused. Things are beginning to make sense, but it's still like a puzzle with missing pieces."

He walked up to me and touched my hand. "I can help you remember, you know? Once, you shared with me that you had to visualize a green light flowing through you and the power igniting in your hand to summon your magic. Focus on it reaching your fingertips," he added. I looked down and did as he instructed. Nothing happened when I thought about this green energy reaching my fingers. I didn't feel anything stir within me. "I'm sorry. I don't know what I'm doing."

"Focus, Mercy!" That time, his voice was harsh and authoritative. It scared me a little, and I flinched. "I'm sorry." His tone dropped and he grabbed my hand. "I'm overwhelming you. We can try this another day."

I frowned. "You look upset with me."

Maurice took my fingers in his, intertwined them, and brought me closer to his chest. "I'm not upset. I'm just worried about you."

Maurice held me in place as he pressed his hands to my cheek, caressing my skin from my cheekbone down to my lips. Then he let his finger slide beneath my chin and lifted it. His lips touched mine again. The kiss was deeper that time, more sensual. My body ached for that kiss as if he were someone I had cared for, for years.

I took a deep breath after Maurice let go, and I noticed boxes down the hallway for the first time. "What is all this?" I asked, trying to catch my breath.

"Oh, I didn't want to bring it up yet, since you're still confused about a lot of things, but we're moving," he explained.

Moving? I didn't even know where I was yet.

"Where are we now?"

"Salem, Massachusetts," Maurice replied. "I wish you could remember all this, but we sold our home last month. Our new home awaits in California. I have business there starting next week, so we're catching a flight first thing in the morning."

I was familiar with the geographical landmarks but had no emotional ties to Salem. I looked out the window, but I only saw the night sky.

"Shouldn't I be in a hospital, Maurice?" I asked. "Not taking a flight clear across the country?"

"It's not as if you have amnesia, Mercy. A witch took your memories away. A doctor could examine you and try to help, but it would be pointless."

I thought about what he said. "But why would someone do that to me?"

"Because you're a powerful witch, darling," he said, running the back of his knuckles along my cheek. You were born years ago, 1671, to be exact."

1671? I'm over three hundred years old?

I've had centuries of memories, and I couldn't remember them.

"You, too?" I asked.

"I'm much older," he explained.

"Are you also a witch?"

He smiled. "No. I'm something else." He opened his mouth, and slowly, his canines protruded into sharp points. I gasped and took a step back, but Maurice caught me by the waist, keeping me from creating distance between us. My heart pounded hard against my chest. I didn't want to fear this man, whom I felt was essential to my life, but I did.

"You're a ..."

"Yes, but I won't hurt you. I've never hurt you," Maurice explained with so much desperation in his voice that I honestly believed he wouldn't. "The only blood I drink is supplied through my contacts at the local hospital."

He retracted his fangs, and my shoulders relaxed. The fear I had felt, though, at seeing him transform into a vampire, still lingered.

I took one more step back to give myself some space from him, but Maurice grabbed my hand and gestured toward the hallway. "Come on, I'll show you around. Maybe the more you see, the more memories will come back."

During the entire tour of the house, my nerves wouldn't settle. Sure, I had memories with him that felt familiar and safe, but my defenses stayed up after he shared with me that he was a vampire. I couldn't relax. I must not have cared, or why would I be dating him? I had hoped the memories of a world filled with dark creatures only seen in movies would flood my mind, but they didn't.

I steadied my breathing as we walked down the hall, taking in my surroundings.

We entered a spacious room on the first floor, which had mainly been packed, other than a few pieces of furniture. Nothing looked familiar to me, though. I spotted a dresser in the corner and opened the drawer. Female underwear and socks were in the first drawer, pajamas in the second, and shorts in the bottom.

"Are these clothes mine?" I asked.

A playful smile pulled at the edge of his lips. "I don't live with anyone else. Of course, they're yours." Maurice walked to the other side of the room and began rummaging in another dresser.

My cheeks flushed with embarrassment, and I looked down again at my clothes, then eyed the bathroom connected to the room. "Maurice?" I called.

"Yes, babe?"

Babe. Darling. I wasn't ready for these pet names.

"Um, would you mind if I took a shower? I feel pretty dirty, so I'd like to clean up and change my clothes."

The truth was, I needed to step away from him so I could absorb everything he had shared with me and try to make sense of the visions I did have.

"Well," he said, taking a step in my direction, "Maybe I can join you?"

I shook my head, tempted, but kept my lips in a flat line.

Annoyance read on his features. "Of course. I understand. Do what you need to do," Maurice said before leaving me alone in the room with my thoughts.

I sifted through the dresser drawer and pulled out underwear, plaid shorts, and a T-shirt before entering the bathroom and turning on the water.

During my shower, I thought about what I had seen. Without a doubt, I knew I was a witch. I felt it, and I saw it in my visions. But I didn't fear it, though. The thought hit me that since witches are real, vampires and whatever else was out there should be just as familiar and normal to me. I shouldn't fear it, right? If Maurice were going to hurt me, he would have done it by now.

After half an hour in the warm shower, I examined myself in the vanity mirror. My skin was lightly tanned, with barely noticeable freckles sprinkled along my arms and across my nose, relatively flawless except for one part. I ran my hand along the top of my chest and paused at the long, pink, knotted scar. I touched the raised flesh and tried to recall how I could have received such an injury. I made a mental note to ask Maurice about it in the morning when things had settled down a bit more.

I put my pajamas on, pulled my hair into a wet bun, and rubbed some lotion I found in one of the drawers on my face. After brushing my teeth, I resigned back to the bedroom, spotting Maurice resting on the side of the bed, closest to the window. He pulled the blankets back, leaving an empty space below the other pillow.

Was I supposed to lie down with him? Of course, he'd assume that if that was our regular routine.

I didn't want to upset him, so I climbed into bed and lay down. "Maurice, I don't … I'm not ready to do anything with you."

His smile was there, but it seemed forced. "I won't touch you yet," he said. *Yet.* "But we've been together for over three years, Mercy. I hope all your memories return so we can get back to where we were before the attack."

I gathered my thoughts, then asked, "Are we really moving tomorrow? Shouldn't we try to find out who took my memories away, and more importantly, why?"

Maurice shook his head. "This isn't new, babe. You've been targeted for centuries. You're a powerful witch, and those who want to hurt you will stop at nothing. That's why we have to leave this place. We need to find a new home where your enemies can't find you."

I looked up at the ceiling, still confused and unsure about everything. Still, Maurice was the only one here—the only one I had even the slightest memories of. Memories filled with love. It showed me I could perhaps trust him. I had to. I had nowhere else to go.

"Okay," I said, smiling and placing my hand on his cheek in a bold gesture. "I'm sorry I don't remember everything, but I promise I'll keep trying."

He leaned in and kissed me on the forehead, the cheek, and the lips. His hands lingered by my hips, caressing my skin, inching under my shirt and up my stomach before his fingers reached my breasts. That arousal was back, and my nerves tingled, my body responding to him as if we had done this a thousand times before.

But then, my body felt distant, as if my mind and body weren't agreeing then, one trying to win a fight over the other. I placed my hand on his, stopping him. It felt good. My God, did it feel good, but I couldn't be intimate with someone I didn't remember, let alone a vampire who frightened me.

Maurice pulled his hand out and ran his thumb along my lips. He didn't say goodnight, only kissed me on the forehead and turned over, his back facing me now.

I shut my eyes, facing away from him until our backs almost touched, but Maurice turned back, wrapping his arms around me, holding me close to his chest. He didn't try to kiss or touch me again, but he held me until we fell asleep.

CHAPTER 30

MERCY

The following morning, I awoke to the potent stench of cooking meat. Bacon, to be exact. I had to swallow back the nausea climbing to my throat as I entered the kitchen. The curtains were drawn tight, blocking out the sunlight. The kitchen was lit with soft gold overhead lights hanging from the ceiling.

"Good morning, beautiful," Maurice said, placing three strips of bacon on my plate. "I'll make you more if that's not enough." His black, tousled hair fell over one side of his face, and his eyes looked darker, covered in shadows as if he hadn't slept.

Of course, he didn't sleep. He's a vampire.

As Maurice leaned back against the counter by the stove with his arms folded loosely over his chest, I sat, staring at the food he placed in front of me.

"What's wrong, darling?" he asked when I didn't immediately dive into my plate. "Is there a problem with what I made?" I blinked, looking up at him. His expression was worrisome, as if my reaction to not eating what he had cooked for me had offended him. "That bacon is only for you. Vampires are a little more se-lective when it comes to our appetite." A touch of a smile on his lips lasted a few seconds before his mouth flattened into a frown. "Fine. Is there something else you wanted me to make you?"

My eyes glanced down at the plate again. "Not this," I admitted. "Sorry, I don't think I ate things like this."

"Meat?" He paused before walking to my side and looking down at me. "Of course you ate meat. This must be from the attack. Perhaps you're not feeling well this morning."

I slid the plate further from me, so I didn't have to smell it so close. "Yeah," I said, unconvinced. "Maybe."

Maurice stepped behind me and placed his palms on my shoulders, his long fingers wrapping around until they rested on my chest. His lips touched my ear. "I can draw you a bath if you'd like," he said. "We still have an hour before we need to leave."

I shook my head as the pressure from his hands squeezed at my shoulders, causing an uneasy feeling in my chest as pain itched at my skin. Maurice was squeezing me too hard.

"I can make you something else," he said. "How about a smoothie?"

The breath I held slowly left my mouth when he eased up the pressure. I looked up, meeting his eyes, before nodding. That hint of a frown was back, but when I smiled, his mood shifted, becoming less intense than before. It was as if everything he did had an agenda, and every reaction that went against that would immediately set him off. It was like walking on eggshells, and everything about him felt fucking wrong.

He pulled frozen strawberries from the freezer, grabbed a glass jar of orange juice from the fridge, and poured them all into a blender.

"Bon appétit," he said as he handed me my smoothie.

"Thank you." I smiled and sipped slowly. It was good. The strawberry blended with orange juice was the perfect combination I had been craving.

"I have a few friends stopping by here this morning, and then a moving company is coming over to help us pack the rest of our things."

"What are we taking?" I asked. "That's quite a trip to take all this stuff."

"Most of it is being sold, and I'll donate the rest. We'll ship a few things to Huntington Beach. We only need to pack our clothes and some personal items."

Maurice's phone rang, and he answered on the second ring.

He flashed me a small smile before he excused himself from the kitchen.

After I finished my smoothie, I stepped outside and took a deep breath, taking in the air around me. I looked over the balcony and saw a few deer running through the nearby clearing.

Where were we exactly? All I saw was a forest surrounding us. No other houses, not even a road.

I turned around, and Maurice stood near the sliding door, watching me, but he didn't step outside. I walked up to him and slid the door back open. "It's nice today. Maybe we can have breakfast out here."

He shook his head. "I can't."

"You can't come outside?"

I looked up. Rays from the morning sunrise shone onto the deck. "Oh, God. I'm such an idiot. Vampires can't go in the sun, right?"

He nodded.

But then I thought about where we were moving. "But aren't we moving to California? It's sunny like three hundred times a year there. Seems a vampire would avoid a place like that."

Maurice looked irritated, keeping his mouth straight and flaring his nostrils when I asked my question, but I couldn't understand why. Was he going to hide inside all day?

He relaxed his expression and grinned. "That's why we're moving there. There's a witch in Los Angeles who's a good friend of mine. She plans to create a more permanent solution for vampires. We lost all hope when we realized we were wrong about the witch we'd thought for centuries would be the key to removing the curse of the sun. So, now, we must figure it out on our own."

As much as I still feared being this close to an actual vampire, the fact that he couldn't enjoy the sun beaming down on him every day made me feel sorry for him. I went back inside the house and slid the balcony door closed when Maurice spoke again.

"I have a meeting with a few of my colleagues. I have a bookshelf full of books you love. How about you read something or watch a show on my computer in the office? Maybe they'll trigger more memories."

I looked past him and saw a man and woman standing in the family room. I didn't recognize them, and no memories came back. They were both beautiful—flawless, like Maurice. An anxious feeling came over me as I narrowed my eyes at them. Maurice being a vampire is one thing. He was someone I remember caring for. Those two in the family room were strangers. Possibly undead strangers. My stomach twisted in knots, and I wanted to hide in my room until they left.

"Please, Mercy," Maurice said, ordering me over with his hand. "Come meet my friends first." I stared at him pleadingly, but he smiled and gently grabbed my hand. "Oh, relax, darling. They won't hurt you."

He escorted me to the front room, where the two stood, and gestured to the young-looking, dark-haired guy with light scruff against his tanned face. "Mercy, this is Julian. He joined my business a few months ago. And this is Jade." I looked at the redhead next to Julian. She had dark auburn hair, and her ivory skin was covered in light freckles, mostly along her cheeks and nose. Her complexion was so pale it almost looked like she had no pigmentation besides her red hair.

They both smiled at me awkwardly, and it made me uncomfortable. Their eyes spoke to me as if they knew something I didn't, and they seemed to take pleasure in that.

"Jade and I have known each other for years. She's been traveling around Europe this last year and joined my company a month ago," Maurice explained.

I swallowed hard and felt a painful lump in my throat go down slowly. Something was off about all three of them.

"What do you do, Maurice?" I asked. "For work?"

He beamed, appearing excited that I was finally asking the important questions. "I run a blood donation corporation," he said, and I looked at him with skepticism. "You see, not every vampire wants to drink from humans," he said. "So, we provide a solution by draining blood from willing donors. Then we sell it for profit."

"They're all willing?" I asked. Just the mere thought of blood made me queasy.

A rumble of chuckling at my question between all three of them echoed off the walls. "Most of them, sweetheart," Maurice said. "You see, that same witch, who we thought could save us, now wants to kill us off. We've also learned of witches who can manipulate someone's face. If vampires don't realize they're drinking from her under this disguise, they will become human again. We can't have that."

I swallowed deeply. "Well, I don't know. I'd think being a human would be a good thing unless you enjoy being this way."

The moment I said those words, I immediately regretted them. They all narrowed their eyes at me and tightened their lips.

I gulped but continued, hoping my voice didn't sound too nervous. "How do you know the donors aren't this witch? In disguise?"

Maurice reached up, brushed the hair from my cheek, and then leaned in and kissed it gently. "We inject them with a potion. If she changes back, then we know. If they don't, we take as much as they're willing to give *without* killing them."

"That ... that sounds wrong," I said.

He inched closer to me, and I backed up. "Which part?"

I looked at the others, then back at Maurice. "All of it."

His frown turned into a side smirk. "What's the difference between a human donating their blood to save another human's life and what we're doing?"

I didn't know how to answer this without upsetting him. Maurice had been kind since I awoke on that couch last night, but I didn't know him, not like he seemed to know me.

Maurice shrugged when I didn't answer. "It doesn't fucking matter," he said, his harsh tone sending me into a wave of panic. "Once we move, I won't be running that business anymore."

I looked at Jade, who snickered under her breath.

"Why not?" I asked, tilting my chin and suddenly finding a thread of courage.

"Because that witch is no longer a problem," he explained, and that was the last thing he needed to say. I was a witch, which meant this other witch Maurice spoke of could be a friend. She could be my family.

"I'm going to go use the restroom. Please, excuse me." I shifted toward the hallway, but Maurice grabbed my arm, and I winced at the pressure of his nails digging painfully into my skin. "You're hurting me, Maurice. Let me go."

His lip came up in a snarl. "Is there something else you'd like to say to me, Mercy?" he asked.

I swallowed down a painful lump. "Nope." I shook my head. "I just really have to pee."

He flashed me a forced smile that made my stomach churn. It was sadistic and unkind. "Be quick. Jade and Julian are taking us to the airport. We leave in less than an hour."

He released my arm, and I hurried to the bathroom. I didn't need to go. I just needed a moment away from those three. I looked in the mirror, not recognizing myself and desperately needing to know if everything he'd told me since I awoke on his couch was true. Why would anyone try to hurt me? That question didn't seem to press Maurice. He should be wondering why the hell this happened and trying to find a solution, not moving across the damn country. I couldn't leave on a plane with someone who was a stranger to me, regardless of these fragments of memories I had of him.

I had to get the fuck out of here.

After I cast my eyes around the bathroom for anything to defend myself with if he or his two minions tried to stop me, I saw the window above the bathroom sink. I double-checked that I had locked the door, moved to the window, unlocked it, and slowly cranked it open. I pulled myself up, climbed out the window, and dropped to the grassy lawn below me. Since it was daylight out, I was able to check around at my surroundings to locate an escape, except there wasn't one. The only relief I felt was that the three vampires were still inside, and even if they wanted to come outside, the sun would stop them.

I snuck around the corner just in case, and when I turned, I ran into a solid chest.

His chest.

Maurice looked down. "Where on earth do you think you're going, my love?" he asked with a sinister grin. I looked behind him, and there stood Jade and Julian. The sun beamed down on them as if my theory were only something you'd see in a movie.

"Magic," Maurice answered the question as if he had read my thoughts.

I blinked. "What?"

"You're asking yourself how we're able to walk in the light, aren't you?"

I nodded.

"You see, when we discovered that this witch couldn't allow us to walk in the light unless she turned us human, we found a witch who created a temporary spell for when we needed it. It only lasts about ten minutes, so we need to get back inside the house."

When I tried to back up, he grabbed my arm and yanked me toward him, slamming me into his body.

"Fuck you," I said.

"Oooh," he hummed. "I sure do love it when you fight back."

His grip tightened.

"I would never be with a sadistic fuck like you," I said, spitting in his face.

Maurice hissed through his fangs; his grip on my arm bit down so hard I knew there would be a bruise the next day. "I know you wouldn't."

That was when I screamed so loudly Maurice had to muffle my mouth with his hand. His other hand reached up and fisted my hair, dragging me back into the house. I flailed my arms and kicked my legs frantically, trying to wrench free. There was no one around to help me. I wailed as I scanned my surroundings. It was just us. The house stood on the property, deep in the forest, surrounded by nothing but trees. No neighbors, no road, nothing. No one would hear me. Maurice told me that my powers came from my hands, so I lifted my hand and focused on this energy I supposedly possessed, but nothing happened.

Shit! This was my chance to escape, and I hadn't a fucking clue how to fight them.

Maurice threw me into a corner of the family room, and Julian stomped toward me. I recoiled the closer he came, my back pressed against the wall.

"Let's try this again, shall we?" Maurice said to Julian. "She is to remember she's a witch, but our attacker took her ability to use her magic. Mercy's too powerful of a witch to not feel her powers inside her."

Jesus Christ. What the fuck is happening?

"She also needs to know about the existence of vampires so she isn't afraid of me," Maurice commanded. "Just make sure she doesn't know *everything* about who she is."

"Her mind is too strong to take away everything," Julian said, "but I'll try."

They spoke to each other as if I weren't in the room. My heart still pounded hard against my chest.

Julian looked down at me as panic filled my entire body. This guy, Julian, wasn't a vampire. He was a witch.

"Oh, and Julian," Maurice added. "Make her fucking want me."

Julian fisted my hair before yanking me down to my knees. He placed his hands over each side of my temples and then chanted. My head screamed in pain, and fear engulfed every part of me ... until it went dark.

CHAPTER 31

CALEB

Dorian's car was on the side of the road at the corner of Chestnut Drive and Parker Road. Someone had broken the front windows, and Mercy's purse was still on the floor of the passenger's side. There was blood splashed down the side of the car and on the road. I turned to Lily and saw Bradley holding her tightly. She cried in his arms, her face buried in his shoulder. Turning to my right, Riley was barely holding himself together. His hands were in tight fists, and if it weren't for Amber caressing his arms to calm him, he'd transform into his werewolf form and go on a rampage. Something he was trying desperately not to do.

I understood this type of rage. Despite the familiarity of the scene, Mercy wasn't off sacrificing herself again. Someone had abducted her, along with Dorian. It must have been an ambush Dorian couldn't stop because he was a skilled fighter and would have fought for her until his last breath. He was likely dead, but not her. I could feel her. I also knew who was responsible.

Fucking Maurice.

This also meant that we were right about it not being him and his cronies who took the dagger. If he had it, she'd be dead, and we would all have felt it.

"That's it. I'm calling the cops," Bradley said, throwing his hands up and reaching into his pocket.

"Lily," I said, hoping she'd stop this nonsense before it got out of control.

She grabbed Bradley's hand to stop him, but when he resisted, she sprawled her fingers out and chanted. Bradley dropped the phone, not able to use his hand.

"Are you kidding me, Lily? You said you'd never use your powers on me!" he scolded. He looked more afraid than upset.

"And you promised to keep my secret after I told you." Lily's face softened. "What do you think the cops will do to us once they find out what's happening here? Huh? What do you think Maurice will do to the cops you plan to call when, and if, they catch up with him?"

Bradley relaxed his shoulders, and Lily released the magic that had kept him from using his hand.

I turned back to Riley. "Go ahead. Shift and see what you can pick up."

Amber, still trying to relax Riley, lifted her hand from his arm, and they both crouched down. After they transitioned into their wolf forms, they sniffed the area around the street. They sniffed the car, her purse, and the glass on the ground and turned to each other. Amber and Riley tapped their noses together as if they were communicating.

Riley quickly turned back to his human form and stood before me, naked as the day he was born. It was a bit awkward, but he seemed not to care, as if it were completely normal to be standing in the buff. "Okay, we have the scent. I smelled both a vampire and a witch. The vampire scent was female."

"So, not Maurice?" I asked.

He nodded. "I didn't recognize the scent of either of them."

"Dammit," I cursed. I then looked at Lily. "It doesn't mean it's not him. He had people who worked for him before. He most likely has a following now."

We got back into our cars, and I called Joel to update him on what we had found out.

⸎

Once back at Abigail's, I entered the kitchen and poured myself a glass of whiskey. It had been a while since I drank hard liquor, but fuck, I felt numb at this point. The extent of Maurice's fury left him willing to do anything to her to seek revenge. The perfect punishment. If he was willing to kill an angel with a sword, with no remorse, what was he willing to do to Mercy?

I sipped my drink as I paced the floor.

"We'll find her," Roland assured me. He'd been standing in the doorway that led into the kitchen. I stopped dead in my tracks when he stepped in front of me. "Look, this is Mercy we're talking about. You know she's going to get herself out of this. She's alive. That you know."

He was right. Mercy was alive, but what had Maurice done to her already? What was he planning? Was she even here in Rhode Island? Had he taken her somewhere else?

I lowered my head and looked at the whiskey, then back up at my father. "I've got to go," I said while handing him my glass. "Here. Knock yourself out."

And with that, I left to find Melissa.

—⁕—

I pounded my fist against the door to her apartment until she opened it. She wore a thin green spaghetti-strap nightgown that came down to her knees. Her tattoos were on display, and her curly hair was pulled back into a low braid. She was breathtaking.

"Hey," she said. "What's going on?"

I stepped in without an invitation and placed my hands on the sides of her neck, staring at her. "Hey, beautiful," I said in a gravelly tone. "Can I stay here tonight?"

There was so much desperation in my voice that I must have come off as truly pathetic.

"Did you find Mercy?" She ignored my question.

I shook my head.

"Is that why you're here?" she asked, raising a thin brow. "You think I can make your pain go away?"

I winced at her question. It stung because it wasn't the entire truth. I cared about Melissa. She was sexy, funny, and intelligent, but I was hurting tonight. I was hurting and needed her to remove that pain so I no longer felt like I was dying inside.

"I don't know," I confessed as I released her and walked toward her bedroom. She looked at me, and her head tilted to the right. She was probably contemplating what she wanted to do.

Melissa sauntered toward me and held out her hand. After I took it, I escorted her to the bedroom. She turned to face me once we reached the bed. I leaned down, kissed her gently on the lips, and my right hand came around and grabbed her ass, lifting her slightly before deepening the kiss.

We kissed for a moment before I realized that just kissing wasn't going to silence my mind. Not tonight. My hands reached down to the hem of her nightgown, lifting it above her head, so she was bare and revealed for me. She placed her hands on my chest and gave me a small smile. It was an invitation that I needed.

Moments later, I was already balls deep inside of her. My thrusts were animalistic and rough, and they couldn't have been further from any form of lovemaking. Her nails itched along my back, and her fingers threaded in my hair. Scratching. Dragging. Pulling. We were both chasing pain that mixed with pleasure tonight, to forget the agony tearing at my chest and the shame she'd feel in the morning, knowing I wasn't entirely with her.

Melissa and I fucked like nothing else mattered that night. It was raw and carnal. Nothing fucking mattered. She was what I needed, and she'd let me have her.

CHAPTER 32

MERCY

California! Maurice was taking me to California. I'd always wanted to visit the Pacific Ocean. I also wasn't just visiting. It was my new home. According to Maurice, our backyard faced the ocean!

Maurice grabbed my hand as we descended the stairs from his private jet. It was eight in the evening, so Maurice and his colleagues didn't need a spell cast on them to avoid the sunlight.

Jade grabbed my suitcase, and Julian waited at the bottom of the stairs next to the limo and opened the door for us as we approached.

It was only a short drive to Huntington Beach. Maurice owned a private runway right outside the city. There was no secret Maurice was wealthy, with a handful of assistants at his disposal, but I wondered if that also included what I needed. Though it felt bizarre to ask anyone to do anything for me, especially something I could do myself.

The flight wasn't terrible, but I was ready to lay my head down and sleep.

Maurice was mostly silent during the drive, but as we pulled into our new driveway, he planted a warm kiss on my lips. His mouth tasted like the dark red wine and chocolate they served us during the flight. Long fingers trailed up my thigh and stopped between my legs, rubbing gently against my nerves.

Oh, God.

"Maurice, someone can see," I said, shifting slightly in my seat.

I felt his lips spread over mine into a smile. "I don't fucking care," he said. "I'm happy we're finally out here together. That's all."

I leaned back and winked. "We can celebrate tomorrow night," I said. "How about that?"

Maurice reached over my shoulder and clicked the door handle. "After you."

I hadn't had the chance to explore our home yet. From what I did see from the pictures online, the home was already fully furnished and ready for us when we arrived. The lights dimly lit the hallway as Maurice led us to our bedroom.

Maurice pulled the blanket over my chest as we snuggled under the sheets. Oh, the feeling of the silky material felt so good against my skin. He brushed the stray hair from my face and pulled me closer to him. "I love you, Mercy." His voice was gentle, and his words were familiar. I was still trying to recall all the memories I had lost, but the sound of his voice, his words, rang familiar and comforted me. I felt safe. "Tomorrow, I have some business to attend to, but I'll have Julian escort you around the city. How does that sound?" He bent his elbow and placed his palm on the side of his head, propping himself so he was looking down at me.

I nodded, allowing him to kiss me again one last time before I said, "Thank you. Night, Maurice."

I closed my eyes, no longer able to fight my exhaustion and let my dreams take me away.

Do I always dream like this?

I assume most people don't remember their dreams. Still, everything around me felt familiar, like I had entered this world in my subconsciousness. Maybe my dreams would help me remember something. Anything, honestly.

A man with features similar to Maurice's walked up to me, holding a red scarf in his hand. He lifted it above my head and wrapped my hair in it. "Tradition," he said.

I looked over, and Maurice stood on a stage. The wind from the open windows around us blew his hair around in a beautiful dance.

I blinked once and was standing outside. A black wolf stood by a light gray one, a little bigger than the other. They slowly crept toward me, but I didn't feel threatened or fear for my life. They were enchantingly beautiful.

The gray wolf was so close I could feel its breath on my arm. It nudged me as I looked over at the other, but I wasn't sure what they wanted me to do. "What do you want?" I asked.

He lifted his snout as the other joined in, howling toward the moon above us. It was dark, and a cool breeze fanned my skin. Their howls echoed in my ears. As their voices rang, I looked down at my hands. They were glowing bright green. The light was shining, and the feeling was so powerful it nearly took my breath away.

I sat bolt upright, gasping for air and clutching the sheet close to my body. Maurice was sound asleep when I looked over at him. I wasn't sure how deep of a sleep a vampire could get. Was he resting his eyes, though, or off into his own dream?

I slid out of bed, entered the balcony attached to the bedroom, and looked out at the water. The waves crashed onto the shore, rolling over each other and thinning out as the tide pulled up and the current brought it back to the deep sea. The full moon beamed down on the water's surface, creating a shimmering glow. The moon was almost as bright as it was in my dream.

I brought my hands up to my body as I had done in my dream. I held my palms out in front of me, focusing on the feeling I had just moments before I opened my eyes. Then my fingertips glowed ever so faintly.

Holy shit.

The more I focused on them, the more intense the glowing became. It grew until my hands radiated emerald green. My body felt a lustful hunger that I didn't know existed.

How powerful am I? What does this power even do?

A noise stirred behind me, and I concealed the light. A moment later, Maurice joined me on the balcony, wrapping his arms around my waist. I thought I would be excited about what I had discovered, but I had a sinking feeling in the pit of my stomach that told me I needed to keep this a secret from him. When I awoke from our attack a few days ago, he had told me I was a witch but that the ability to use those powers was taken from me.

No. It's all a lie.

Unless whatever happened to me was no longer working. I could use my magic again. My God, it felt incredible. The surge of strength from the power was intoxicating, and I felt a part of me come back to life in that light.

"What are you doing out here, babe?" Maurice asked. His grip tightened around me, pulling me closer to his body as his hands brushed up against my breasts through the silk of my nightgown.

I stared at the moon as if I were drawn to it, like a moth to a flame. There was a world out there that I didn't fully know or understand. Slowly, memories began coming back to me about my life with Maurice, but that was it. Everything outside that box was still missing. I knew my name and places I had been to with Maurice, but what about me? I had no memories of who *I* was. Who was Mercy beyond this relationship? What did I do as a hobby? Was I funny? Serious? Kind? Do I have a family?

Why were memories of activities I'd done with Maurice and my feelings for him there but nothing else?

"I couldn't sleep ... bad dream," I explained, looking over my shoulder.

Maurice's fingers trailed over my bare skin, brushing my scar and sending a shiver through my body. I had once asked him about the scar on my chest, but Maurice just shrugged and said it was from a car accident when I was twelve. He had refused to talk about it since then.

He held me close, pulling my backside toward him. It was no secret that it was one of the parts of my body that he loved the most. I could feel his hardened cock press against me. It was an effect I seemed to have on him often.

"Do you want to talk about it?" he asked.

I shook my head. "I'm going to grab some water and go back to bed." I wiggled out of his grasp. "I'll be right back up."

When I turned around, it was hard to decipher the expression that flooded his face. It was an odd mixture of hurt and anger, but I didn't stop to make him feel better. I left him standing on the balcony and headed inside.

Upon entering the kitchen, I grabbed a glass from the cabinet and filled it with filtered water from the fridge.

I looked around the fully furnished family room. Maurice had told me that a local furniture company had set up the house a week ago, so we didn't need to worry about unpacking anything aside from our personal belongings that would show up from the moving truck in a few days.

I hadn't been able to explore the new house yet. We got in last night and turned in early due to the exhaustion brought on by our travels.

The house was dark and not just because it was three in the morning or because all the lights were turned off. They had painted the walls a deep gray, the furniture was all black, and the dark cherry floors were highly polished. From each window hung black, thick drapes, which I assumed were to black out the sun for Maurice's benefit.

I didn't mind the dark colors—they felt warm and inviting—but they created a haunting feeling around me. A strange, dark home I had never been to. It wasn't mine, not really. Maurice wasn't my husband. I didn't work. I was a stranger in *his* space, whether he wanted me there or not.

There was a thick door at the end of the hallway. It differed from the others—dark brown with three silver locks, and there wasn't even the tiniest crack between the bottom of the door and the floor. The handle resembled a car's steering wheel but was made of metal.

A vault?

I stepped toward the hall that led to the door right before I heard someone clear their throat behind me. I jumped.

"Maurice doesn't like to keep his money in a bank. The safe is off limits," Jade said in a harsh tone.

"I was just curious," I said, hoping she'd leave me alone. "Besides, it's secured. I'd need a key, which I obviously don't have."

Her face grew hard. Jade did *not* like me.

"I didn't even realize you were in the house with us. This place is enormous. Did I wake you?" I asked, hoping if I appeared that I cared about her feelings, she'd back the fuck off.

"Does that bother you?" she asked. Her question didn't sit well with me, but I didn't want to argue with her at three in the morning.

I'll talk to Maurice about it.

"No. I just didn't expect you here, that's all," I said. "You startled me."

She giggled like a little girl and took a step toward me. "You're not the only one Maurice wants."

I knew what she meant, and it made me sick. I didn't want to be here. Not standing in front of her, not even in this damn house.

"Jade, what the hell are you doing?" Maurice asked her, his voice filled with fury and disgust.

"Nothing, Master. I was only stopping her from snooping. She asked about the safe."

Maurice glared at her. His jaw was clenched, and if looks could have killed ... well, Jade would have been long gone. There was no question about the fury that was apparent on his face. "It's not snooping when it's your own damn house," he said through gritted teeth. The moonlight streaming through the windows cast a garish glare on his protruding fangs.

She stopped, her face frozen with fear, and a familiarity with her words struck me like a ton of bricks.

Master.

Where had I heard that?

"Forgive me," Jade said. "I just came to the kitchen to grab some blood from the fridge. I'll be leaving now."

She was afraid of him. No, not *scared*. She was terrified.

As Jade left, Maurice wrapped his arm around my waist, drawing me in closer as he looked down at me.

"Are you okay?" he asked, placing one hand on my cheek and running his thumb along my jaw. The calming sensation of feeling safe finally came to me. I exhaled slowly as he inched his way closer to me. He removed any free space between us—I could clearly feel his cock, hard and ready for me, as it brushed in between my legs. A tingling sensation spread through me instantly; I loathed the way my body reacted to him when he was this intense. I couldn't tell the difference between being afraid of him and being protected. "However, though I don't mind you wandering the house, Jade is right. You're not to ask about that safe. Understand?"

Maurice, forbidding it with such intensity, made me want to know what was inside even more.

His hand dropped, inching its way to my thigh before his fingers slid underneath my gown. I stilled in my movements, and my breath hitched in my throat. "Maurice, Jade is awake. She could walk back in here."

He clicked his tongue. "Always so careful," he said, stepping back to give us space. "You're dating a vampire, darling. Perhaps let loose a little. Or do I have to remind you what life used to be like between us?"

Desire itched beneath my skin, and yet I was terrified.

I craned my neck to look up into his dark eyes as he stepped toward me again. There was something unreadable in his gaze, something that I couldn't quite put my finger on. He reached out, his long fingers running between the strands of my hair right at the back of my scalp. With a slight tug, he pulled my neck back, keeping it still.

"Years ago, before my father died," he said, his tone low and dangerous. "He taught me two things that I've never forgotten."

I searched my memories of our life together, and I couldn't remember any moment he had spoken of his family. He was born near Rome in the thirteenth century, but that was it. Everything else came to me in small slides through my memory, like a film.

Maurice swallowed, drawing me closer. The heat behind his eyes looked desperate and hollow, as if I were the only thing keeping him together. If one of us cracked, the other would fall.

"My father was a well-respected warrior," he continued. "He fought to protect my mother, me, and my brother Colin until his last breath. Though he was not a kind man, often beating my mother until we could no longer recognize her face, he loved me and would have died for all three of us if he had to."

"That doesn't sound like someone who loved their wife," I pointed out the obvious.

"It would appear that way," he said, chuckling. "Now, wouldn't it?"

I shook my head. "Why are you telling me all this?" I asked.

"Because ..." He licked his bottom lip, and his eyes turned away for only a moment. "I need you to understand me."

"I do—"

Maurice silenced me by placing his finger over my lips.

"My father told me that if I couldn't become something as a man, then my purpose in life meant nothing. I was only six." His eyes glistened as if recounting the memory was almost too difficult to bear.

"And the other?" I asked, my voice barely a whisper. "What else did he teach you?"

A smile pulled at his lips that stretched from ear to ear.

"On his deathbed when I was eighteen, my father had dismissed my mother to the hall so we could speak alone." Maurice softly ran his finger down to my lips, and his eyes looked to my mouth. My heart hammered, my body aching to be touched by just that one look. "In the darkest nights of war, you must be willing to show no mercy and give out the consequences to those who do you harm." I swallowed and tried to turn my gaze away from his when his expression grew too intense. He gripped my jaw, forcing me to look at him. "And until this day, Mercy, I've never allowed someone to go unpunished."

Maurice lashed out and gripped my throat. His cold grip on my neck was tight, momentarily restricting my air supply. I made a feeble attempt to wrench free, but my strength could never match the power of a vampire. He pushed me back against the island, his free hand wrapping around my wrists and pinning them above my head.

"Maurice ..." I murmured, squirming underneath him, but he left little to no wriggle room.

"Shhh," he shushed me, easing his grip on my throat. His lips found mine, kissing me gently, as if he attempted to offer some form of comfort with his lips.

I didn't know what all this meant. My mind screamed at me—warning me I was in danger, yet my body refused to move as that soft, tickling sensation spread through my body, erupting between my legs. His mouth soon abandoned mine, drifting lower to my neck. His fangs protruded, leaving a sharp sting on my tender flesh, but he didn't bite down. The coolness of his icy breath tickled my neck, making me tremble underneath him.

"You smell so fucking amazing," he murmured, inhaling the scent of me.

"Are ... are you going to bite me?" I asked meekly. I couldn't recall him ever doing this before. "Is that something we did before or—"

"No," he said sharply. "I'll never drink your blood." His predatorial gaze looked up, locking with mine, as he inched closer. "But I will fuck you."

Maurice's hand clutched the delicate fabric of my panties, yanking them down my smooth thighs so my heated core was revealed to him. His nostrils spread as he drew in a sharp breath, the corners of his lips twitching. He was holding back a smile.

"So wet for me, aren't you?" He could smell it. I wanted to deny it, but what was the point? Any signs of fear that roamed through my body moments ago were gone, now replaced by desire and need.

Maurice's mind was dangerously somewhere else tonight.

His lips found mine once again, but his kiss was different now. It was hungry and desperate, rough in comparison to how he usually kissed me. A small moan escaped my lips, coming out muffled against his mouth as he devoured me.

That sound seemed to trigger something within him; his free hand fiddled with his pants, pulling his cock out. It was as if he was in a rush to be inside of me, with no time to remove his pants fully.

His shaft slid in between my folds, teasing me up and down for a moment as he panted.

"Maurice ..." I murmured against his lips, arching my back underneath his body. I was already throbbing for him. His other hand was still pinning my wrists down against the island, as if he wanted to ensure his claim on me.

"Tell me how much you want me," he demanded, his tone hoarse as he breathed. His cock lingered at my entrance, positioning itself, but he didn't enter just yet. "Beg for me to be inside you, Mercy."

"Maurice," I said with a soft moan, my head tilting back as my lips parted. "Please, I—"

My words cut off as he rammed himself inside of me in one rough, deep thrust. My entire body tensed, my inner walls convulsing around him as they adjusted to his thick size. It was clear that no begging was needed on my end—he wanted this as much as I did.

Maurice released my wrists from his clutch, settling his hand on my hips instead to guide me into his harsh thrusts. With each movement, he seemed to enter me deeper and deeper, sending waves of pleasure mixed through my body.

The sensation was unlike anything I could remember ever experiencing before.

I clutched his back, clawing my way over his icy, bare skin, hoping it would help me stay anchored through the rush that roamed within me. The sound of my small, panting moans, mixed with his heavy breathing, echoed through the room.

"Oh, God," I cried out. His length moved inside of me at a curved angle, hitting that spot inside of me that made the world momentarily sway. My eyes began to close over, and my head tipped back, but Maurice's hand reached for my throat, gripping it.

"Look at me while I fuck you, Mercy," he demanded, momentarily tightening his grip around my throat, wanting to remind me I breathed the air that he allowed. "Eyes on me."

For whatever reason, I obeyed, my gaze locking on his. His eyebrows were furrowed in bliss, and his lips parted as he fucked me. Hard and relentless, owning every part of my being.

With each thrust, I could feel myself approaching that point of no return. The pleasure of it all was almost too overwhelming for both of us. Maurice's hand drifted from my hip to my thigh, holding it open for him as I soaked his cock in my arousal.

As my orgasm rippled through me, hard and fast, I gasped for air. Maurice tightened his grip on my throat, only increasing the intensity of the bliss that crashed through my body, leaving no fragment of my being untouched. My pussy pulsed around him, triggering his own orgasm. He tensed above me as he exploded inside of me, his hand releasing my throat to support his weight against the island he spread me out on.

We exchanged no words between us as he pulled out of me, leaving me sore and throbbing. An odd tension rose between us that I couldn't quite understand—he must have felt it, too. His hand slowly trailed over my cheek, an odd contrast to how hard he had just fucked me.

So uncharacteristically silent, he turned on his heels and left me alone with the mess of my thoughts.

CHAPTER 33

MERCY

My body didn't feel sore when we awoke, which surprised me. The way Maurice railed me against the kitchen island was brutal and violent, despite how my body responded to it. I expected to be bruised along my back and thighs, but there was no trace.

What the fuck is wrong with me? Was it normal for Maurice to treat me like that during intimacy?

I decided not to ask Maurice about the safe or why Jade called him *Master*. Honestly, I didn't want to know. Whatever twisted, fucked up relationship the two of them had or have, I wanted to bury it in my mind like the rest of the memories I couldn't recall. I didn't want to know.

True, there was a rollercoaster of emotions that conflicted with each other, and you'd think I'd be jealous, but I wasn't. One moment my heart ached for the man who cared for me when I awoke from that spell. The other, I feared him and what he'd do to me the next time I got out of line.

My instincts told me everything they'd been feeding me was a lie.

"Can you pour me some more coffee?" I asked Maurice, who held the coffee pot, pouring his own mug. "I didn't sleep very well last night. As you well know."

A warm smile reached his lips. "Did I hurt you?" he asked. Maurice's eyes were tired, defeated. He almost looked as if he felt sorry for me.

Maurice walked to my side, topped off my coffee, and leaned back against the counter after setting it back down on the warmer.

"A little," I admitted. The smile I gave him seemed to put him at ease.

I sipped my coffee slowly, shifting my gaze up at him. He only stared at me as if he were waiting for me to speak again. But I had nothing to say. I only wanted to see what was inside that safe.

I need to know.

"I'll be in Los Angeles for the remainder of today, setting up my office. Julian will be in and out, and if you want to explore the city, make sure he's with you, though," he said. "You're not to be alone. Understand?" It wasn't a request. It was an order.

"What about Jade?" I asked. "Is she not around today?"

I almost wanted her to be here. Jade may have shown her dark side last night, but if I could get her alone, perhaps she'd slip up in the moment and share more with me than she intended.

"You'll be out in the daylight too long, darling," he reminded me. "The spell Julian creates is only temporary; you know that. So unless you want her to suffer a cruel, painful death ... Jade will need to stay indoors until dusk."

"Oh, right," I said, pretending to have forgotten. Perhaps staying inside the home with her would be wiser than venturing out with Julian. He alone made my skin crawl with each penetrating gaze he threw at me.

He came around the corner again, leaned down, and kissed the top of my head. I didn't look up. Just the feeling of his lips on my head sent a wave of uncertainty coursing through my mind. After last night, something wasn't right, and I was going to find out what it was.

Maurice was dressed in a blue silk suit this morning, with a plaid tie, and had even trimmed down his nails, which seemed like sharp little daggers most of the time. He was strikingly handsome, much different from most vampires I remember. At least the ones from the brief memories that seem to creep into my thoughts whenever I'm about to panic again. There was a fleeting moment when he looked back at me by the door, a moment that spoke of power with a threat of violence if I got out of line. His eyes darkened, but he still wore that playful smile on his face that I couldn't determine if it was friendly or deceptive.

With his hand placed on the door handle, he said, "Oh, and Mercy?" I watched him intently. "Sorry if Jade made you feel uncomfortable last night. This is your home, too. You are to tell me if she gets out of line with you again so that I can punish her properly."

Punish her. Maurice wanted to punish Jade, and though she was not someone I knew or trusted, it bothered me he'd even consider that.

I nodded in understanding, and as he left me in the kitchen, I said, "Wait, did Julian cast that spell, so you can walk to the car safely?"

Why do I care about his safety? Wait, of course, I did, or should. He was my boyfriend. I should love him and care about his well-being.

He chuckled under his breath. "Yes, my love. I only need Julian's help from the house to the car. The limo has tinted windows, and we're parking in an underground structure at the office. It'll be dark when I leave the office tonight."

"Oh," I said, not realizing he had planned to be home so late. I'd be at home alone all day.

Alone with that safe down the hallway.

"Okay, well, get lots of work done today, I guess," I said with a smile. "I'll see you tonight when you get back."

He gave me a soft smile and exited the home. I hurried toward the front, stared out the porch windows, and watched Maurice drive away.

Where is Julian, anyway?

As if I had summoned him with my thoughts, Julian strolled into the kitchen moments later, just as I placed my plate in the sink.

"I need to run a few errands in town for Maurice. Would you like to join me and get some sun?"

No, I said in my thoughts, but for all I knew, Maurice had security cameras around the home and property. If I were going to snoop around, I wouldn't get far.

The house really was suffocating.

"Let me put on my shoes," I said as I rushed to get ready.

After ten minutes, I met Julian at the front door. "Okay, let's go." My tone came off a little too excited. I didn't want Julian to report to Maurice how I was already hating it here.

Or that I was acting weird as fuck, because I was uncertain and reluctant about every goddamn thing that they threw at me.

We drove only a few blocks until we hit Main Street. There were people everywhere. A few street vendors lined the boardwalk on the crowded sidewalks, and couples walked hand in hand on the pier. I could see a few young skateboarders and even a man playing his guitar for money on the corner of Pacific Coast Highway and Main. It was very different from Salem.

Julian parked along the street, and we headed toward the pier. "I need to speak to a colleague and pass off a few items," Julian said. "Enjoy the beach. But stay within sight."

Really?

I saw a man looking at us on the pier, wearing a polo shirt and khaki pants. He held a cell phone in one hand and a briefcase in the other. As curious as I was about this brief exchange of theirs, my eyes shifted to the waves crashing onto the shore. The view was stunning at night, but through the daylight, with the sun shining against the surface of the water, it was something else. I stepped onto the sand, and vague memories washed over me. Perhaps I used to live by a beach near Salem.

The grainy sand between my toes felt a little funny. I dropped my shoes at the perfect spot and sat down, crossing my legs underneath me. I closed my eyes, and a single tear fell.

I didn't understand it. Why was I crying? I kept them shut and took a deep breath in.

"Lily, you're too close to the water," a woman called, and my eyes shot open.

Lily?

A little girl, maybe four years old, ran toward her mother, who sat on a beach towel, carrying a bucket of salt water. "Sorry, Mommy," she said. The mother pointed her finger at her daughter and then toward the shore as if teaching her the dangers of getting too close to the water when she wasn't next to her. I couldn't hear what they were saying, but I could see the worry in her mother's eyes.

Lily. It was a beautiful name. A familiar name at that. Maybe I had a friend back home by that name.

I made a mental note to ask Maurice about it.

Just as I made myself at home on the beach, Julian cleared his throat behind me. "Don't worry. We'll come back. It's nice out here, isn't it?"

"It's beautiful," I said, keeping my eyes on the ocean. "Have you been to a beach before?"

He laughed. "Yes, Mercy. There are several beaches on the east coast. My coven had a beach house up at Cape Cod at one point, too."

"Did I have a coven?" I asked.

He shook his head. "No."

Julian's answer was so abrupt that it gave me pause. But then he reached out his hand, and I took it for him to help me to my feet.

"Why not?"

He wrinkled his nose. "Mercy, I have some business to attend to. Come on, let's go."

I didn't press the issue. Julian obviously didn't want to answer me. Even though it was a logical question.

"Ouch, Mommy. It hurts," the same little girl cried, and I stopped to look back at them. Her mother held on to her daughter's foot. There was blood.

Oh, no.

Her mother ruffled through her purse and looked scattered while her little girl screamed and cried, holding her bloodied foot.

I didn't hesitate before rushing toward them.

"Mercy, stop," Julian cried out. "It's none of our fucking business." There was so much detest and hatred in his tone that it agitated me.

What an asshole.

Julian caught up and grabbed my arm, but I yanked it away. "What are you doing, Julian? Don't touch me!"

If looks could kill—that was how furious he looked. His eyes blazed like fire, and his hands were in tight fists.

I looked back at the mom and daughter, not caring about Julian, and approached them. "May I?"

Tears rolled down the mom's face. "She stepped on broken glass. There's so much blood, and I can't find my Band-Aids."

"It's okay," I said as I grabbed the girl's foot. I had no idea what I was doing. I didn't have any Band-Aids either, but I felt I could help her somehow. It was like little whispering voices calling to me, but I couldn't hear them.

I placed my hand on the little girl's foot and focused on the power I had ignited in the middle of the night. It was easier that time because I didn't have to think about it. My magic came through and wrapped around her tiny foot, and when I removed my hand, the laceration had disappeared as if it had never been there.

Holy shit. Okay, now I know what that power does.

The little girl stopped crying, and when I looked at the mom, her jaw dropped, and she began to shake.

"Oh shit. Hey, it's okay, miss," I said, but she quickly grabbed her daughter, cradling the child tightly against her chest. There was no "thank you," because I had frightened them. The woman stood up to run with her daughter in her arms, but Julian intervened, placing his hands on both their heads, causing the woman to fall to her knees. They both kicked and struggled with him, but he held on to them firmly until they relaxed and went into a trance-like state.

I cast my eyes around the beach, seeing if anyone around us had been watching. Everyone was so preoccupied with their lives that no one had witnessed the spell he'd done on them.

"What the hell are you doing to them? Let them go."

He did but then bent down, grabbed the beach bucket of ocean water, and poured it over the blood on the little girl's foot, washing it clean.

When he finished cleaning her foot, they opened their eyes and looked at us. "Who are you guys?" the mother asked. "What are you doing here?"

"I'm sorry," Julian said, "but your daughter was screaming. We came to make sure everything was okay."

"We're fine," she snapped back as she pulled her daughter close.

"We'll leave," I said. "Sorry to bother you." Julian was right behind me as I turned on my heel to walk away, but I didn't get far before his hand wrapped around my elbow and pulled me back.

"What the fuck were you thinking?" he seethed through his teeth.

"Excuse me?" I said, turning around to face him.

"Don't ever use your magic like that in public. I don't give a fuck if someone is dying. I forbid it!"

I yanked my arm from his hold. "Forbid me? Who the hell do you think you are? Shouldn't you be happy I have magic back?"

Julian's jaw tensed. "We'll talk about it when we get back to the house." He stomped off, and this time, I staggered behind.

"So, your power is that you can take memories away?" I asked, then stopped again. My feet wouldn't move anymore as I realized what that meant.

Blood drained down my face as I backed up, watching the heated glare from his eyes. He knew that I knew what he did to me.

"It was you," I gasped, backing up another foot. "You took my memories. Didn't you?"

I held up my hands when he tried to approach.

He chuckled, holding up his own hands in defeat. "Fine," he said, his voice eerily steady. "Yes. I did this to you. You're still coming back to the house with me. I think I'll cut my errands short today."

"I'm not going anywhere with you," I said. "Back the fuck away!"

When I turned to run, he was at my back and fisted my hair, dragging me under the pier while I thrashed my legs. Julian slammed me against the wooden post holding up the dock. I placed my hands on his chest and blasted him across the sand until he hit the water.

Alright. My powers also do that.

What the fuck was I doing, though? I needed to run, but I just stood there like a statue.

Run, you idiot!

But I didn't. Julian was still knocked out, and the water covered his face. He'd drown if I didn't pull him out.

"Fuck," I cursed out loud.

I'll pull him up to the sand, then run.

I grabbed his legs and pulled him farther onto the sand. I wouldn't be responsible for someone's death, even if they were a piece of shit.

Once Julian was safe from drowning, I turned toward the parking lot to run, but I felt his grip on my ankle, and he yanked, pulling me down onto my stomach. I lifted my hands, but he was already at my temples, chanting.

Ah ... not again.

CHAPTER 34

CALEB

It had been almost three weeks since Mercy disappeared. A week where we could still feel her within our own souls and subconscious, as if she had been calling to us, but we didn't know where she was. It was as if there was another power blocking us, keeping our bond from truly connecting. The power that bound us was there, and yet, it wasn't.

Melissa squeezed her arms around me, her head resting peacefully on my naked chest. I turned the television off and looked down. Melissa didn't last an hour before she slipped into a slumber, and my mind drifted to the thought that Mercy might be suffering somewhere. Afraid.

Anger brewed inside me when I saw Maurice's face in my mind. It had to be him, and I wished to God I would be the one to take him out.

I rubbed Melissa's arm gingerly with the tips of my fingers, kissed her on top of her head, and slowly wiggled out of her grasp. After laying her head carefully on the pillow next to us, I pulled the blanket over her before heading toward the liquor cabinet. I poured myself a glass of whiskey right as Simon walked into the kitchen.

As a coven, we had decided to stay together at all times, given the circumstances. At Abigail's mansion, there was plenty of room and a security system in place if anyone were to breach the walls again. I just had to remember to set the alarm.

"How about one for me, too, yeah?" Simon asked.

"Happy to oblige." I poured him a glass, and we clinked our drinks together. "Cheers, brother."

"I'm going by Melissa's tomorrow to pick up a few more of her things," I told him, taking a sip. "I'm not okay with her being alone until we can release Kylan from Cami's body and the killer in East Greenwich is caught."

"It's been quiet," he reminded me. "Like the fucker is playing with us now."

"Yeah, I noticed that too." I looked toward the stairs. "Is everyone else asleep?"

He nodded. "I can't shut my mind off. It's crazy that when you lay your head down and your dreams appear, the first thing you see is her face. Like, she's here, but not."

I placed my glass on the counter and folded my arms across my chest. "I know what you mean."

Even with Melissa in my arms, the image of Mercy's face haunted all of us. I don't even know if wherever she's at, she even knows she's doing it—but she's there, silently reaching out to us to save her.

And we can't do a fucking thing about it.

"What time does Roland want us downstairs for the meeting?" he asked.

"Nine."

Simon looked up at the wall clock, and my eyes followed. It was three in the morning. "Fuck," Simon cursed, finishing his drink before placing the glass in the sink. "Maybe that will do the trick. I need to crash."

After Simon resigned upstairs, I picked up Melissa from the couch, cradled her in my arms, and carried her to my room.

I tapped my coffee mug impatiently with my index finger as we waited for Roland to speak. He took a call right as we finally sat down for the meeting, so now we had to wait even longer. Ezra was the most impatient in the coven, so he tapped his foot against the floor as loudly as possible so Roland would hurry the damn call and get on with it.

"Caleb," Melissa whispered, sitting down beside me. She bit her bottom lip and looked around. "Are you sure Roland even wants me here?"

"It doesn't matter what Roland wants. You've helped us out more than most," I said. "You're a part of this family as long as you want to be."

My words didn't ease her discomfort. I could tell as she pressed her lips into a flat line and clasped her palms together, interlinking her fingers. I wanted the coven to know that she wasn't going anywhere.

"Did you mean what you said last night?" Melissa asked, bringing my thoughts back to the conversation we had about being exclusive.

"Yes," I said honestly. "When I told you that you were mine last night, and though it's taken me this long to figure it out, I know in my heart it's real. You're who I want."

There was no desire within me to date anyone else, and Melissa and I cared about each other. Still, given the fact that she was sitting in a room with a coven of powerful witches, she wouldn't truly feel welcomed. As much as I tried to convince her that she was part of us, she may never feel like she truly belonged.

Roland finished his call and stood, placing his palms flat against the table. "Sorry about that," he said, leaning forward. "We have a lot to discuss, so I'll get right to it." He glanced around the table, noting that everyone was accounted for. "When the vampires learned what Mercy's blood would really do, Maurice orchestrated a team to find another solution."

Hearing that monster's name caused a lower, almost inaudible growl in my chest.

Ezra and I both exchanged glances before I said, "There isn't another solution. It's impossible."

Roland shook his head. "That we know of."

"What are you saying?" Leah asked. "That Maurice found a way to do what he *thought* Mercy could do?" She looked around the table, her eyes stopping at me as if I had more answers or a better explanation than my father had.

"When Maurice was in Salem, he built a business supplying blood to vampires for profit," Roland continued. "He's acquired quite a client list, and according to Alexander, he was working on locating a specific coven of witches, who aren't the easiest to find, to help him create a potion that, when given to a vampire, would block the UV rays from the sun and prevent them from burning to ash.”

My jaw dropped, and when I looked around, everyone else at the table appeared just as dumbfounded as me. “How is it,” I asked, “that I’ve never heard of a spell that has the power to do that? And how do you even know this information?”

“Marcus,” he said. “He heard Maurice talking about it before Maurice left the clan. Marcus brought it up to me a few months ago, but until I had more information, I didn’t want the coven involved.”

I slammed my hands down on the table, rattling it, and Melissa jumped beside me. “Are you fucking serious?” I said, heat from rage warming my cheeks. “This could be the very reason Maurice took her.”

Roland shook his head at me. “Mercy can protect herself. There are more vampires and witches involved in this than we know. This is the only way to find the covens who have turned to the dark side and take them out. I’m confident Mercy will be able to escape and help lead us to where they’re at. We need to know what they’re up to. Perhaps she can even take them down from the inside.”

I was about to punch my own father in the face. I stood up, balling my hands into fists. “So, you allowed her to be fucking bait?”

“Relax, Caleb,” my father said. “I’ve always done what was best for the coven. Sit. Down!”

Fire ignited in my hands, and I held my palms up.

“Caleb, oh my God. He’s your father. What are you doing?” Melissa cried as she placed her hand on my arm, trying to calm me, but I only brushed her hand away. I hated pushing her back like that when I knew I was frightening her. My own actions were about to push her completely away.

"You're a fucking traitor, is what you are," I threatened. "Twice now, you've put Mercy's life in danger. I swear to God, if anything happens to her, you're dead to me. I should have known all those years with those monsters would eventually turn you into one. You're not the man I thought you were. That trust we all had to rebuild after you returned … is gone!"

The trees rattled outside the windows surrounding us as Ezra stood and pulled his hands out, brown light radiating from his palms. "Traitor," he growled through his teeth.

Simon stood, slightly slower than Ezra, and pulled his hands out as a white glow radiated from them. A gust of wind whipped through the windows and into the kitchen.

Leah remained sitting. She looked up at us with fear shining in her eyes, but she was loyal and would always have the coven's backs, so she, too, stood and glared at Roland. She pulled her hand to her side, and balls of water hovered over her palms.

Melissa pulled her hands over her mouth and gasped. She didn't get up and run. She must have been too terrified to move.

"You've betrayed this coven," I told my father. "We could have protected Mercy and found another way because there is always another way. You just never take a moment to consider that. It's always the fucking extreme decision with you." I dropped the fire in my palms, but only enough for me to clench my fists, flame wreathing through my fingers. "You're a traitor, *Roland,* and no longer my father. Get the fuck out of this house."

I couldn't stop those words, even if I wanted to. I had to protect our coven, and Roland couldn't be trusted. I ached at the thought of losing my dad, but we had no other choice. It was up to us to get Mercy back.

The coward didn't even try to defend himself. He had fucked up, and now we had to pick up the pieces and do it all on our own. Roland gripped his phone and stormed out, slamming the door behind him.

When he reached the courtyard, he lifted his phone to his ear and spoke to someone on the other line. He turned to me one last time before leaving the property grounds.

Everyone lowered their powers, and I turned to Melissa. "Oh, God. Melissa, I'm so sorry. I didn't know that was going to happen." I inched toward her, but she lifted her hands, putting her palms out in front of her to stop me.

"I ... Caleb, I can't do this," she said, tears welling up in her eyes. She grabbed her purse from the back of her chair and hurried out the door.

Fuck!

CHAPTER 35

MERCY

"What time is your meeting?" I asked Maurice, who was adjusting the buckle to his suit pants. "You look sexy in that suit, by the way."

Maurice smiled and leaned forward, kissing me softly on the lips. His long finger trailed down my chest and between my breasts. *Damn.* I wanted to be caressed all day by those hands, but he had already told me what a busy week he was going to have, and once again, I'd be left in this home ... alone.

"How did I get so lucky to have someone as beautiful as you?" Maurice said as he pulled back from our kiss and dropped his hand. My cheeks warmed, but my body ached at the loss of his touch.

After he adjusted his tie, he grabbed his keys and wallet from the dresser and inched toward me again. "The meeting is in two hours, but Los Angeles traffic is a nightmare." A playful smile flitted across his lips. "We can continue what we started the other night when I get back, okay?" His hand touched me one last time, wrapping around the back of my neck in a tight grip and pulling me toward him. His forehead pressed against mine. "I'll miss you today."

I gave him a tiny smile. "I'll miss you, too."

He brushed his lips against mine again, then dragged his lips under my ear, trailing his tongue up to my earlobe and nibbling slightly. "And I'll miss this," he whispered.

I smiled back and bit my lower lip. "I'll be sure to be naked when you return."

Maurice sucked in his bottom lip, and a low growl buzzed in my ear before he pulled back. "See you tonight, darling."

After he left, I hurried to the shower, taking my time as the warm water hit my skin. This week had been exciting but also exhausting. Julian had given me a tour of the city, and I'd spent most days and nights hanging out by the beach, and each night when I stood under the moonlight, I was drawn to the light that shined down on the ocean. It was as if the moon was pulling me in, but it was just out of reach.

I had thought I'd be alone today with my thoughts. I was mistaken.

At least Jade kept her distance from me. I wasn't sure what her problem was. It was as if she hated me, but I couldn't figure out why. She watched me sometimes from the other side of the room, and every time Maurice put his hands on me, she'd scrunch up her nose and walk out of the room. Did she not want me to be happy, or were her feelings more personal regarding Maurice? Had she loved him?

After a day at the beach, I met up with Julian for a smoothie on Main, and he took a call once we sat down at the outdoor tables.

"Yes, I have her," he told the caller on the other end, then paused. "Are you sure?" He pulled the phone away from his ear and muffled the bottom of his phone. "Will you be okay if I take you to

Santa Monica with me? You can see the city on the drive and sit in the lobby while I take care of some business with Maurice."

This sounded exciting. I mean, not sitting in a lobby, but since I had been here, I hadn't been to any other city. Los Angeles was where Hollywood stars lived, and maybe they'd take me to all the tourist stops.

"I'd love to, actually," I said, trying to hide my excitement. It always seemed like I annoyed Julian, so I didn't want to do anything that could set him off. So, I appeared more neutral about the situation.

"Okay, see you in about an hour or so," he said to the caller on the other end.

"Was that Maurice?"

He shook his head. "No."

No?

No other explanation, just ... *no.*

We drove for over an hour, and I peered out the window, watching the cars zoom past us and cut each other off. We reached an industrial building near the Santa Monica pier. I walked into a fancy lobby trailing behind Julian, and I eyed the receptionist, smacking gum with a wide-open mouth. She hustled to stand when we approached the counter.

"Julian, sweetheart. It's nice to see you," she said, leaning in to kiss him on each cheek. She had a beautiful accent, but I wasn't sure from where. The woman with short blonde hair, blue eyes, and freckles on her crooked nose sized me up. "Who the hell are you?"

And ... she's a bitch.

"I'm Mercy," I said confidently, trying to match her brazen re-mark. "Who the hell are you?" Her jaw dropped right before Julian gripped my elbow, pulling me from her and into a hallway.

"Don't you mind Emma," he said once the door shut behind us. "She's grown a crush on me after a one-night stand two weeks ago and probably believes we're together now." He gave me a wink and gestured for me to move forward. Julian seemed to be hurrying me, and I wasn't sure what the rush was.

Julian wouldn't answer any of my questions on the drive to Los Angeles, either. He was someone I thought I could trust, yet he seemed so cryptic most of the time.

He led me down the hall, which was framed with glass windows, and I saw beautiful purple plants growing inside a greenhouse through the glass. The plants lined several racks along the walls and in the center. Whatever plant they were growing, they needed plenty of it. We entered a spacious room with tall ceilings. The room was massive, but it wasn't the size that caught my attention, but the equipment inside.

"Julian, what is this place?" I asked.

"This is where we operate our business," he replied. "We've been developing Freedom Corporation for a year now, and we're about to launch our first product. We're still working out a few kinks and last-minute ingredients, but once we do—" He stopped as we both looked up at a large steel tank in front of us. "It will change their kind forever."

"Vampires?"

He nodded. "Yes, Mercy. Vampires never had to seek out the ability to walk in the light, because they depended on a witch to save them from that curse. But when they learned that was a lie, the vampire race joined forces with my coven to create a spell, a potion that, when given to a vampire, would enable them to walk in the light forever. Not just a temporary solution like I've been able to provide."

I placed my hand on the cold steel of the tank and looked back at him. "But ... how?"

This baffled me. From what I'd learned this last week, vampires could never walk in the light. Could something as simple as a potion work? Could Maurice finally join me on the beach during the day? God, that would be a dream.

"Dark magic," he said. "It's the only way, because witches are forbidden to help vampires. You were one of the loyal ones, Mercy. You wanted to help. You knew there was good in them, which made you fall in love with Maurice. The two of you, though vastly different, understand one another."

I blushed. Surely, I felt a powerful connection with Maurice. Did I *love* him? I wasn't sure anymore.

"We are short a few ingredients, though. Once it's complete, we can start testing it on vampire subjects."

Test trials. But what if it didn't work? Would they all die? No, Maurice wouldn't put his own kind in danger like that.

I cast my eyes around again. There were machines, tubes, and cases all over the place. On the right-hand side sat several computers and technology that looked far too complicated for me to understand. Right as I approached the computers, Maurice walked in. "Hey, babe," he said with a smile so wide it reached his eyes and creased the dimple on his left cheek. "Exciting, isn't it? Now you can finally see what we're doing here."

He walked up, kissed me on the lips, and pulled back when I heard someone clear their throat. A woman with short black hair and stunningly beautiful features stood behind Maurice with her arms crossed over her chest.

"So, this is Mercy," she said. "How delightful it is to meet you. I'm Clara."

Would she reject me, too, like that bitch, Emma?

I held out my hand. "Hi. Nice to meet you, Clara."

She grabbed my hand and shook it with a firm grip. "Welcome to Freedom Corp." She let go and looked at Maurice with an odd grin. "I hope you like what we're doing here. It's been quite a year developing this potion, but once we're finished, we'll be able to help so many lives. Just think about it. This potion will create a barrier on vampires' skin to protect them from the UV rays that destroy them. Wouldn't that be delightful?"

I nodded, except an unexpected trail of nerves slithered down my spine. "Yes ... yes, it would," I said. Then I looked at Maurice, desperately wanting to be anywhere but near this woman. Something was off. "I'd love to see the rest of the factory."

Maurice ran his hand through his black hair before reaching out and taking my hand. "Come, I'd love to show you something, Mercy."

"Okay," I said as he led me out the door and down the hall. We entered another room, which had clear stalls toward the back, and ... *people* were inside.

The lump in my throat got stuck, and I found breathing almost impossible.

What the actual fuck?

My stomach twisted before I asked, "Maurice, what the hell is this?"

With one smooth glide, he stood behind me, slinking his powerful arms around my waist and pulling me into his muscular chest. "Don't worry, darling," he purred into my ear. "Their sacrifice is going to save us."

"But they're prisoners," I said, suddenly feeling sick about him touching me. "What are you doing, Maurice? This doesn't seem right."

He chuckled in my ear before planting a gentle kiss on my cheek. "I don't care."

The room spun around me as my nerves took over. Did Maurice want me to hate him? Why was he acting so cruel? Did I really date, maybe even love, someone like this? I wished so badly I could remember everything.

He gripped my arm firmly, and I immediately attempted to wrench free. I had no strength over a vampire, though; I barely budged.

Maurice leaned down to whisper in my ear again. "Do you have something you want to say to me?" My heart raced, and it nearly exploded in my chest. I couldn't speak. I just shook my head and looked down at my feet.

He let go of my arm and walked over to Clara as she entered the room. "We have all five, now. Alexander came in last night," she said.

Alexander.

That name sounded familiar.

I stalked closer to the first clear stall and looked in. A young woman who looked about my age sat with her knees to her chest, rocking back and forth. How long had she been in here?

A man in his forties stood in the corner stall, his arms folded across his chest. He looked straight at me, but his face was fierce like he wanted to rip me to pieces. I wanted to tell him I had nothing to do with this. Next was an older woman. Her silver hair was matted, and she was curled up in the fetal position. I couldn't tell if she was sleeping, but she wouldn't look up, either. The fourth was a beautiful blonde woman who stood against the glass and stared at me. She put her hand up and tapped. She was saying something, but I couldn't hear it. Her eyes grew wide as she threw her hands up and screamed at me while hitting the glass. It startled me, so I backed up, my back slamming into Maurice's chest. He wrapped his arms around me again, pulling me further back.

"That is Abigail," he said. "She's a wild one, isn't she?"

I shook my head. "She's trying to tell me something, Maurice."

He leaned down to my ear. "Would you like to see the last one, my dear?" The coolness from his breath tickled my skin until each hair stood up on my neck. I didn't want to be here anymore, but I nodded anyway.

When we reached the fifth stall, I looked at a middle-aged man, handsome, with dark brown hair, and the look he gave me was pained. His eyes searched mine as if something connected us in some way. I placed my hand on the glass, and he put his hand flushed with mine on the other side.

"Who is this man?" I asked.

Maurice was now by my side, but this man behind the glass only held my gaze.

"His name is Alexander." He fisted my hair and pulled my head back. I winced.

"Maurice!" I cried out. "What are you doing? You're hurting me!"

Once he released my hair, he straightened his back, attempting to control the beast inside him. I could see the anger contorting his features before he regained his calm. "We need their sacrifice to complete the spell. Then, we'll need *you*."

He straightened his suit and bore his eyes into mine.

"Me?" I repeated.

Maurice grabbed my right hand and traced my palm with his index finger. "We need your beautiful green light to activate the potion as the last ingredient. You'll be helping millions of vampires experience the freedom of the light."

I shook my head. "But I don't have any magic. You told me it had been taken from me."

Clara stood in front of me now. "Julian," she ordered. Julian was directly next to me, grabbing my arm and pulling me into the last stall at the end of the room. I tried to pry away his hands, which held me tightly, but he was too strong.

"Stop, Julian," I cried. "Get the fuck off me!"

He slid open a glass door and threw me in. I landed on the hard floor with a thud, my knees crashing against the tile.

No.

Julian slid the door shut, raised his hands over the glass in a circle, and black smoke trickled from his fingers. He swirled it around until the door was sealed on the right side. I pulled at the handle, but it wouldn't budge. I slammed my fist against it hard, but it wouldn't break.

Shit! I'll not be kept in a cage.

What is happening?

CHAPTER 36

MERCY

At least two hours had passed, and I clambered to my feet with a sudden urge to pee.

"Hello?" I called out, banging my fist against the glass, but no one came. "I'm going to pee myself if you don't open this damn door."

Julian appeared in front of the glass and moved his hands around until I heard a click. As soon as it opened, he grabbed my arm and escorted me to the bathroom. After I relieved myself, I took my time washing my hands.

I cannot go back into that stall.

Julian knocked on the door. "Hurry your ass up."

When I opened the door, I flipped him off and moved past him, but he grabbed my arm again. "Watch it!"

"Fuck you!" Without thinking or caring about the consequences, I spit in his face. "And go to hell."

Maurice entered and let out what sounded like a hiss. "Enough, Julian. Don't put her back in the stall. We're ready for her."

Maurice grabbed me this time, and when I looked back at the glass stalls, they were empty.

Oh no.

My aching heart felt like it was crumbling into pieces. Not only was I a prisoner in this hellhole, but the man I thought cared about me was a monster. My enemy. I had to be willing to fight and defend myself if the opportunity arose.

We walked into the main room with the large tank, and standing on a platform were the other five people that were kept as prisoners here. These criminals had tied their hands behind their backs. It was clear someone had drugged them as they swayed from side to side, the older woman almost falling down.

"Maurice, what's happening?" I asked. "What is this?"

He gestured to the people on the platform and said, "They're going to be our sacrifice." He turned and smiled. "The world comprises five Universal Elements. Centuries ago, five families represented these elements. Other witches had to use spell books to harness those powers. But not those families. If that wasn't special enough, an angel came down and gave them each a child, their spirit being the element itself. It allowed them to have a direct connection to Earth. Pretty extraordinary, don't you think?"

I clamped my mouth shut, afraid to say anything, as fear and horror drained through me.

Fuck him. Fuck these people and this place. I had to find a way out and take those other prisoners with me.

"These five are descendants of those families," Maurice said. He then climbed up onto the platform.

He moved over to the first prisoner, pulled out a sharp knife, held it to her throat, and sliced it in one swift motion.

Oh my God! I held my stomach, holding back the bile rising in my throat.

"Water," he said as her blood spilled from her wound. I shielded my eyes away.

He killed her. Holy shit. He killed her!

"Hold her head up so she can watch," Maurice commanded Julian, who pulled at my hair and yanked my head up to stare in their direction. Maurice walked behind the man with the fierce eyes, who had been in the second stall and slit his throat, too. "Air." Then to the older woman. "Earth."

I let out a loud sob and gasped for air as terror filled my body. Once Maurice reached the young blonde woman, I tried to step forward, but Julian yanked me back. "Please don't do this, Maurice."

The woman looked me straight in the eyes and called my name. "Mercy!" she called.

She repeated my name, but the second time, she screamed it. Maurice slapped her hard across her face. "Shut the fuck up, Abigail!"

Abigail, I said the name in my head.

"Mercy, you need to use your powers," she said. "Use them now!" Panic rose in my chest as he slit her throat. She let out a choked cry, "Mer ... cy!"

"Stop! Please, Maurice. No!"

Tears welled in my eyes as she fell to the floor.

This isn't happening.

"Fire," he said as her body collapsed at his feet.

The last one stood, keeping his eyes glued on mine. He rocked from side to side. I hoped the drugs they had given him would take away his pain. They were sick. Monsters. Sadistic pieces of shit.

I thought about what the woman they had called Abigail had said to me. Use my powers? I didn't have any. Maybe I did, but I didn't know how to use them.

He held the knife under the last man's throat. They called him Alexander, and I felt like he was someone I knew. Someone I *loved*.

Maurice reached into his pocket with the other hand and pulled out a necklace with a black stone dangling from it. His thumb ran over it with one stroke. "This used to be yours, you know," he said. "My men found it in a safe house after you had carelessly left it there. It used to protect you from monsters like me." His fingers wrapped around the stone, and he squeezed. I watched the gem turn to powder in his palm, sprinkling down like rain onto the platform around the man he held at knifepoint. "Now you have nothing."

I stepped forward, but I winced as Julian pulled me back again.

"Say goodbye to your father, darling." He slit his throat, and blood poured out of his neck. "Spirit."

My father?

I looked up in horror as Maurice stepped down from the platform. I watched their blood ooze out of their necks and flow to the center until their blood mixed in a pool of misery and death.

Maurice gripped my hands and squeezed. "Focus, now. It's your turn."

He pulled my hands out, palms facing the five bodies in front of me. "Let me go!" I screamed.

"I need your power now," Maurice said. "Use it, dammit!"

"I don't know how," I explained. "What's supposed to happen?"

Maurice gripped my waist and leaned in close to my ear. "I just killed your father. I've made you believe you belonged to me for the last three weeks. I've tricked you into loving me." He kissed me on the cheek. "I've *fucked* you over and over again these last three weeks, and each time you screamed my name as if I was the only thing that mattered to you." He stepped back with a huge grin. "Focus on how that makes you feel and then use that anger. How are you feeling at this moment, *dear?* Focus on that rage."

Angry. That made me feel so fucking angry. It was all a lie. I knew I couldn't love someone like Maurice, but I wouldn't let my anger give these assholes the power they needed. I wasn't going to let them use me this way.

Except, I felt something stirring inside just then. I felt these powers Maurice had spoken of. They rushed through my body and reached for my hands. I looked down and saw the green light for the first time, but I wasn't going to give them the power they needed. Instead, I reached out, yanking at his collar and pulling him down. I then flung my head back and head-butted Maurice so hard I heard a crunch.

As I bolted for the door, Julian grabbed the collar of my shirt and yanked me back. I threw my hands forward and blasted him across the room as soon as he stood over me. Once I reached the door, Clara was standing in front of it. I lifted my hands to blast her too, but the moment the power landed in front of her face, she caught it in her hand and threw my magic toward the bodies on the floor.

No!

I backed up into someone, and a needle pricked my neck. Immediate dizziness took over me, and I sagged against the body that held me.

They pulled me toward the platform, and I watched in horror as my power, which she had directed their way, swirled in circles. The blood of their victims circled around like a tornado until it was mixed as one. The blood flowed up in a single crimson stream, green light crackling throughout it. I tried to concentrate, tried to recall the magic back to me, but nothing happened. Nothing worked. Despair racked through me. I had given them what they wanted.

Clara walked up to the platform and moved her hands from side to side, directing the liquid up to the large tank in the center of the room and lowering it inside.

She was a witch, and that scared me more than being around Maurice. She just took my own powers and used them against me.

Clara smiled and stepped toward me, but I couldn't attack anymore. The drugs they'd given me had taken over.

And I shut my eyes.

CHAPTER 37

MERCY

The chains around my wrists and ankles burned my skin. I cast my eyes around the room and realized that I was back at the house, in the master bedroom. I yanked on the chains, which only burned more.

Oh, come on!

I looked at the open door and called out, "Maurice!" But he didn't come.

I huffed, laying my head back down and closing my eyes. I focused on the power that dwindled subtly over my palms.

Did he really think I wouldn't try this?

The powers hovered over the chains, and I focused, hoping it would penetrate the metal, but nothing happened.

"Morning," Jade said as she walked in. "I'm not supposed to take those off, so I have to feed you and give you the drugs that are keeping your powers stabilized." Her voice was laced with annoyance, like I was a huge inconvenience to her.

She carried a tray of food and a glass of orange juice. She set the tray on the nightstand and stuck a straw in the drink. "Here."

"No, thank you," I said, turning my head away from her. "It could be poisoned."

Jade laughed. "Ha! Not like it would kill you. Drink it. You're going to dehydrate."

"Then give me a bottle of water," I snapped, turning back to her. "Cap still sealed."

Her face hardened. "Look, you stubborn little shit. Drink and eat what I give you, and I'll leave. If you don't, Maurice will punish me."

I smiled. "Then let him punish you. You deserve it for being such a nasty bitch."

Her fangs appeared, and she lurched toward me but stopped before she reached my neck. Her breath was heavy against my skin. She was so close, but she wouldn't bite down. I laughed in her face.

"I dare you," I whispered.

Most likely another thing Maurice would punish her for.

Jade let out a frustrated growl, grabbed the tray, and stormed out.

She left me alone again, which I was both thankful for and worried about. How long were they going to chain me up like this? What if I had to relieve myself?

The clock on the nightstand read ten in the morning, and when I looked back at the ceiling above me, the door opened again.

Maurice.

He kneeled at the side of the bed, staring at me. "I'm heading back to the lab today to start preparing the vials of potion you helped us make last night. Thank you, by the way. After learning about what you did last year, I found you worthless, but really, you actually were the key to helping us, just in a different way."

He rubbed the back of his fingers against my cheek, and my skin crawled. "What are you talking about?"

His devilish smile grew wide. "You and I have done this before, but in a different setting and circumstance." He kept stroking my cheeks, and it was pissing me off.

"Why?" I asked. "Why do all this? The relationship was obviously fake. You kissed me. Violated my body—"

"Oh, come on. You enjoyed it just as much as I did."

My face hardened. "Enjoying sex under false pretenses does not and will not ever equate to when you love a person honestly. You're truly pathetic, using me to tell yourself you had control, that you actually matter. You're the worst possible thing on this Earth, and I hope and pray that whatever you have coming, it's me who raises that hand."

Maurice finally removed his fingers from my cheek, and I hadn't realized I was tensing up the entire time. I relaxed my shoulders on the mattress. "True, we were never in love. But just because I made you believe you cared for me doesn't mean I didn't feel something for *you*."

I rolled my eyes. "Bullshit!"

The wry smile on his face made my skin crawl. "Clara wanted me to put you back in that cell," he said. "She wanted to keep you there until we located the dagger and then end you with it." His eyes looked to the floor. "I told her no. You see, vampires may struggle with human emotion, and my humanity was stripped from me, but you're the only one I found quite enjoyable to be around in centuries. I've been hunting you since the seventeenth century. The thought of all that ending ... well." His voice trailed off, and his beautiful eyes looked back at mine. "You can believe what you want. But I craved you then, and I still want you now."

I didn't know what to think about what he had just told me. I hated Maurice, and none of that would change.

"You think you want me?" I asked. "I'm a possession to you, Maurice."

"That's good enough."

I looked away, not wanting to stare into his eyes any longer. "You wanted to use my powers. That's it. You're incapable of caring about anyone but yourself."

His face grew fierce before his hand lashed out, and he squeezed his hand around my throat. "I already got what I wanted. I could let you go back to your coven, but you're too dangerous with them. With the help of Julian to remove all the negative feelings and memories you have of me, you and I could have a future together. It's a shame you can't die, or I would turn you into a vampire. Maybe then you'd see that a powerful man needs a powerful woman at his side."

"I'd rather choke on my own vomit," I spat out. As I turned to look away, his fingers lifted from my throat.

I didn't want to see the look on Maurice's face, but I could only imagine. "Eat when Jade brings you food!" His voice was harsh and authoritative.

I didn't watch him leave, but I heard the door shut. "You didn't get anything from me, dick. Not a fucking thing."

I must have laid in bed for over three hours or so.

Waiting.

Bored.

Thirsty.

The door creaked open again, and I thought it was Maurice coming back, but it was Jade. She didn't have food this time, but she was carrying a bottle of water. "Open it," she instructed. And I did begrudgingly. I can't remember the last time I had been so thirsty.

After I drank the entire bottle, she undid my chains with a key and stepped back. I rubbed my wrist.

My brows furrowed. "Why couldn't I break the chains with my magic?"

"Julian put a spell on it, but I'm still able to open it with the key. Go on, use the bathroom," she commanded. I hurried to the bathroom quickly and relieved myself as Jade sat on the bed, waiting.

I could have taken her out right then and there if I wanted to. With a flick of my wrist, I could have shot my powers out toward her and ran.

I wasn't sure if anyone else was in the house, but I had to try at least to escape. I took a deep breath and opened the door.

"If you're thinking of hurting me, please don't," Jade said as I came back into the room.

"Are you going to tie me back up again?" I asked.

She shook her head. "Come. Follow me to the library."

I didn't understand what was happening. Jade seemed like she didn't hate me at that moment. She was being ... kind.

I followed her to the library, which I had only been to a few times. Her coffee mug sat on a small table, and next to it was a copy of Shakespeare's play, *Romeo and Juliet*.

I snickered.

"What's so damn funny?" she asked.

"Oh, I don't know, Jade. You seem like you'd be reading something darker. Like *Dracula* or *Salem's Lot*."

She laughed softly that time, picking up her book. "Yeah, I don't come off as the romantic type, do I?"

I shrugged. "Well, there is a tragedy in that story, isn't there?"

She smiled solemnly, set the book back down, and strode toward me. "I love him, you know?"

I knew who she was talking about. It wasn't Julian. It was Maurice. "Did you two have an intimate relationship?"

She nodded. "A long time ago. Now, I only work for him."

I looked down, gathering up my thoughts. "Maurice is my worst enemy, isn't he?"

Jade nodded again. "Yes, but he's become obsessed with you," she said. "It's bad for business."

My stomach twisted into knots at those words. Love wasn't scary. Hatred wasn't even scary. Both love and hate still allow you to feel free. But *obsession*. That was something you'd have to escape from.

"What am I?" I asked her.

She turned, and she had a stony expression. "You're *our* worst enemy."

Jade sauntered to the bookshelf, pulled out a book, and opened it. It wasn't a book, though. It was a box with a small cut-out. She pulled out a large vintage gold key and walked up to me.

"What does that open?" I asked curiously.

She placed it in my hand. "The other answer to your question."

I looked down at the key, then eyed the hallway connected to the library. The hallway led to that thick door they had forbidden me to open since I arrived.

"I'll be in my room for a while," she said.

I nodded my head, and she moved down the hall toward the stairs which led to the second level, and I walked to that door. I slipped the key in, and it unlocked. It worked on all the locks of the door. I turned the wheel, and it opened.

It wasn't a safe. The only thing inside was a coffin, which stood at the center of the room.

Slowly, I entered, placed my hands on the lid, and lifted it. There was a young, handsome man inside. Honestly, he looked dead but no different from Jade or Maurice.

I placed my hand on his chest, and I felt it rise. He was alive, or rather, undead.

A vampire.

He looked so familiar to me. I pulled my hands up to his face and closed my eyes. I didn't know what was wrong, so I didn't know how to help this man, but I allowed my powers to come through me and into him. After a few moments, his eyes opened, and he looked right at me.

"Mercy, you're okay!" he cried out with pure desperation in his voice. The man sat up and reached for me, but I stepped back, almost stumbling over my feet.

"Who ... who are you?" I asked, my voice trembling. "Do I know you?"

The handsome man's eyes glistened, and his tortured stare answered my questions. I was someone he cared about. A flutter went through my heart.

I must know and care for him, too.

He climbed out of the coffin and walked toward me, holding up his hands. "I won't hurt you."

When he reached for me again, I didn't step back. Instead, I moved toward him, touching his ice-cold fingers. "My name is Dorian. And we were in love centuries ago. They ambushed us when I was driving you home. I was subdued and forced into this coffin. All I remember is Maurice telling me that he needed me as leverage if you refused to cooperate. It was a witch that put me under a spell in here. You can't trust them, Mercy. You can't—"

"I know," I said. "I don't remember who I am, but I know all of this was a lie."

Dorian's eyes looked heavy; he didn't look well. "I think you might be sick," I said to him.

"I need to *feed.*"

"So, you're a vampire, then?"

He answered with one nod.

"Here." I pulled my hair to the side, not even hesitating to help him. "Please, it's okay. Drink."

Dorian shook his head. "I can't. Not *your* blood. I need to be able to use my vampire strength to help you."

I creased my brow. "I don't understand."

His eyes stared into mine. He inched closer, and for a moment, I hesitated and started to step back, but I stopped. Dorian leaned in, placed his lips on mine, and deepened the kiss.

The fire that burned inside me leaped to the surface, aching for more of his touch. His taste was familiar; his touch was a memory. My mind was in the moment; then it wasn't. I remembered the first time our lips touched, but it was a different life. *We* were different. But the feeling remained unchanged, unaltered by the centuries that passed.

Dorian! I remembered him.

Julian did this. He took Dorian away from my heart and replaced it with Maurice.

I felt the heat and hatred behind my eyes. The murderous rage built up so fast that I found my powers exploding inside me.

The memories of how it all happened came flashing before me. Julian had placed his hands over my temples outside of Dorian's car. I grabbed at his wrist and tried to use my powers, but it happened so fast. He pulled at my hair and yanked me down until my knees crushed the pavement on the side of the road. Dorian had screamed for me in the distance. Then there was only pain and darkness.

When I came to, I looked at Dorian and smiled with relief. I was back.

"You remember?" he asked with urgency and hope.

I nodded. "I remember."

He grabbed my hand, pulling me behind him as we heard the floorboard creak outside the room. "You have ten minutes to get as far away from here as possible," Jade said. "Julian is on his way back."

"We have to go," Dorian said, turning to me. "Now!"

"Wait," Jade said.

"What is it?" I asked.

"The sun," Jade reminded me. "Dorian can't leave."

I looked at him, and my eyes widened. "You have to turn back, then," I said. "You don't have a choice."

He shook his head.

"You're going to be dead when Julian gets here. You can't help me fight if you're dead," I said as panic rose in my chest.

Dorian hesitated but grabbed my hand. "Okay."

I felt my heart pounding against my chest as I held my wrist up to his lips. Then he bit down.

I closed my eyes, feeling the blood drain from my veins and enter his mouth. The feeling of euphoria took over, and tears welled in his eyes when I opened mine back up. Dorian released his bite, trying desperately not to spit out the blood. He swayed a little before he took a deep, long breath.

Heat warmed his skin as he came back to life.

"You don't have time to have a moment, you two. Go," Jade said.

My smile was faint as a tear ran down my cheek. I never thought Dorian would ever choose to be human again, even when faced with life or death, but he had.

He had for me.

"Come on," I said, taking his hand while we rushed to the door.

When we reached the exit, I turned to Jade. "He's going to kill you for helping us."

"I know," she said, "and I don't care."

No. This wasn't right. "I can turn you back, too. Right now. You can come with us. You don't deserve this."

Jade laughed. "Yes, I do. I've done a lot of fucked up things, to say the least. And I deserve to die because of it. Maurice doesn't love me; he was the only reason I allowed myself to stay alive all these years. I don't want to be a vampire, but I also don't want to be human, because I know that the moment my soul returns, I will be haunted by the guilt of everything I've done. I'm ready to die."

I turned to Dorian and shook my head. "No!" I turned back to her. "No!"

"We have to go, Mercy," Dorian said. "Please."

"I can't leave," I said. "Jade, let me turn you."

She shook her head, a tear running down her face. "Get out of here. Now, or I'll put you both in that coffin."

Dorian grabbed my wrist, yanking me out of the house as I resisted him the entire way. I'd force her if I must. She wasn't going to sacrifice herself like that. I didn't know why I cared so much, but I did. Nothing about this was right. Maurice would not be the cause of her life being taken from this earth.

I yanked free from his grip, running back to the house, but she was already on the porch, the sun beating down on her fair white skin. The sun would be the weapon to take her life.

"No!" I cried out as I watched her body burst into flames. It didn't last long. Not for a vampire. She was ash before she could scream.

I fell to my knees. I had never seen a vampire die by the sun before. It was always so quick, with a flick of my wrist and the pierce of the stake through their heart. This was something else. This wasn't a sight I was prepared for.

"Now, Mercy. We have to go. Now!"

I felt Dorian's hands on mine again, pulling me away from the prison they had held us in. A prison that, hours ago, I believed to be my home. I thought it to be the place I shared with a man I loved. An ugly lie. A fantasy created by a demented narcissist. He wouldn't win today. Not with me. Not with Dorian. And not with Jade.

We took off down the road. We had no money, no phone. I had no idea where we were going to go.

We hurried down to the beach, and I spotted a couple sitting on the sand. "Excuse me. We have an emergency. Can I please use your phone? I have no money to give you. I'm sorry."

The man shook his head, put his arms around the woman, and walked away.

Okay, I get it. We're strangers. Not everyone will be that skeptical, though.

I pointed to a teenager. "There."

This time, Dorian spoke. "Excuse me. We have an emergency. Can we borrow your phone for just one minute?"

She nodded and smiled. "Um ... sure, here."

"Thank you," I said, grabbed the phone, and dialed Joel's number, and he picked up right away. "Hello?"

"Joel, it's Mercy," I said, relieved to hear his voice.

"Mercy!" he shouted in reply. "You guys! It's Mercy on the phone." I heard shouts and commotion in the background.

"Who's there?"

"Lily and Bradley came over tonight," Joel said. "Oh, kiddo, we've been so worried."

"Look, we don't have much time," I said. "Dorian and I are on the north side of the Huntington Beach Pier. We need you to teleport us home."

"Give me five minutes. I need to grab a map to pinpoint the exact location."

"Okay, see you soon."

I hung up the phone and handed it back to the girl. "Thank you again."

The girl continued down to the pier, and we waited for only a few minutes before the entrance to the vortex opened, and we stepped inside the portal. It zipped us through faster than it took for us to blink.

We landed in the front living room, but no one was there. I called out, "Joel? Lily?"

"I'll check the kitchen," I said.

Dorian eyed the back door. "I'll check out back."

We split up, and I called for them again but heard nothing. I looked for Dorian near the back door but didn't see him, so I walked out to the backyard.

"Dorian?" I called.

I then spotted the back of …

"Bradley?" He turned around, holding the carved-out end of our missing dagger.

Well, fuck.

I stared at him; confusion clouded my senses, and my heart pounded hard against my chest. "Oh, you guys found the dagger?" My question was stupid. No, that's not what this was, especially after seeing the hardened expression that Bradley was giving me.

His face read hatred and disgust.

"Where is everyone?" I asked, swallowing down my nerves and attempting to stay neutral. He gestured with his other hand to the right. Sitting under the willow tree were three bodies sprawled out. I could see their chests rising and falling. They weren't dead.

I looked back at Bradley. "Who the hell are you?" I asked. "What did you do to them? Are you a witch, too?"

My questions came out fast, one after another, without skipping a beat. I didn't understand any of this, but I was shaking with growing rage, and I was ready to kill this asshole as soon as I had answers.

"I honestly didn't think we'd ever see you again, but I'm glad I've kept the dagger with me everywhere I went, just in case," he said, snickering. He spoke in a slight British accent that I hadn't heard from him before. "What a great opportunity to catch you off guard once you came through that portal." Before I could speak again, he continued. "You're just as dimwitted and careless as your father."

What? This is about my dad?

"You knew Alexander?"

He pulled his glasses off and tossed them in the yard. His face was hard and furious. "A vampire killed my wife, Mercy. I could only watch as she slipped away in my arms, but before she died, she gave me a name: Alexander Winchester."

I was stunned silent for a second. I remembered my father's story about the woman he had accidentally killed. He couldn't stop before he took too much of her blood. He escaped before the husband returned, but he watched the man through the bedroom window, holding his wife until she slipped away in his arms.

"I'm sorry about your wife, Bradley, but what does that have to do with me? Your quarrel is with my father, and he died yesterday. Maurice slit his throat right in front of me."

I understood the need for revenge, but no one would go through this much trouble for revenge. Why kill innocent people for one person?

All of this. All the death couldn't be because my father killed his wife unless it fucked up his head so badly that he was acting with no remorse.

Bradley stepped toward me, and I raised my hands, ready to use my powers.

"Ah. Ah. I wouldn't do that if I were you," Bradley warned. Then he gestured toward Dorian and my family, lying on the ground. "There is magic connecting me to them. They'll die in less than a minute if you kill me."

"How?" I asked, my voice steady. Finally, I was regaining composure.

"I'm not going to tell you how the spell works, my dear."

I cringed at the sound of him calling me "dear."

"No, how did you do it? The killings? Was there a vampire doing your dirty work?"

He stepped toward me, and I moved back. "No. That was all me." He pulled something out of his pocket and held it up, smiling. A proud grin tugged at his lips. "I designed this after I mastered my plan to draw you out. How to entice you to kill your own father."

I narrowed my eyes, focusing on an object that looked like vampire fangs. Two metal prongs, a little over an inch apart from each other, connected by black rope or string.

"It makes the perfect bite mark into one's neck. Once I subdued my victim, I used these fangs to pierce their artery, causing them to bleed out."

He was fucking crazy.

And I was pissed. Bradley's need for revenge was so powerful that he took innocent lives.

"But they were innocent. You killed *humans*. People who had families who cared about them. Have you no shame about what you've done? All for what? So that I'd think it was my father and kill him to avenge your wife? I told you, my father is dead. You can't have your revenge, because someone else did it for you."

He placed the fang device back into his pocket, and I could see him adjusting his grip on the dagger in his other palm. "No one is innocent, especially not you. After you turned your father back into a human, I knew I couldn't continue with the original plan. But me killing his daughter? Now, that's rich. The perfect revenge. An eye for a fucking eye. You're the one person he loved on this earth." He stepped closer, and my backside hit the patio post when I moved back. "At first, I was hesitant because we witches would be without Spirit again, but then I thought about it." He tapped the dagger on his thigh, just as I had seen Kylan do at the cove a year ago. The gesture was unnerving. "Would the powers really leave this earth if a witch kills them? If I killed your coven, I would gain your powers, right? You kill a witch, and you get their power."

"I don't think it works like that with the Chosen Ones."

"Your mother thought so, didn't she? Isn't that why she tried to kill you?"

Bradley was right. It wasn't a scenario that had really crossed our minds since this all started. We were so worried about vampires coming after us that we didn't think about other witches desiring our powers.

"It doesn't matter," I said. "You'd have to get close enough to me first." I held up my hands, ready to fight him. But I couldn't kill him until the spell on my family was released. I had to disable him somehow.

Before he took a step closer, I released my energy, blasting him up into the air and throwing him back toward the back fence. Once he hit, the dagger flew from his hands.

I dashed for it.

But I didn't get far. Bradley lunged out and grabbed my legs, pinning them to the ground, and yanked me closer to him. I punched him hard in his face, but he barely flinched. He grabbed my head, and I felt a whirl of dizziness take over. The power he had was something I hadn't encountered before from other witches. Even Julian's magic didn't cause me to feel faint. He created a sense of vertigo in my head, and I was on the verge of throwing up, but I kept my hands steady as I tried to tap into my powers. I attempted to summon the surrounding earth, the dirt, the trees, the air, and fire, but nothing worked. I couldn't focus enough with the pounding in my head to conjure up my magic. He was crippling me, making me feel like I had overdosed on drugs.

"Stop it, Bradley. You don't want to do this," I cried. "My powers will kill you if you take them. You can't handle this amount of magic."

He just laughed at me while continuing to distort my mind.

My pleading was pointless, but I had to try something. I brought my knee forward and up, kicking him in the groin and causing him to fall to his side. I was on my feet before he could grab me, and I side-kicked him, causing him to fly through the air and slam into a tree.

I blasted my powers toward him, keeping him pinned to the ground. I jumped onto him, gripped his throat, and threw a punch, but when his hands lifted, he shot back powers I hadn't seen coming, and I flew back, landing on my side.

Just as I looked up, I saw Bradley's face in doubles and triples, a blur of confusion. He was now on top of me, pressing his hand to my head, causing another wave of extreme vertigo, and I could no longer use my powers on him. I tried to lift my fist, but I missed his body, and he gripped my arm, pulling it back down. I struggled against his grip and kicked out, but I couldn't connect. Then I remembered what I had done to Maurice at the lab. I jerked my head upwards and slammed my forehead into Bradley's face. His grip slipped, and my arm came loose.

Once my hand was free to strike again, I mustered up every ounce of power I had in my body, not from my magic, but from my own physical strength. I lifted it up, slowly brought it back down to my body, and trust my fist forward with every ounce of strength that I had in me until my fist broke through his chest.

I felt his skin, muscles, and sternum crushing right before my fingers wrapped around his heart in a firm grip. I held on, his eyes wide open, blood pouring from his mouth, but before I could move, the piercing sound of a dagger plunged into my stomach. A cold sensation bloomed around the wound and started to spread.

With the dagger still in me, I looked into Bradley's eyes. "I'm sorry about your wife; I really am. But you failed in your revenge. And you hurt Lily. You killed Sarah. I can't forgive that." I squeezed his heart with my hand and yanked it out of his chest. Hot blood washed over my stomach and legs, soaking me through. I tried not to vomit from the smell and from my own numbing body.

Bradley fell over me, which caused him to push the dagger deeper into my belly, but I was able to push him off so I could sit up, but barely. Blood spewed out of my mouth, and I felt like I was choking.

I eyed my family and Dorian and moved as fast as possible, though my body was weakening by the second. I covered each body with my hands and started to chant a spell, bringing them back from the brink of death. They'd all started to fade away after I ripped Bradley's heart from his chest, their breathing becoming shallow. I focused my energy into bands of light that tied around each person. The light then touched Bradley's spell and burned it away. The spell's connection snapped, and everyone's strength came rushing back.

I watched all three of their chests rise and fall. They were alive, thank God. I sighed with heavy relief, but I couldn't hold on anymore. The power from the dagger was taking my life.

I was going to die.

"Mercy!" Dorian cried as I fell into his arms. My name was the last thing I heard before I slipped away.

CHAPTER 38

MERCY

I looked down a long hallway where the walls were bright white.

Was this the spirit world?

I continued down the hallway until I reached a door, but when I placed my hand on the knob, my hand went through it, and I stepped onto the dark pavement beneath my feet. The air was thick, and the only things I saw in front of me were bodies walking shoulder to shoulder like a crowded street in a city. Most of the people walking looked lost, sad, or frightened to be there.

No, this wasn't heaven.

"Excuse me," I said to a young woman with golden blonde hair. She stopped and turned to me; her eyes widened, and her face looked terrified.

"It's you. That means ..."

I died. The woman was going to say that I had *died*.

Failed.

I nodded. "I think so. What is this place?

She looked around as people passed by, ignoring us. "The Unclaimed World. Some call it 'Purgatory.' It's the realm where the essence of our lifeforce go when our bodies are still connected to the human world in some way. A part of me is a vampire up there. The ugly, monstrous part, killing without remorse. You were here not so long ago."

I thought about her words. Vampires were undead, but their souls were taken from them when they were turned. Was this the place where those souls ended up?

"We're tethered to our physical body, so we can't move on until it completely dies on Earth. Or you help resurrect us with your blood. We all hoped for you to save us; bring us back our bodies and humanity. But ... since you're here, it means we are all doomed."

I looked again at the people walking around in their lost state and asked, "What did you mean by me being here before?"

"Of course, you don't remember. After the village hanged you at the gallows, you came here. You're bound to your coven, so your spirit doesn't truly move on unless they all do."

I thought about how Caleb had finally found a way to bring me back twenty-two years ago and how difficult it must have been for him to find my soul. It could only be done by a special kind of magic. It was magic that could only be done once.

Was I doomed to be in this place forever? What would happen to me if I were truly bound to the earth, and now my body was dead again? What about these souls that were stuck here?

"I'm sorry," I said. "I tried. I tried, and I failed you."

She smiled for the first time since I'd stopped her. "You can still watch over them."

"How?" I asked.

She smiled one last time and faded into the crowd without answering me. I now stood alone.

I kneeled on a grassy lawn near a tall tree with beautiful amber leaves breaking off the branches and falling around me. Looking ahead through the crowd of people in front of me, I could see through them, like a window had been opened for me. My body lay in Joel's backyard, with Dorian holding me in his arms. And he was weeping.

I wished they could hear or see me, so I could comfort them in their pain. Lily buried her face in Joel's chest, sobbing over my death.

I really was gone.

CHAPTER 39

CALEB

"No!" I gasped out all the air in my lungs. Every part of my being prayed that I didn't just feel that. The coven stood still, their eyes wide open, and we couldn't move. Another surge rocked through me, making me collapse to the ground.

"Oh my God!" Leah screamed. She held her chest, and we all cried out in agony, feeling a deep sense of sorrow and pain we hadn't experienced since the witch trials.

We felt it. We felt Mercy die.

"Let's go. We need to move. Now," I yelled to the coven as we bolted outside and into Leah's car.

Joel had just texted me that he was teleporting Mercy and Dorian to his home after they escaped. But minutes later, we felt her life be taken from us. Did the killer find her and use the dagger?

I drove as fast as I could, not caring if a cop tried to pull us over. Not caring about the hundreds of laws that I was breaking to get there.

"Caleb, she's already gone. Slow down before you kill someone," Ezra said.

I ignored him. I had to get there.

We pulled into the driveway, jumped out, and hurried inside. We didn't see anyone in the kitchen or even the family room. "Joel!?" I shouted. The voice that followed wasn't his. It was Lily's.

"Caleb, come quickly."

Once we entered the backyard, the first body I saw was Bradley, lying lifeless on the floor with a hole in his chest and his crushed heart on the ground beside him. I cringed, but my attention immediately pulled to Lily sobbing under a willow tree. She and Joel held each other tightly. They kneeled next to Dorian, whose back was facing us. When we walked around to face him, he held Mercy's lifeless and bloodied body in his arms. Lily gripped the dagger in her hand, then placed it on the ground when we ran over to her.

"No!" I screamed, kneeling beside them, the coven following behind me.

I felt numb. We couldn't lose Mercy again.

We all held hands, sobbing and shaking, our hearts aching over her loss. Not again.

Not again.

I leaned down and kissed her on the forehead. "I'm so sorry, Mercy. I am so, so sorry." Everyone took turns kissing her head, and we sat in near silence. The only sounds were those of agony-filled weeps.

I looked up at the coven. "We're bringing Mercy back." I didn't even think about my words. I knew what we had to do, but I had to convince the other three it was our duty to do it. We had to.

"What the hell are you talking about, man? She's gone," Ezra said. "The spell won't work again, but we can keep looking until we find another way."

I shook my head. "There is another way."

Their eyes met mine, and I knew they were confused. I was the only one who knew the other way to bring her back. When I had found the spell to resurrect her twenty-two years ago, the witch who helped make the spell had used the last remaining bark of the original tree on Gallows Hill. The same tree that took the lives of our fellow Salem witches centuries ago. Once it was gone, there'd be no more left. But he explained something else to me. He explained that if this were to happen again, a sacrifice would need to be made. It was the only way to give her enough power and magic to bring her back.

"Leah, Ezra, Simon," I said, pausing to gather the words. "Our powers are the only thing that can bring her back."

Leah lowered her brow. "Then we join hands and conjure whatever spell we have to in order to share our powers with her. Just tell us the spell, and we'll do it."

I shook my head. "Sharing our powers won't be enough."

Simon looked up, his eyes widening. He understood.

He turned to Leah. "We have to give up our elements," he said.

Leah's breathing picked up the pace. "If we give up our elements, we die, Caleb."

I nodded slowly and hesitantly; she nodded back in understanding.

"Well," Ezra said, "we've lived a long life. I think I've done everything on my bucket list." We chuckled quietly to ourselves, everyone shedding a tear at the realization that we were all on the same page. Spirit couldn't be retaken from Earth, and Mercy was the only one strong enough to hold on to all five elements.

"Okay," Leah said, wiping her eyes.

Lily and Joel stood, and we embraced them and said our good-byes. Lily leaned toward me. "We will find a way to make this right somehow. I promise we won't give up."

I squeezed her hand, and the four of us gathered around Mercy's body, kneeling. Simon gripped Leah's hand, and Ezra grabbed mine. Dorian laid her down gently. He had been quiet the entire time as tears rolled down his face. Before he stood, he leaned closer to me and said, "Thank you."

Dorian stood back with the others while Leah, Simon, and Ezra kneeled with me. All four of us gripped our hands together in a circle, and I chanted the spell the witch had taught me years ago. They mimicked the chant, and I felt my power as it sparked inside of me. It was more powerful than I had ever felt.

We stopped chanting, and Leah lifted her hands above her head. "I am Water. I give Spirit my power."

Simon followed her lead. "I am Air. I give Spirit my power."

"I am Earth. I give Spirit my power," Ezra said.

Finally, I spoke my last words. "I am Fire. I give Spirit my power."

As soon as the last word left my lips, we all collapsed to the ground.

... Darkness had claimed us.

CHAPTER 40

MERCY

My eyes opened, and I looked at the gray clouds forming above. My eyes felt watery, and I rubbed the tears away before I sat up and saw my coven lying down on their backs, circling me on the grass.

I had seen everything. I witnessed what they did for me, and there wasn't anything I could do to stop it. They couldn't see me or hear me scream for them to let me go. I couldn't get them to stop.

I felt the warmth of Fire, the flow of Water, the comfort of Earth, and the fresh breath of Air within me circling my soul. They circled Spirit as if the five of us were one. My body didn't just conjure the power; it *was* the power. All five elements were inside me.

Their vessels, the bodies that walked with them, lay dead, but were they really dead if the elements that gave each person life, to begin with, were still empowered and thriving?

I looked to my right, and Dorian kneeled with me. He reached out his hand, and I clasped it in mine.

Caleb's body was a few feet from where I kneeled, and I inched toward him, dragging my knees against the prickly grass. After I placed the back of my bloodstained fingers on his cheek, caressing his skin, I looked at the others.

"Joel?" I said. He had stood silently by the tree, holding on to Lily, waiting for me to speak. His and Lily's eyes were puffy and red from crying when they had thought I was gone forever.

This wasn't a moment to embrace each other and celebrate because I was alive.

No.

An evil man lay dead behind us with his heart ripped out. A man Lily loved, and she now knew he had lied to her to get to me.

There was nothing to rejoice about at that moment. Four members of my family—my coven—lay dead before us. They had sacrificed themselves for me.

Joel was now by my side, and Dorian moved over, allowing Joel to bring me to my feet. "We need to find four coffins," I said. "The three of us will perform a spell that will preserve their bodies until the day I find a way to bring them back."

Joel nodded. "My spell book has one, but it's *dark* magic, and I've never performed it before. The spell will last as long as their spirit is tied to the earth."

"Then we do it," I said. "We do it, Joel."

I didn't care that it was dark magic. They were not leaving me.

"We'll keep the coffins locked in our family's mausoleum on 34th Street in Salem," I said. "We'll do it tonight before their bodies decompose."

Lily walked toward me and brought me in for a hug. I squeezed her tightly in my arms while the tears I held back now fell freely down my face.

"You're alive. I know that means nothing to you right now, but it does to me. I couldn't lose you, too," Lily said as she released me and turned to face Joel. "We need to do the spell now. I'll help you gather what's needed."

While Lily and Joel went into his house, I turned to face Dorian, who was now by my side.

We watched each other for a tiny, still moment before I said, "It's gone, Dorian." I placed my hand on my chest.

He tilted his head slightly. "What's gone?"

"The spell," I said. "When I died, the spell I did died with me."

It took him a moment to realize what I was saying. Then his eyes grew wide. "All of it?" A faint smile pulled at his lips.

I walked closer to him and brought my hands to his cheeks, caressing his jawline with my fingers. A tear rolled down my face, and he wiped it with his hand. Slowly, I reached out, wrapping my hands around his neck to pull him closer to me until our lips touched. Dorian gently placed his hands on each side of my face, drawing us deeper into our kiss. It was passionate, loving, and filled with centuries of undying love. The feeling in my heart showed me I could never take it away again.

I wanted to embrace the emotions my body was screaming for, but my heart also ached from losing my family.

I would search for a way to bring my coven back and continue the mission to save this world from creatures like Maurice. My archenemy was still out there. Kylan's spirit was still out there too, and lives would be lost for as long as they walked this earth.

But at *this* moment, it was only us.

Me and Dorian.

And I was in love with him.

EPILOGUE

MAURICE

I looked down at a pile of ash at my doorstep and shrugged.

Fucking Jade. I should have killed her years ago. Then a realization struck me.

A slight panic rose in my chest, followed by anger. Would Jade be so stupid to have let Mercy go?

I turned toward the limo outside my home and held up my finger, signaling to Clara that I would be back in a minute. I couldn't see her through the tinted windows, but I assumed she had seen me, knowing that crazy bitch was always watching my and everyone else's every move.

I walked into my house and sniffed. Not like it would have mattered. Mercy was still under that infuriating spell her uncle had cast upon her to mask her intoxicating scent.

I strolled down the hall and stopped dead in my tracks when I saw the safe's door standing wide open.

My nostrils flared.

Where the hell is Julian?

When I neared my bedroom where we were keeping Mercy, I saw she was, indeed, gone. Her unlocked chains lay on the bed, and the syringe filled with the drugs I'd needed Jade to administer to her was full.

If Jade weren't already dead, I'd kill her.

I balled my hand into a fist, feeling the pressure build around my eyes, and my fangs protruded. I hissed as Clara walked into the bedroom.

"While you were playing house with her, she should have been locked up in a cage," she said in a huff. "Doesn't matter anymore. We got what we needed from her."

"*You* got what you needed from Mercy." My jaw tightened. "I wasn't done with her. Not by a long shot."

Clara walked past me and picked up the syringe. "You really are a sadistic son of a bitch." She squeezed the syringe and emptied its liquid contents onto the floor. "But we have more pressing matters to address." She tossed the needle into the trashcan in the corner of the room.

I followed her, and as we neared the front door, Julian entered the foyer. "She's at the factory. We have her bound in stall number five."

"Good," Clara said. "Vampire trials for the potion will start tomorrow. Our test subjects will be brought to the office at seven in the morning." She turned to Julian. "Maurice is in charge, and you'll obey him from now on. Once the subjects are brought in, we will proceed with the ceremony. Be there at nine," Clara ordered before looking back at me. "Oh, and Maurice?"

My eyes met hers, waited for her order.

"I expect a proper goodbye in my bed before Kylan leaves Cami's body and takes over mine."

ABOUT THE AUTHOR
D.L. BLADE

D.L. Blade grew up in southern California and studied at the California Healing Arts College, working as a massage therapist for thirteen years, then on to real estate. D.L. and her family moved to Colorado in 2015, where she now writes full-time.

Blade always loved writing, concentrating on poetry and music rather than novels when she was younger. That changed, however, when she had a dream one night and decided to write a book about it. Aside from reading and writing, she enjoys hosting parties, wine tasting, rock concerts, and spending an enjoyable weekend in her cul-de-sac with her neighborhood besties, drinking cold sangrias.

In the future, D.L. hopes she can continue writing exciting novels that will captivate her readers with twists and turns and all our favorite tropes.